● ● ● ● ● ●

"What's up, shorty?"

She shrugged. "Nothing. What's up with you – besides the fact that you don't know how to spar?"

He chuckled. He had a nice smile and beautiful brown eyes. "How you figure that?"

"You not supposed to hit your sparring partner in the face like that," Nisha said, "unless you wanna spar by yourself from now on."

"Huh." Lonzo smirked. "Like you know something about it."

"I know a lot about it. What you think, I'm just some hoochie who came in here to see some hot guys?" That was pretty close to the truth, but Lonzo didn't know that. "My daddy was a fighter. I probably know more about boxing than you."

He grinned. "Oh yeah? Who's your daddy?"

Nisha liked the way he said that. She had her first sexual fantasy about him right then.

Who's your daddy?

Ohuh! You baby!

"Walter's my daddy," she said.

Lonzo's eyes widened, and he straightened his posture. "For real? Ay, yo, your pops is the real deal. He a legend. He fought all kinds of greats back in the day. I wanna be like him when I grow up. Real talk. Except I'm gonna be a champion – no disrespect."

"It's cool," Nisha said. "I saw your fight the other day. You're 3-0. You got a long way to go before you can fight for the title."

"You saw me fight?" Lonzo said and smiled brightly. "I wish I woulda knowed that. I wouldn't have hit my sparring partner in the mouth, if I knew you already seen me fight."

She giggled. "So, you did that for me?"

He shrugged. "If I was a peacock, I'd show you my feathers. But I ain't got no feathers. I got these." He held up his fists.

● ● ● ● ● ●

BLOW BY BLOW

KeithWalkerBooks Edition

KEITH THOMAS WALKER

KEITHWALKERBOOKS, INC
This is a UMS production

KEITHWALKERBOOKS

Publishing Company
KeithWalkerBooks, Inc.
P.O. Box 250626
Plano, TX 75025-0626

For information write
KeithWalkerBooks, Inc.
P.O. Box 250626
Plano, TX 75025-0626

ISBN-13 DIGIT: 978-1-7320624-4-3
ISBN-10 DIGIT: 1732062447
Library of Congress Control Number: 2019906967
Manufactured in the United States of America

Second Edition

Visit us at www.keithwalkerbooks.com

This book is for Regina

MORE BOOKS BY
KEITH THOMAS WALKER

Fixin' Tyrone
How to Kill Your Husband
A Good Dude
Riding the Corporate Ladder
The Finley Sisters' Oath of Romance
Blow by Blow
Jewell and the Dapper Dan
Harlot
Plan C (And More KWB Shorts)
Dripping Chocolate
The Realest Ever
Jackson Memorial
Sleeping With the Strangler
Life After
Blood for Isaiah
Brick House
Brick House 2
One on One
Brick House 3
Jackson Memorial 2
Backslide
Threesome
Backslide 2
Threesome 2
Election Day

NOVELLAS

Might be Bi Part One
Harder
Primal Part One
The Realest Christmas Ever
Hotline Fling

POETRY COLLECTION

Poor Righteous Poet

FINLEY HIGH SERIES

Prom Night at Finley High
Fast Girls at Finley High
Bullies at Finley High

Visit www.keithwalkerbooks.com for information about these and upcoming titles from KeithWalkerBooks

ACKNOWLEDGMENTS

Of course I would like to thank God, first and foremost, for giving me the creativity and drive to pursue my dreams and the understanding that I am nothing without Him. I would like to thank my mother for always pushing me to be the best I can be. I would like to thank Janae Hafford for being the best advisor, supporter and little sister a brother could ever have.

I would also like to thank (in no particular order) Beulah Neveu, Deloris Harper, Denise Fizer, Michele Halsey Hallahan, Priscilla C. Johnson, Kim Tanner, Tia Kelly, Edwina Putney, Melissa Carter, Cathy Atchison, Lanita Irvin, Ramona Weathersbee, Cynthia Antoinette Taylor, Jason Owens, Ramona Brown, Johnathan Royal, Sharon Blount, BRAB Book Club, and Uncle Steven Thomas, one love. I'd like to thank everyone who purchased and enjoyed one of my books. Everything I do has always been to please you. I know there are folks who mean the world to me that I'm failing to mention. I apologize ahead of time. Rest assured I'm grateful for everything you've done for me!

BLOW BY BLOW
CHAPTER ONE
FIGHT NIGHT

The crowd at the Will Rogers Coliseum became restless midway through the third fight. The arena, which hosted rodeo events on most evenings, had been transformed to accommodate a standard boxing ring. Stadium seats were erected for the throngs of fans who had come to support and possibly revive the dying sport.

There were only three hundred people in attendance, maybe three-fifty if you counted the trainers and coliseum staff hired to serve beers and keep the peace throughout the night's festivities.

Nisha's dad, Walter, told her basketball and football were the main reasons for boxing's demise. Most athletic black men were dribbling a ball or sweating it out on the gridiron nowadays. Spectacles like LeBron and Odell Beckham Jr. were to blame. They made it look so enticing.

Who wants to get hit in the head for twelve rounds when you can chill in the paint and snatch a rebound off the rim? Who in their right mind would want to end up like Muhammad Ali, when it was less dangerous and just as profitable to run a quick pattern and catch the game-winning touchdown?

Yet boxing lives on.

And every now and then, every decade or so, a guy comes along to breathe life into what may be the most ancient of all sports: A gladiator will step into the ring and pummel his opponent so thoroughly, everyone in the stadium will rise to their feet and stare in wonderment, their mouths ajar. They'll scream victoriously when the ref raises the warrior's glove.

They'll feel a pinch of sympathy for the defeated man, wondering if he will ever speak or walk the same after the ass-whooping he endured. But for the most part, they'll want to see the gladiator in action again. They'll leave the stadium shaking their heads, asking their buddy, *Did you see that, man? You see the way he cracked that guy's jaw? He's going to the top. He's gonna make it, watch. That's the baddest mo-fo in the country!*

And *that* was what the crowd at Will Rogers wanted to feel this Friday night. They didn't come to see the featherweights who had enough energy to throw 300 punches per round but didn't have the strength to knock out or even stumble their opponent. And they didn't come to see the fat heavyweights currently in the ring. These walruses were doing more hugging than virgins at the prom, and even Lonzo's brother Leo, who wasn't into excessive brutality, started to complain a little.

"Damn, I wish they would just *fight*!"

Most of the folks in the arena were dressed in tee shirt and jeans, the same attire you'd find at a baseball game. But Leo was always a snappy dresser. He stood out in slacks with a button-down and a sleek pair of snakeskin shoes. He didn't wear lip gloss that night, but his nails were glistening, and the effeminate way he sat with his legs crossed was a dead giveaway.

"I know," Lanisha groaned. "That's why don't nobody want to come see the fights no more."

She sat with her regular crew, cradling Little Lonzo to her chest. To her left Leo watched the ring with growing impatience. He sighed and waved at the fighters passively.

"This is a mess, right here. They need to go on home and eat a cake or something. That's all they been doing anyway. They damn sure can't fight."

To Nisha's right, her father Walter paid closer attention to the match, but that was to be expected because he was once a boxer himself. Walter was a tall man, dark like molasses. He had big hands, full lips, and a big nose that had been broken a few times.

Lonzo's sister Shay was there as well as Nisha's sister Shonda. These two ladies were around the same age. Neither of them knew much about boxing, but they did know a good fight when they saw one. And Simpson vs. Turner didn't come close.

"Why don't he *hit him*?" Shonda whined. She didn't address any boxer in particular. From the way things were going, she could've been referring to either one. "All they doing is hugging!"

"They tired," Walter said knowingly. "Both of 'em. Look at the way Simpson got his mouth open. He can get his whole jawbone knocked off, messing around like that."

"Which one's Simpson?" Nisha asked her father.

"Blue trunks," Walter said. He had a soft, smooth voice no one expected to come from his 6'3, 240 pound frame.

"Why don't the other one knock him out?" Nisha wondered.

"He tired too," Walter explained. "Ain't got enough energy to push him off and tag that chin. That's the problem with heavyweights: Got all that muscle, but no cardio. The best you gon' get from guys like this is the first round and the last thirty seconds of the final round."

"I know," Leo interjected. "I like them *little* boxers, the skinny boys."

Nisha chuckled. She knew Leo liked skinny boys in general – not just boxers.

"That's why your man's special," Walter went on. "What Lonzo got, you don't see too much in heavyweights. He got the speed and quickness of a small fighter, and he got that knock out power. He wouldn't be standing there with his mouth open in round three. That boy's a real fighter. Something special."

Walter had a twinkle in his eye that made his daughter smile. Lonzo had a lot of people in his life who believed he could make it to the top, but only a handful of them were *one hundred percent positive*. Nisha knew it was rare to have a father who was so supportive of her man.

"I thought Lonzo never went past two rounds," Shonda said.

"He hasn't," Nisha confirmed.

"But I check him out in the gym all the time," Walter said. "Lonzo can go twelve rounds if he has to. That boy's ready. He would murder either one of these clowns." Walter looked back to the ring in disdain as the referee stepped between the lummoxes for the umpteenth time and pushed them away from each other.

"Come on, break it up, fellas," the ref urged. "These people wanna see a fight! Come on. Let's get it on!"

Nisha and her crew were sitting three rows from the ring, but the stadium was small, and everyone in attendance had a great view. A couple of men near the back got up to leave, and an aging white man looked back at them in surprise.

"You guys leaving?"

"Yeah. This some bullshit," one of the men said.

"My kids fight more than this at home," his friend agreed.

"You can leave if you want," the first gentleman said, "but The Champ's on his way out, and you don't wanna miss that. No sirreee!" He shook his head. "You don't wanna miss that."

The would-be fans looked at each other and decided to wait it out. They took a seat next to the older man.

"You talking about that Lonzo cat, right? I heard he be busting skulls."

"Most definitely," the Caucasian said with a delightful grin. "I've been following him for three years now. He's 16-0. He won all of his fights by *knock out*. Tonight he'll be 17-0. You wait and see."

The men he was talking to wore basketball jerseys with baggy jeans. The first guy was sixty years old, sporting tan slacks with a striped button-down. The trio meshed together as a group because they were all there with a single goal in mind: Everyone in the building wanted to see Alonzo Ingram send some poor sap to Sleepy Land. The posers currently in the ring were holding up the show, like a teacher who stands silently at the front of the classroom, refusing to go on with her lesson plan until the students notice her demeanor and quiet down.

"I wish they would hurry up and bring him out," one of the younger men said. "This some bullshit. These niggas can't fight. *BOOOO!*" he shouted with his hands cupped around his mouth. "I wanna see The Champ! We want Lonzo!"

Nearly everyone in the auditorium heard him, but Nisha was surprised when someone on the opposite side of the ring repeated the yell.

"YEAH! WE WANT THE CHAMP!"

Within seconds the roar reverberated around the stadium as it gradually dawned on the masses that they paid good money for their seats, and they deserved better than what Simpson and Turner had to offer. They wanted quality entertainment, like they had in the eighties; back when kings like Sugar Ray Leonard and the Hitman Hearns gave everything they had on fight night. Those fighters were class acts. They wouldn't disrespect the fans by grappling for round after boring round. No, they wouldn't dare.

"**WE WANT THE CHAMP!**" someone else yelled, and then another, "**WE WANT THE CHAMP!**"

The chant picked up momentum, and soon almost everyone in the stadium was on one accord. They stood and rocked their fists. The referee looked over his shoulder with uncertainty, wondering if there was something he should do to restore order.

"**WE WANT THE CHAMP! WE WANT THE CHAMP!**"

Nisha stood and looked around in amazement. Her father was smiling at her when she returned her gaze to him.

"Oh my God," she breathed.

"How does it feel?" Walter asked. "How does it make you feel, baby girl?"

Nisha didn't know how to put her feelings into words. She felt exhilarated and proud and awestruck at the same time. This is how Lonzo told her it would be. And if he was right about this, maybe he was right about other things too; like wearing a championship belt one day. Lonzo said he would fight for *millions* in the not so distant future. Nisha had never stopped believing in him.

Her smile was ear to ear. "Oh my God," she repeated.

With her eyes wide, she handed Little Lonzo off to her father and quickly made her way down the aisle.

"Where you going?" Leo asked as she scooted by him.

"To see Lonzo," she said, but her voice was barely audible over the three hundred blood-thirsty fans in the arena.

Somewhere near the ring, the final bell rang, putting an end to the Simpson vs. Turner fiasco, and the crowd yelled in earnest – not in approval for the nonsense they just witnessed, but because the bout was over, and there was only one fight left on tonight's card.

"WE WANT THE CHAMP! WE WANT THE CHAMP!"

"I'm going to see Lonzo!" Nisha shouted in Leo's ear.

"They not gon' let you back there!" he yelled back, but Nisha only saw his lips moving.

He didn't know what he was talking about anyway. There were only two people in the auditorium who had Lonzo's heart unconditionally. One of them was the little bundle of joy stirring in Walter's arms. This child's mother was the other. Nisha would be allowed into Lonzo's training room because anyone who tried to stop her would face The Champ's wrath.

And *no one* – not even the sucker Lonzo was scheduled to demolish tonight – wanted any parts of that.

Lanisha Michelle Elder was twenty-six years old. Tonight she wore denim Capris with a blouse that was mostly unbuttoned, revealing cantaloupe-sized breasts concealed by a white tank top.

Nisha's skin tone was a few shades lighter than her father's. She wore her hair in a pony tail on most days. Today it was layered, hanging down to her shoulders. Her eyes were large and dark, seemingly innocent. She thought she resembled her father more than her deceased mother. She was not a thin girl, but no one thought she was fat either. She had shapely hips that garnished as much attention as her perky bosom.

She navigated the underbelly of the arena with no hesitation because the majority of Lonzo's fights took place there; she knew the place like the back of her hand. She encountered quite a few people in the well-lit tunnels but didn't come across any opposition until she neared Lonzo's training room.

"Hey, where you going?" A tall man she didn't recognize stepped forward and blocked her progress with his girth. Nisha noticed the word STAFF stitched on his shirt.

"I'm going to see Lonzo."

He shook his head. "You can't go back there. You'll see him when he gets to the ring."

"I'm his girlfriend," Nisha said. "I always see him before he fights."

"Yeah right, lady," the man told her. "Everybody's Lonzo's girlfriend. Go on now. You need to get back upstairs."

"I'm his baby-mama," she offered, not for the first time a little vexed that she didn't have anything more substantial to identify herself as. One day she would be able to thrust her hand forward and show off a wedding ring. One day...

"I'm sorry, ma'am..."

She looked over the employee's shoulder and spotted someone from Lonzo's camp.

"Trey!" she hollered. "Tell him to let me in."

Trey was another up and coming fighter who worked out with Lonzo at the gym on Belknap. The lanky boxer approached the staff member with a grin.

"Hey, that's Lonzo's girl. Let her in."

"Oh." The guard backed up and stepped to the side. "Sorry about that. Just doing my job. You'd be surprised what kind of stories people come up with."

"It's okay," Nisha told him as she passed. She didn't harbor any ill-will for anyone trying to protect Lonzo, and she didn't question his *Everybody's Lonzo's girlfriend* comment.

Nisha and Trey walked together for twenty paces until they came to a closed door on the right. Trey opened it, and Nisha was hit with a scent that perked her tongue with a taste for war. It was the smell of adhesive tape, Vaseline and a distinct mixture of sweat and adrenaline that made her heart skip a beat.

There were half a dozen people in Lonzo's room. They were all clamoring around The Champ. Nisha's man wore new red trunks with his black Adidas boots laced up tightly. His trainer, Fats, stood before him with a focus mitt on each hand. Lonzo already had a solid game plan for the fight, but Fats always took him through a few combinations before they stepped to the ring.

"Head, head, head," Fats urged, and Lonzo complied with a series of right and left hooks that connected with the mitts in almost a blur.

WHAP! WHAP! WHAP!

"*Body! Body!*" Fats instructed, and Lonzo fed him two half-uppercuts to the desired region.

POP! POP!

Lonzo's cut man watched carefully, while a rapper named Slick stood to the side, looking down at the floor, bobbing his head to a rhythm that was only in his head for now.

The rest of the crew were Fats' assistants. Nisha wasn't sure what their jobs were. Collectively they made up Lonzo's entourage – or his *niggas*, depending on what neck of the woods they were in.

Lonzo's eyes were quick. They darted and settled on his woman as soon as she entered. He lowered his gloves and blew out a pent-up breath.

"Hey, baby."

"Hey," Nisha said, and her smile widened by degrees. *Mmm. Look at my man.*

Alonzo Ingram was 6'1, two hundred and thirty-two pounds of chocolate thunder. He was a heavyweight, like the men who just got booed off the stage, but you could not put Lonzo in the same league as those buffoons.

Nisha's man was dark chocolate with a beautiful bald head that glistened with sweat. His pecs were hard and massive. Fresh off his light workout with Fats, every muscle in his upper body was primed; like dynamite waiting to explode.

Lonzo had thick eyebrows and dark brown eyes. The muscles in his arms and shoulders were delectable. The definition in his six-pack was jaw dropping. His nipples looked ripe for sucking. Nisha felt herself slipping into a daze. She closed her mouth and focused on his eyes.

"What's that?" Lonzo asked. He cocked his head and listened to the uproar upstairs.

"That's for you, baby," Nisha said.

The chants from the crowd were barely audible down in the training room. Everyone listened quietly for a moment. A smile crept to Lonzo's lips.

"Damn, it's like that?"

"What's that they saying?" Fats asked. He went to the doorway and stuck his head out.

Nisha always thought Lonzo's trainer had the most uninventive nickname *ever*, but she couldn't argue with the accuracy. Fats was well over three hundred pounds. Nisha never saw him turn down a meal of any kind.

"They calling for you," she told her boyfriend.

By then everyone could hear the chant clearly. Lonzo nodded with a chuckle. "Is that for real?"

"Aww, that's *tight*!" Slick said as he made his way to the door. He turned back and grinned at Lonzo with a mouthful of gold teeth. "Man, they *is* calling for you! I told you it was gon' be like this one day! I told you!" Slick slapped Lonzo on the shoulder. "I can't wait till I blow up like you. I'ma have a whole crowd cheering for me too, watch. I'm a be just like you, man!"

"Alright, baby, we about to head out," Lonzo told Nisha. He stepped to her and put two padded hands around her waist. He drew her close and she nearly swooned like a southern belle.

"Gimme a kiss for good luck," he said.

"You don't need luck," Nisha replied, but she kissed him anyway. Lonzo's lips were moist and warm. With her, he was as gentle as a teddy bear, but she knew his demeanor was about to change drastically.

"I'll see you in a minute." He let go of her and watched as she backed away.

"In a minute?" Nisha said, her heart thudding.

"In a minute," Lonzo promised, his smile completely gone now.

The crowd was booing again by the time Nisha made it back upstairs. She was confused at first, but she realized the announcer was introducing Lonzo's challenger for the evening. Jimmy Crenshaw was a slightly muscular journeyman from Louisiana. He won more fights than he lost, but he entered the ring a 16-1 underdog.

The crowd didn't stop giving Jimmy the business until someone flipped a switch and a tune they recognized boomed through the loud speakers. Both fighters had the option of coming to the stage with music of their choice, but only Lonzo took advantage. Not only did Nisha's man have his very own song prepared, but Lonzo had the rapper performing live.

Nisha made it to her seat in time to see Slick lead the procession from the tunnel. The rapper wore blue jeans with a black hoodie. He sported a thick, gold chain with a twinkling medallion affixed to it. His song had an up-tempo beat and thudding baseline everyone could get into. His eyes looked menacing, his face set in a sneer. He brought a cordless mic to his mouth and belted the first line of his song, and everyone was immediately electrified.

"Here come The Champ!"

"YEEAAAHHH!"

The screams were so loud, they nearly overpowered the rest of the song, but Nisha had heard it so many times, she could recite it without music. Everyone in the stadium was on their feet. Lonzo emerged from the tunnel with his head down, his eyes low. His trainer followed close behind. The rest of his crew swung towels in the air and pumped their fists to Slick's song.

"Here come The Champ!
Hook! Jab! Knock him out!
Ready to battle? Wanna rumble?
Lonzo's here, boy! Ain't no doubt!
Step in the ring! Raise yo gloves!
Sucka, buck if you ain't scared!
We bringing the ruckus! You better duck, cuz!
Whop, whop, whop! Better watch yo head!"

Slick bounced down the aisle like Tupac in his prime, and the crowd loved it! People started to dance and jump up and down. Somewhere in the middle of the ring, a chump named Jimmy Crenshaw peed in his shorts – just a little bit. No one noticed.

"Here come The Champ!
Run, nigga, run! Sprint like a cheetah!
Cause Lonzo gon' pop 'em, and Lonzo gon' drop 'em!
He gon' buck 'em-buck 'em-buck 'em
Like a nine-millimeter!
Yeah! Here come The Champ!"

The Champ made it to the ring and casually mounted the stage. Fats held the ropes open for him as Lonzo entered his place of worship. He locked eyes with his opponent and began the stare-down. Jimmy Crenshaw avoided eye contact; an automatic sign of weakness. Lonzo bounced on his toes and shook the tension from his arms as the announcer gave the particulars for their fight.

His opponent was 36 years old, hailing from Shreveport. Crenshaw brought to the table a record of 23-18, with nine wins coming by way of knock out. Alonzo "The Champ" Ingram was a 25-year-old Overbrook Meadows native. His record was a pristine 16-0. All sixteen of his wins came via knockout.

Nisha was always nervous before her man's fights, and tonight was no exception. Crenshaw didn't look like much, but Lonzo told her plenty of times that *anyone* could get knocked out if they weren't careful. All it took was one punch thrown at the right moment. When your brain bounces around in your skull, even the strongest man has no control over how his body will respond.

Lonzo's woman remained standing for the entirety of the bout.

The fight began in The Champ's usual fashion. For the first twenty seconds the boxers circled each other, throwing little pop shots to test each other's defenses. Lonzo scored with three out of his first five jabs. Crenshaw's counter punches were slow and telegraphed. Lonzo easily bobbed away or blocked them with his gloves.

"This'll be over quick," Walter told his daughter.

Nisha's heart thudded. She didn't respond.

One minute into the first round, Lonzo was in control of the fight. He bounced on the balls of his feet like Tyson and tagged his opponent's nose at will. The Champ had a way of luring reluctant challengers into mounting an offense. He lowered his hands in a show of confidence, and Crenshaw took the bait.

The journeyman threw a sloppy right hook. Lonzo ducked and came back up with a tremendous body shot that rattled Crenshaw's entire frame, like someone chopping down a tree. Crenshaw grimaced and lowered his elbows to protect his ribs from the second body blow, but Lonzo had no intention of targeting that area again.

With the deftness of a surgeon, The Champ came back upstairs with two stiff jabs and a beautiful left hook that all landed flush.

POP! POP!
WHAP!

The blows stumbled Crenshaw. Sweat sprayed from his face, and the crowd began to shout.

Little Lonzo didn't appear to mind the noise. The baby was nine months old. Nisha sensed he knew when his daddy was getting down.

Big Lonzo clenched his teeth and pressed the attack with another jab and a looping cross. Crenshaw was dazed and confused. He held his gloves by his ears, and the jab slipped between them seamlessly. Expecting a double jab, Crenshaw moved his gloves in front of his face, and Lonzo's cross connected right on the button; the crucial spot between the ear and the forehead. Crenshaw's knees buckled. The crowd gasped.

Before the journeyman could hit the ground, Lonzo growled and stood him up with a brutal uppercut that landed hard on the mouth. In the split second it took Crenshaw's lip to tear and leak, Lonzo finished him off with his signature punch; another deadly uppercut to the temple.

The last blow sounded off like a gunshot, and everyone's eyes grew as large as quarters. The ref rushed in to save the wounded warrior, but there was no need. Lonzo was already backing away as Crenshaw slowly dropped to the canvas. The journeyman landed hard on his butt and slid to his back, with one leg pinned under him at an awkward angle.

"Oh my damn," Leo said and turned away from the carnage.

Here come The Champ!

A conscious man would've responded to the position of his leg right away, but Crenshaw's head rolled to the side. His arms lie limply at dead man angles. He was feeling no pain.

The ref dropped to his knees and threw his hands in the air, waving off the fight with no need for a ten count.

Lonzo thrusts his fists in the air, his mean mug still in place. The crowd responded with a deafening roar.

Nisha closed her eyes and exhaled and took in what felt like her first breath since the fight started.

CHAPTER TWO
TILL THE LAST BELL

The crew went to Pappadeaux after the fight. Lonzo loved to celebrate there after a win, and the staff loved him. They had photos and newspaper clippings of The Champ's exploits posted all over the restaurant. The manager hurried to greet him as soon as he heard they were in the building.

"Hey, Champ!" He grabbed Lonzo's hand and shook it fiercely. "I heard you took out another one! Man I hate I missed it! How was it? You gotta tell me all about it. How many are eating with you tonight? You know I'll take care of you guys. Nothing but the best! How many bottles of wine you want? Huh? Come on, Champ! Tell me about the fight!"

Lonzo laughed and Fats did too. Everyone was in a great mood.

The Champ wore a black, silk shirt with dark slacks and his favorite square-toed dress shoes. His shirt was unbuttoned halfway down his chest, revealing a sexy crease between his smooth pectorals. He brought with him the scent of Versace cologne. Nisha thought her man glowed under the spotlight.

"Aww," he said modestly, "You know how I do, Nick."

"Heard you got him out of there quick," the manager said. "Damn, I hate I missed it! How long was it, Champ? One minute? Two?"

Nick still had a strong grip on Lonzo's hand. The manager's eyes were twinkling. It never ceased to amaze Nisha how people could get so excited about an ass-whooping.

"I don't know." Lonzo shrugged, grinning. "A minute thirty, forty..."

"One minute and *twenty-two seconds*!" Fats clarified. He stepped forward and slapped Lonzo on the back. "Champ took care of business, as usual! I'll put the video on YouTube tomorrow. It was the best left hook I ever seen!"

"That whole combo was sweet," Slick said. He shadowboxed in the restaurant's lobby, mimicking what The Champ did in the ring. At other restaurants, someone might've called the police, reporting an aggressive black gangster. But the manager at Pappadeaux couldn't have been more pleased.

"Aww, man! I can't wait to see it. I'll be stalking your YouTube page all day tomorrow," he told Fats. "Y'all ready to eat? How many you got with you?"

"It's eleven of us," Lonzo replied.

"Great!" Nick said. "That's just great, Champ."

A hostess appeared with a stack of menus in hand. "Would you like a high chair for the baby?" she asked Nisha.

"Yes, please."

"Okay, right this way..." The woman walked away, and the manager finally let go of Lonzo's hand so they could follow her.

"Anything you need Champ, just holler at me!" Nick called after them.

"Thanks." Lonzo put an arm around Nisha's waist and gave her a squeeze. "What you thinking about, shorty?"

"Thinking about you," she said and batted her eyes. "The way you beat up that poor, old man."

"He started it," Lonzo said with a grin. "He hit me first. Everybody saw."

"You don't have no bruises on your face," Nisha noticed.

"What, you wanna take up for him?" Lonzo joked. "Maybe I should beat you up too."

She giggled. "You'd hit a girl?"

"Nah," Lonzo said and lowered his voice. "But I am gon' beat it up tonight. I know that much."

Nisha's heart grew warm, and she felt a shudder in her lower belly. Lonzo always abstained from sex for two weeks prior to a fight because some old fogey told him he needed all of his *manhood* when heading into battle.

Nisha got so desperate the first time he shut her down, she pulled out her phone and researched the topic. She found several scientific sites that disputed the theory.

"Everybody says that's just a superstition," she told him.

"How is it a superstition?" Lonzo had asked. "You know I feel weak after I bust a nut."

"That only lasts for, like an hour," Nisha argued. "We can have sex the day before you fight – or at least two days before."

"*No we can't*! That man told me my balls make my testosterone, and the longer I let sperm build up, the more testosterone I'll have. The more testosterone I have, the more aggressive I'll be. How is that superstition, Nisha? That's basic biology. I don't know what sites you looking at, but I ain't doing it!"

And that was the end of that.

Since then Nisha learned to be patient during their abstinence, but it wasn't easy. Lonzo was always at his sexiest when he trained for a fight. That was when he'd do push-ups and sit-ups all the time. He'd shadow box in the living room and come home from the gym with his wife-beater clinging to his muscles.

"I wish you *would* beat it up," she told him as they followed the hostess.

"You talk shit now," Lonzo muttered, "but you know I'll have you crying."

The shudder descended from Nisha's womb and settled between her legs. "Boy stop, before I drag you to the restroom *right now*."

Their victory meal was wonderful. Nisha lost track of how many diners stopped by their table to congratulate her man. It used to feel weird; being with a local celebrity, but she felt good about it now. She couldn't wait until Lonzo achieved fame on a national level.

"I tell ya," Fats said, sucking the meat out of a crawfish tail, "ain't nobody out there who can hold a candle to you, Lonzo. I keep a close eye on your contenders. You would murder any of 'em."

Fats was Lonzo's trainer slash manager *slash* promoter *slash* personal friend. In the beginning, Nisha questioned giving so many responsibilities to one man. But Lonzo was a good judge of character, and he trusted Fats completely. The two met after Lonzo's first fight. On that day, Fats promised he could get a championship belt around Lonzo's waist, if he adhered to his tutelage. Five years later, the duo was going strong. Lonzo hadn't lost a bout, and he was now within three or four fights of a title shot.

"When am I gon' start making some real money, though?" Lonzo asked. His plate was filled with gutted crab legs and lobster tails.

"You don't have to worry about that," his manager said. Fats was short and fair-skinned, of black and Columbian heritage. He had a pencil thin moustache and scraggily hair that was rapidly receding from the top of his head. Nisha thought his lips protruded from his face too much, like a duck.

"When we win these next couple of fights," he said, "I got some people in Austin who will get us on TV. When we–"

"Cable?" Nisha's dad interrupted.

"Naw, not on cable," Fats said. "*Regular* TV. I'm talking channel four, five or eight. That fight will pay some big chips. And when we win *that* one, they gotta give us a shot at the title."

Slick was a great rapper, but math wasn't his strong suit. After counting on his fingers, he looked up with a smile. "That's three more fights!"

"Once we get on TV, that purse will be a few hundred thou'," Fats informed them. "And when we fight for the title…" He shook his head and wiped sweat from his forehead. "A title fight will be a million or more."

Everyone at the table let that sink in, and then the ruckus broke out.

"Damn, man!"

"A million dollars? No shit?"

"Don't forget about us!"

"Yo, for real," Slick said to Lonzo. "You ain't gon' forget about us, is you? You *gotta* let me roll to Austin with you. I'll take all the curse words out my song to make it good for TV. Hell, I'll write you a *brand new* song. You gon' let me lead you to the ring when you get big, Lonzo – or you gon' hire somebody that's already famous?"

Nisha giggled. Slick's eyes were wide and hopeful, like a bastard waiting for his dad to pop in on his birthday.

"Man, you *know* you coming with me," Lonzo said. "What I look like turning my back on my peeps? When I blow up, shit, we *all* blow up!"

Everyone laughed and held on to Lonzo's words for dear life.

"You already blowing up," Walter said to Slick. "I heard your song on the radio the other day."

Nisha frowned at her father. "Daddy, you don't be listening to those rap stations."

"I like to get my thug on every now and then," Walter said with a smirk. "You was number nine on the countdown," he told Slick. "Even the DJ was singing it; '*Here come The Champ!*'"

Slick cheesed, his gold fronts shimmering. "Yeah, I be hearing it on the radio too sometimes."

"You selling any CD's?" Walter asked.

"I got that song on a mixtape," Slick said. "It get a lot of downloads. Plus my girlfriend put it on Apple Music. *Here Come The Champ* sell for ninety-nine cents. I made two thousand since it came out."

"That's a lot," Nisha said.

"Not really," Slick countered. "But don't none of my other songs be selling like that one. People love Lonzo. I'm trying to get a deal, so I can make some *real* money."

"As long as I'm fighting, you got a job," Lonzo assured him. "You'll probably be the one to forget about me, when Jay Z call yo ass."

"What about me?" Gillespie asked. This was Lonzo's aging cut man. He always seemed foul-tempered, but Nisha learned that was just his way. "You don't never get cut," he told Lonzo. "What I gotta do to hold on to my job?"

Everyone laughed, but Gillespie was serious.

"What you want me to do?" Lonzo asked with a chuckle. "Let somebody hit me?"

"Sometimes," Gillespie said honestly. "Wouldn't hurt."

That brought another round of laughter.

"Look, y'all," Lonzo said and leaned with his elbows on the table. "If y'all down with me now, I'll be down with you when I make it to where I'm trying to go. I got love for everybody at this table. I'm not gon' pull a Hammer and go broke; supporting a whole *gang* of niggas, but I wouldn't never turn my back on y'all."

That settled things. Nisha's heart swelled with pride. Her father stood and stretched his back like a Tom cat.

"Well, I got love for y'all too, but I'm tired; gotta go to bed."

Lonzo checked his watch. "It's only eleven o'clock, Mr. Walter."

"Yeah, Daddy," Nisha said. "The restaurant's closing in an hour. Why don't you stay till then, have some more wine?..."

"Nah, I'm getting old," Walter said. "Y'all have fun. I had a good time tonight. I really appreciate it." He grabbed hold of Lonzo's hand and shook it heartily. "Great job tonight, son. You keep taking care of business, ain't no limit to where you can go."

Lonzo nodded. "Thank you, sir."

Nisha turned and plucked her baby from the high chair. "Daddy, do you mind–"

"Not at all." Walter took the child with no hesitation.

"Hold up," Lonzo said. He stood and gave his son a kiss on the cheek. "See you later, lil man."

The baby grinned and farted politely.

"Thanks, Daddy," Nisha said. "I love you."

"Love you too, pumpkin. See you tomorrow."

"He gon' buck 'em-buck 'em-buck 'em like a nine-millimeter!" Nisha laughed, and Lonzo did too. They were both a little tipsy, feeling good. Lonzo closed the door and locked the deadbolt. Nisha backed him against the door and pressed her body close to his.

"What you say, baby?" he asked.

She looked up at him. "I said you gon' buck 'em-buck 'em-buck 'em like a nine-millimeter." She stood on her tiptoes and kissed him slowly.

His hands slid down her sides and found a home on her hips. She placed her hands on his chest and undid the shirt buttons.

"You like that song, don't you?" he asked.

He palmed her ass with both paws. Nisha's hot lips traced down his chin. She sucked his Adam's apple and nibbled his jugular.

"What girl wouldn't like a song about her man?"

She pulled his shirt off and groped his pecs. She ran her palms down his stomach, loving every ripple of his six-pack. She sucked his collar bone and traced her tongue down the center of his chest. She kissed one nipple while squeezing the other and then switched sides.

Lonzo's throat caught. *"Damn, baby."*

His hands drifted up her sides and caressed her neck. He ran his fingers through her hair. Nisha quickly undid his trousers. They fell to the floor, and Lonzo's manhood pushed against his boxers. She looked into his eyes, and he returned the gaze. She kissed him again. She slipped a hand into his boxers and marveled at the warmth and size of his erection. Lonzo parted his lips, and she sucked his tongue while she massaged him.

He grew steadily in her hand. She sighed heavenly as she dropped to her knees and pulled his boxers down. The sight of his piece made her mouth water. She took the head into her mouth without hesitation. She worked her tongue and jaws while squeezing and stroking the shaft with both hands.

Lonzo's stomach tightened. His fingers disappeared in her hair. He guided her face further down his erection. Within a couple of minutes, she tasted his pre-cum. She swallowed it graciously, savoring every bit of his essence. When he started to pulsate in her mouth, she sucked harder and faster, but he pulled out at the last moment. She looked up at him while his penis throbbed before her nose. Lonzo's breaths were quickened. Her lips were wet.

She gobbled him up again, loving the taste and texture and the feel of each throbbing vein along his shaft. She backed away and stared at his dick. One droplet of his juices lingered at the tip. She licked it off slowly, while watching Lonzo's eyes, fully aware of her seductive prowess.

"You want me to stop?"

Lonzo shook his head but said, "Yeah. For a minute."

She stood. "Alright. How come?"

"I, I got something for you."

She smiled. "What you got for me, big daddy?"

"It's, uh…" He took a deep breath. "I, uh…" He looked around the room. "I can't even get my head together right now. It's supposed to be special."

Her heart fluttered. "You got me something special?"

He nodded. "You know you deserve it."

"Okay." She backed away. "How about I go take a shower and put on something special I got for you? While I'm gone, you can get your head together."

"You got something for me?"

"You know you deserve it."

"Alright," Lonzo said. "Go take your shower. I'll be ready when you get out."

"Okay, baby. It's a date."

Nisha stepped out of the shower ten minutes later. She could hear music when she turned off the water. It was The Isley Brothers *Baby Makin' Music*. She smiled wistfully. Lonzo only put that CD in when he was down for some serious pipe-laying.

She dressed in a new Victoria's Secret outfit she bought two days ago. The lingerie probably would've stayed in the shopping bag if Lonzo lost his fight, but thankfully Lonzo *never* lost his fights. The outfit was mostly red with black trimming. It featured G-string panties, stockings with garters and a half bra that put her puppies on display like never before.

When she exited the bathroom, she caught the scent of raspberry from one of the fragrant candles she kept in the bedroom. Lonzo wasn't a caveman, but he wasn't the kind of guy who went around lighting romantic candles either. That, plus the music, made Nisha feel like she was in for a special night indeed.

Her boyfriend lounged on the bed wearing only his boxers. They locked eyes when she emerged from the bathroom. His gaze intensified, and he mouthed something she didn't hear. On the stereo, Ron Isley crooned about taking his lover way up, past the clouds.

"What'd you say?" Nisha asked.

Lonzo cleared his throat and made it to his feet. "I said you're the most beautiful woman I've ever seen in my life."

She giggled. "I didn't expect that."

"Why not?" He approached her slowly and wrapped his arms around her waist. He kissed the side of her neck and hugged her tightly.

"I don't know." Nisha spoke softly in his ear. "I guess I expected something more, you know, *freaky.*"

He backed away smiling. He eyed her cleavage and raised an eyebrow. "Well, I also think you're quite tittylicious."

She laughed.

He spun her around slowly. "Quite bootylicious, too."

"Which do you like more?" Nisha asked when they locked eyes again.

"I love that you're such a good woman," Lonzo said. Again, that wasn't a bad response, but Nisha's man wasn't a hopeless romantic.

"What's up with all the lovey-dovey?"

He chuckled. "You don't like that kind of stuff?"

"You know I do. I'm just, curious."

"I can't believe your pops didn't tell you."

"Tell me what?"

"I thought y'all were so close," Lonzo went on. "I asked him not to tell you, but I thought he would anyway."

"Tell me what?" she asked again, her heart starting to quicken.

Lonzo raised his hand, revealing a ring box. Nisha knew this day would come *eventually,* but that didn't lessen the surprise. She brought a hand to her mouth. Her eyes glistened.

"Oh my God, are you for real?"

"I wouldn't play about this." He opened the box, revealing a rock so big it had to be a cubic zirconia.

"Is that, is that real?" she gasped.

"Course it's real."

She shook her head, her eyes watering. "But we, how, how can you afford that?"

"I got a loan," Lonzo said. "The owner of the jewelry store; he helped me out. I told him I'd pay him back after the fight. I made seven thousand tonight. I'm paying this ring off tomorrow."

"But, what, what about the bills?" Nisha asked. They were always behind on something, sometimes multiple bills at the same time. The electric company had been threatening termination for two weeks. It was a wonder the lights were still on.

"We gon' be alright," Lonzo promised. "Now is you gon' take this ring, or not? I already asked your daddy for his blessing, and now I'm asking you: Nisha, will you marry me?"

The tears spilled from her eyes. She nodded.

He grinned. "I can't hear you, baby."

"Yes, Lonzo! Yes, I'll marry you! You know I will!"

"That's more like it." He plucked the ring from the box. Nisha's fingers were trembling badly, but he managed to slip it on her third finger. The ring had a gold band with a princess diamond in the center and two smaller diamonds nestled on either side. Together, the three diamonds produced a dazzling sparkle, even in the sparse lighting. Right away the ring was Nisha's most prized possession.

"Do it fit?"

Nisha nodded absently.

"It's too big," Lonzo said. He worked it back and forth on her finger. "It's too big, ain't it?"

"A little," she admitted. She wiped her eyes with her free hand.

"I'll take it tomorrow to get it sized up," Lonzo said. "I don't want that bad boy to *ever* fall off your hand."

"It won't," Nisha promised. "I love you so much!" She wrapped him up in the biggest hug imaginable. "I love you so much, Alonzo."

"I love you too, baby." He hugged her back. His embrace was like a warm security blanket. "I can't wait to move you out of this shithole," he said. "I'ma get you a big house in Plano or Dallas, or wherever you want to live."

Nisha looked him in his eyes hopefully.

"Our baby is gonna go to some *good* schools," Lonzo said. "He's going to learn something. He ain't gon' drop out like I did. He gon' graduate and go to college too. All our kids will."

Nisha never knew what it was like to be overwhelmed with joy, but Lonzo's words put her on cloud nine.

"Do you like your ring?" he asked. "Do you really like it?"

"Yes, baby! I love it."

She went to the bathroom so she could admire it under the brighter lights. She held her hand up and watched her reflection in the mirror. In all honesty, she didn't think she was worthy of such a treasure.

Lonzo followed her into the restroom. She watched him in the mirror as he touched and then groped her ass in earnest. His hands moved from her waist to her belly and then up to her chest. He pulled her to him until her shoulder blades rested on his chest. He kissed under her ear while he fondled her breasts.

"I still like these better," he said.

Nisha threw her head back on his shoulder. "I know you do, baby."

He slipped a hand under her bra while the other inched down her stomach and disappeared in her panties. He caressed her mound tenderly, parting the lips with his middle finger.

"You so wet, baby."

"I know," she breathed.

"Come on."

He took her hand and led her to the bedroom. He flipped the light switch, but they still had a little illumination from the flickering candles. He slipped off his boxers and took a seat on the bed. Nisha slid out of her panties and crawled on top of him. She straddled his lap, and they kissed, more passionately than she ever remembered.

Lonzo lie flat on his back and stared up at her longingly. Nisha raised her hips and inhaled deeply as she took him into her. She could never take his full length, but she tried her best. Lonzo's manhood was like a lightning rod, sending slivers of electricity down every extremity, all the way to her fingers and toes.

Nisha gripped his chest as she rode him, undulating her stomach and hips like a serpent. She had her first eruption within a couple of minutes. Lonzo rolled her over, and he was still bone hard. He entered again, and her whole body shuddered. She never thought she could experience complete happiness and absolute pleasure at the same time.

"Are you crying?"

She said, "No," but then she felt a tear slide into her ear.

"I told you I was gon' have you crying," Lonzo said with a grin. He planted his hands on the mattress and lifted his upper body. He looked down at her while he worked his hips, stirring her juices.

"You not, *uhh*. You not so tough," she whispered. "I can make you cum right now, if I wanted."

Lonzo shook his head. "Nuh uhn. If you couldn't do it while you was on top, you can't – Aww. *Shiiiit*..."

Nisha dug her heels in the mattress and threw it back at him with perfect timing.

Lonzo's eyes ran out of focus. His erection throbbed, and his strokes became more and more erratic. "That ain't, *oh*... That ain't fair..."

"I know you got another one in you," she said with a wicked smile.

Lonzo's arms trembled, and gradually he gave up the fight against gravity. He stared into his woman's eyes when they were chest to chest. "Alright. So you won round one..." He panted lightly. "But I ain't through. We still, we still got eleven rounds to go. You down?"

"Till the last bell," Nisha promised. "Forever, baby."

CHAPTER THREE
BLOODLINE

On fight night Lonzo and Nisha were on top of the world. But after a couple of weeks, they settled into the groove of their *regular* lives, which was nothing to jump up and down about. For his day job, Lonzo worked in a refrigerated warehouse. His duties included driving a forklift, stocking products and unloading the delivery trucks.

Nisha worked as a pharmacy tech for the only black-owned pharmacy in Overbrook Meadows. Lonzo made fifteen dollars an hour, and Nisha made two dollars less than that. Their combined income was enough to eat, pay the bills, and raise a baby as best they could, but it was by no means an ideal situation.

Lonzo Jr. was growing fast, and their apartment was getting more cramped by the day. And Lonzo's car was on its last leg. The transmission was noticeably slipping each time he drove it. The repairs cost $2,800, which was more than the old Buick was worth.

The bill collectors were constantly ringing their phone. It seemed the only time Lonzo and Nisha could relax for a minute was when Lonzo had a fight. In the early days, Lonzo was lucky to get a couple thousand for his time in the ring, but now he was getting five to ten thousand a pop. That kind of money went a long way in easing their financial woes, but it wasn't enough for Lonzo to quit his day job. Not yet anyway.

Nisha woke up early on a Tuesday morning and ironed her work clothes while she fed the baby. She took a shower and started on a breakfast of bacon, eggs and grits. She heard Lonzo get out of bed when the bacon started to crackle. The Champ entered the kitchen twenty minutes later, freshly showered and dressed in his work uniform.

"Hey, baby." Nisha took his plate to the table and gave him a kiss on the jaw when he sat down. "How'd you sleep?"

He shrugged and sighed. He stuck a whole bacon strip in his mouth and gnawed on it vacantly.

Nisha sat across from him with the baby in her arms. Lonzo was as handsome as ever, but his demeanor made her heart sigh. If he used drugs, she would think his low eyes and lack of energy was indicative of marijuana. But Lonzo was completely sober. It was exhaustion eating away at him like termites.

"You going to the gym today?"

He shook his head. "Can't do it. Too tired. When I get off, I'm coming home and going to bed."

"When's your next fight?"

"February 7th."

The date was November 1st.

"You got three months. Why you been hitting the gym so hard lately?"

"I'm not working out," Lonzo said. "It's Fats. He worried about this next dude I'm fighting. He want me to watch a bunch of videos, but I can't hardly stay awake after work. Training is one thing, but sitting there watching fights..." He sighed and rubbed his eyes.

No further explanation was needed. Nisha knew her fiancé wasn't the brightest student in the world. Lonzo lost interest in school in the ninth grade when his math teacher introduced him to Algebra. He made it to his sophomore year before dropping out, but as far as aptitude tests were concerned, Lonzo's education level peaked in the eighth grade.

One would think he would be a better student of boxing, and he was, in some ways. Anything Fats wanted to teach him while they were on their feet was good. But whenever he sat Lonzo down and started talking for too long, it began to feel too much like school.

"Who you fighting next?" Nisha wondered.

"Cat named Michael Veston," Lonzo muttered.

"Is he good?"

"He a'ight. Toe to toe, he ain't got nothing for me. But he tricky. He be doing some stuff Fats wants me to pay attention to;

some stuff to make his opponents get tired fast. Plus he got real good defense. Fats say he won't fight me straight up. He'll try to rope-a-dope me."

Nisha knew a lot about boxing because her father was a contender when he was young. The rope-a-dope strategy was invented by Muhammad Ali and used successfully against a brutal puncher named Big George Foreman. Possibly knowing he couldn't beat him in a normal fight, Ali kept his back on the ropes for round after round. He leaned away from the majority of Foreman's head punches and didn't start fighting back until Big George was visibly fatigued. Ali won that fight by K.O. He later called Foreman a "dope" for falling for the strategy.

"You too smart for that," Nisha told her man.

"I know," Lonzo said. "But Fats said I never been in the ring with somebody who won't fight back. He don't know how I'll react."

Nisha didn't know either. Lonzo was all about *show time*. If Veston was a smart fighter, he'd find a way to exploit that.

"What's his record?"

"19-4," Lonzo said. "He only got three knockouts."

Those numbers made Nisha's stomach turn. Lonzo never made it past round two, but Veston won sixteen fights by decision.

"I think you need to watch those tapes," she said. "Why don't you take some time off work? I'll try to work some overtime to make up for it."

"Ain't that much overtime in the world," Lonzo said knowingly.

"If you take two days off a week for the next month–"

"Bullshit," Lonzo said. "You got any idea how much overtime you'd have to work to cover two days of my pay – for a whole month?"

Nisha knew the math didn't add up.

"I wouldn't never see you," he said. "The baby wouldn't see you neither. And ain't yo arm still hurting?"

Nisha reached for her wrist instinctively. It didn't hurt today, but she had a nagging pain that came and went. The doctors couldn't figure it out. Nisha tried to forget about it whenever it wasn't hurting.

"Your arm could fall off any minute," Lonzo teased.

She shook her head grinning. "Well, it's got to be *something* we can do."

"It is," Lonzo said. "I go to work. And if I ain't too tired when I get off, I'll go to the gym. When it's time to start training, I'll make it work like I always do."

"I know you always do," Nisha said. "But sometimes I don't feel like *I'm* doing enough."

"You do plenty," he assured her. "You make me happy."

"Real happy?"

He smiled for the first time that morning. "I'm real happy, baby. Trust me."

Nisha believed what Lonzo said about her making him happy, but she wanted to do something to let him know how much she appreciated all the sacrifices he made for the family. Without spending money, her options were limited. She hoped surprise fellatio would relieve some of his stress.

When he went to the bedroom to fetch his gym bag, she pulled him into the bathroom and took a seat on the toilet lid. She guided him between her legs and unbuckled his britches. Lonzo offered minimal resistance.

"Whuh, what's going on?"

"Nothing, baby. Just stand there." She pulled down his pants and boxers at the same time.

"Wait, baby. I gotta, I gotta go to work."

"This will only take a second."

By then Lonzo was getting hard, but he was only halfway there. Nisha took him into her mouth completely, which was something she couldn't do when he reached critical mass.

"Whoa, baby. This is, I gotta..."

"Mmmm mmmm." She worked her neck and cupped his balls, and Lonzo was soon poking the back of her throat.

He grunted. "But I, we ain't got time, baby."

She stopped sucking long enough to tell him, "We don't have to get back in bed, Lonzo. I'm doing this for you. And then you can go."

She swallowed him up again, and he shuddered.

"You, you don't wanna have sex?" he asked.

She shook her head. "Nnnn nnnn."

"I can, I can cum? It's okay?"

She nodded. "Mmm hmm."

"Aww, shit, well, that, that's just fine," Lonzo said, and Nisha had to stifle her laughter.

He placed his hands on her head and worked his hips like he wanted to, and the deed was done in less than ninety seconds. Nisha spat rather than swallowed, and Lonzo left for work with a dopey grin.

Before Nisha left the house, she got a call from her sister Shonda.

"Hello?"

"Hey, girl. You still at home?"

"Yeah..."

"I can't watch Baby Lonzo today," Shonda said. "Something came up."

Nisha's heart sank. "What? What came up?"

"Blue came over here last night," Shonda explained. "He still here. He say he gon' stay all day."

Nisha shook her head in disappointment. Blue was Shonda's on-again-off-again boyfriend of four years.

"I thought he was in jail."

"He got out last night," Shonda informed her.

"So you just gon' lay up with him all day?"

"He *just* got out," Shonda said. "You know how it is."

"It's almost seven-thirty. Why you call me five minutes before I'm about to walk out the door?"

"I'm sorry. I'll watch him tomorrow."

Nisha sighed. "Don't you watch three more kids over there? I thought you was trying to start a daycare business or something."

"I cancelled them, too. None of them was tripping – except you."

"That's cause you leaving me hanging over some *dick*," Nisha said. "That's not good business, Shonda. You ought'a be ashamed of yourself."

"Yeah, whatever. Bye, girl. I'm sorry." She disconnected.

Nisha fumed for a few seconds and then called her father.

"Hello?"

"Hey, Daddy."

"Baby girl. What's going on?"

"Shonda just called and said she can't watch Baby Lonzo today. Can you keep him for me? I gotta go to work."

"Sure," Walter said. "What time will you be here?"

"In about twenty minutes."

"Alright, Pumpkin. I'll be here."

"Thanks, Daddy."

Nisha hung up only moderately relieved. Her father was a lifesaver, but Walter lived all the way in Arlington; versus Shonda who lived right around the corner from the pharmacy. Nisha called her boss and told him she'd be late.

Walter still lived in the house Nisha grew up in. It was a modest three-bedroom flat with a big front yard and two sprawling acres in the back. Her dad bought the house in 1987. He paid cash for it, using the winnings from a successful boxing career that spanned a decade and a half.

When he was a fighter, Nisha's dad was known as Walter "The Sledgehammer" Elder. He was the first boxing celebrity from Overbrook Meadows. A few older restaurants and coffee shops in the area still had photos on their walls from his days of yore.

He was a skilled fighter, but it seemed he was always one step away from glory. When he was 24, he almost made it to the

Olympics in Montreal, but he was beaten out by a scrappy, young slugger named Michael Spinks. Six years later Walter finally got a chance to fight for the heavyweight title, and he was knocked out by Larry Holmes, a man now regarded as one of the greatest boxers in history.

Without ever wearing a championship belt, Walter was pleased with the way his life turned out. He got out of the sport before succumbing to DP (dementia pugilistica), and he invested his money wisely. He was 59 years old now, and he never had to work another day in his life. He went to the gym regularly to keep up with the new prospects, but he wasn't interested in training or managing fighters. Being a spectator was fine with him.

Walter took his grandson from Nisha's arms and grinned at the expression on the baby's face.

"How many months is he now?" Walter asked. "Ain't it about time to get him some boxing gloves?"

"No it is *not*," Nisha said with a smile. She stood in her father's doorway while her car idled in the driveway. "He's ten months. Who said he's gonna be a boxer anyway?"

Her father laughed. "No it is *not*," he mocked. "Look at you; acting like you don't want your boy to be a fighter."

"What makes you think I do?"

"Like you got a choice."

Nisha shook her head. "I don't care what he wants to be, Daddy. It's his choice. But I won't push boxing on him when he gets big. For all you know, he might wanna be a dancer."

"Naw. This baby ain't gon' be no dancer. Look, his feet aren't good for dancing."

Nisha tried to look, but she remembered Baby Lonzo had booties on.

"You can't even see his feet."

"It don't matter," Walter said. "This boy's got boxing in his blood. His daddy's a boxer, and his granddaddy's a boxer. It's his destiny. Just like you going with Lonzo is your destiny."

She cocked an eyebrow.

"I know you don't believe in stuff like that. But I know what I'm talking about."

"You told me *not* to go out with Lonzo," Nisha recalled.

"I know. And you defied me – because it was destiny."

Nisha laughed. "I gotta go, Daddy. And I didn't defy you. Stop saying that."

"It turned out for the best. I was wrong to try to come between you two in the first place. I understand that now."

"Okay, Dad. I'll see you later."

"Alright. Bye, Pumpkin."

Nisha got back in her car and saw she was supposed to be at work one minute ago. This was actually better than having ten minutes to spare, because she would've sped down the highway trying to make it in time. But when you're guaranteed to be late, you might as well take your time and drive safely.

She listened to a slow jam station on the way to the pharmacy and thought about when she first met Lonzo. Her dad was right about her not believing in fate, but Nisha couldn't deny there was something special about her and Lonzo's relationship from the very beginning.

The year was 2013. Nisha was 19 years old, fresh off a recent breakup with her high school sweetheart who decided to join the marines so he could help make this world a better place. Nisha was all for tracking down foreign terrorists, but she was deeply in love with Ellis, and his departure hit hard.

After a few months of sulking around the house, Walter finally talked her into going to see a boxing match with him. Her dad was mainly interested in a middleweight named "Paco" Serrano, but Nisha couldn't help but notice a dark chocolate warrior who entered the ring with only two fights under his belt. Lonzo was ridiculously fine, even back then, and his flashy style and ring dominance was a big turn on, especially for a boxing fan like Nisha.

"Daddy, do you know him?" she asked her father.

Lonzo had just won his third fight by first round knockout, but Walter wasn't impressed.

"Yeah, I know him. He trains down at the gym with Paco."

"He's good."

Walter noticed her demeanor and shook his head. "He's not all that. He has potential. He *could* be a good fighter, one day. But he's a hot head. And he's as dumb as a post. Got too much street in him. He'll probably do a driveby when he leaves here tonight. He's no good, baby girl."

But unbeknownst to Walter, his discouragement only made Nisha more interested in the young man who had enough balls to call himself "The Champ" despite not wearing a championship belt. Nisha kept up with her father's comings and goings for the next week, and when Walter returned to the gym, Nisha showed up unexpectedly a few minutes later. Her story was that she couldn't find her cellphone and maybe she left it in her father's car. Walter didn't buy the ruse. He tried to cut her off when she walked through the doors.

"Baby girl. What are you doing here?"

"I can't find my cellphone," Nisha said, looking around the gym. "I was gonna ask if you saw it, or if I left it in your car."

"Why didn't you call to ask me?" Walter wondered.

"I just told you, I can't find my cellphone."

"You coulda called from the house phone. I can't see you coming all the way over here to ask me that. And..." He looked around. "Who are you looking for?"

"Nobody, Daddy. I'm just checking the place out. You act like you don't want me here."

"I brought you here plenty of times," Walter said. "I'm just–"

"Hey, Walt!" One of the trainers wanted help spotting a weightlifter. "Can you give me a hand over here?"

Walter turned in that direction. "I, hold, hold on, Mac." He almost didn't go. He looked back at Nisha and sighed. "I don't have your phone, honey."

"Okay."

Walter waited. "So, uh, are you going home?"

"In a minute," she said, looking around. It was the middle of summer, and she was dressed for the occasion in short shorts and a little tee shirt that had the word "*SPOILED*" sprawled across her chest. She had legs and boobs for days. Half the men in the gym were peeping her out of the corner of their eyes.

Walter shook his head. "Nisha, what are you doing?"

"Nothing, Daddy." At that moment a sound emanated from her purse. Her mouth fell open as she dug for it with a surprised look on her face. "Oh," she said, producing her cellphone. "Here it is."

Walter brought a hand to his face and rubbed his forehead. "I'll be right back," he said and went to help with the weightlifter.

Nisha told her friend she'd call her back and went on the prowl. She found her man-to-be sparring with another boxer. She stood innocently next to the ring and caught Lonzo's attention right away. The Champ had on a tank top with shorts. He looked very nice. Nisha smiled at him, and he smiled back.

And then Lonzo did something that should've let her know everything her father said about him was true: He turned back to his sparring partner and started to *fight* him, literally. His partner complained about the hard blows to the body, and when Lonzo hit him in the mouth a couple of times, his friend had had enough.

"Man, what the hell you doing?" he asking, rubbing his swollen lip with his glove.

"What?" Lonzo said. "What's the problem?"

"Nigga, you *hit* me. We *sparring*, Lonzo! Why you hitting me like that?"

"Man, a fight's a fight," Lonzo quipped. He checked to make sure Nisha was still watching. She was.

"This ain't no fight, you dumb ass nigga!"

Lonzo's face darkened, and he went after his friend again. "What you say, cuz? What the hell you call me?"

The other guy hastily got out of the ring. "Say, leave me alone, Lonzo. Why you starting shit?"

"I'm saying a fight is a goddamned *fight*," Lonzo spat. "Keep yo pussy ass out the ring, if you can't take it!"

Lonzo glared at his partner until the man disappeared from sight, and then he turned back to Nisha. He approached her and leaned with his elbows on the ropes.

"What's up, shorty?"

She shrugged. "Nothing. What's up with you – besides the fact that you don't know how to spar?"

He chuckled. He had a nice smile and beautiful brown eyes. "How you figure that?"

"You not supposed to hit your sparring partner in the face like that," Nisha said, "unless you wanna spar by yourself from now on."

"Huh." Lonzo smirked. "Like you know something about it."

"I know a lot about it. What you think, I'm just some hoochie who came in here to see some hot guys?" That was pretty close to the truth, but Lonzo didn't know that. "My daddy was a fighter. I probably know more about boxing than you."

He grinned. "Oh yeah? Who's your daddy?"

Nisha liked the way he said that. She had her first sexual fantasy about him right then.

Who's your daddy?

Ohuh! You baby!

"Walter's my daddy," she said.

Lonzo's eyes widened, and he straightened his posture. "For real? Ay, yo, your pops is the real deal. He a legend. He fought all kinds of greats back in the day. I wanna be like him when I grow up. Real talk. Except I'm gonna be a champion – no disrespect."

"It's cool," Nisha said. "I saw your fight the other day. You're 3-0. You got a long way to go before you can fight for the title."

"You saw me fight?" Lonzo said and smiled brightly. "I wish I woulda knowed that. I wouldn't have hit my sparring partner in the mouth, if I knew you already seen me fight."

She giggled. "So, you did that for me?"

He shrugged. "If I was a peacock, I'd show you my feathers. But I ain't got no feathers. I got these." He held up his fists.

Nisha liked his analogy, and she could tell he wasn't as dumb as her father said he was. Lonzo was rough around the edges, and he was also confident, strong and handsome. And the fact that he beat up someone to get her attention was also a turn on – even though Nisha knew it shouldn't be.

Walter searched for his daughter when he finished helping the trainer, but by then it was too late. When he found Nisha, she was with Lonzo; saving the roughneck's number in her cell.

Walter didn't approve of his daughter's new friend, but he wasn't the type to interfere with his children's relationships. Nisha was nineteen years old, a grown woman by anyone's standards, and she had to figure life out on her own.

And thankfully things didn't turn out as Walter had envisioned. Once Lonzo started training with Fats, he gained more discipline and respect for the sport. Not only did he continue to win fights, but he became a technical boxer, a smart fighter, even.

Lonzo still had problems in the streets in the early days. He was raised poor, and hustling had always been a part of his life. As an adult, Lonzo sold drugs and did some dirty work for the most notorious crime boss in the city. But after his son was born, he settled down and got what he called a "lame" job.

Not only did Walter take back all the bad things he said about The Champ, he was one of Lonzo's staunchest supporters. Nisha didn't know if she and Lonzo were *destined* to be together, but she did believe he was the only man for her.

Their life wasn't perfect. There were plenty of trials and tribulations over the last six years. But each time, they came through the storm stronger. There was nowhere left for them to go but up.

CHAPTER FOUR
TOYA AND DR. COATES

Dr. Thomas Coates owned and operated the only black-owned pharmacy in Overbrook Meadows. His store was located on the south side of town. This wasn't necessarily a good location, considering the gangs and drugs and rampant crime in the neighborhood. But the south side was a predominantly black area, so Dr. Coates was in the perfect spot, as far as his customer base was concerned.

Nisha went to a trade school for four months to become a pharmacy tech. She thought about getting a job at one of the larger drug stores, but when she interviewed for her position, Dr. Coates was friendly and eager to have her on board. He told her bluntly he would only hire a black person in his pharmacy because, "The white man never tried to help me, so I'm not doing anything to help them."

Nisha probably should've been turned off by his reverse racism, but she wasn't. At the time, she thought Dr. Coates was a pioneer of sorts. He was a role model and an entrepreneur. He was a black man with a doctorate. Given her background, that was as rare as a white track star. She was honored to take the job. She felt like she was going to work for Charles Drew. Her opinion of Dr. Coates diminished a little over the years, but she never felt the need to seek employment elsewhere.

She pulled into the parking lot twenty-two minutes late for work. She didn't rush to get to the time clock, because there was no such thing at Dr. Coates' pharmacy. There were only three employees in the whole building (the pharmacist and his two techs), and Dr. Coates kept up with attendance himself. When

Nisha walked through the doors, he looked at his watch and then back up at her; indicating her tardiness had been noted.

"I'm sorry I'm late." Nisha pulled on her white lab coat as she walked.

"It's okay," Dr. Coates said. He stood behind the register counting the money in the till. The doctor was tall and dark-skinned. He kept his head shaved bald. He was fifty years old, but he could pass for forty. He had thin eyebrows and no beard or moustache.

The pharmacy wasn't very large; less than half the size of an average Walgreens. Nisha stepped behind the counter and deposited her purse in a cubby hole. Her co-worker Toya was busy filling prescriptions. Nisha sidled next to her and got started on the same task.

"Morning," Toya said.

"Hey," Nisha said. "Sorry I'm late."

"Your sister flaked out on you again?"

"Yeah," Nisha said with a sigh.

"I told you; you need to get you a *real* babysitter. Family will treat you any kind of way."

Toya was short in stature, high-yellow with big lips and a slim waist. She wore bright, red lipstick but no other makeup. Her hair was braided to her scalp in eight neat cornrows.

"I tried to find one when I first had him," Nisha said. "Remember? Them people wanted a thousand dollars a month to watch a newborn. That's what I make in two weeks."

"Yeah, but them people are guaranteed to be there every day," Toya countered. "I don't depend on my family for shit."

Nisha didn't say anything. It was fine if Toya wanted to live her life that way, but Nisha depended on her family for a lot of things. And Shonda only flaked out on her once a month, tops.

"Are you staying late today to make up your time?" Toya asked.

"I need to," Nisha said. She lowered her voice because Dr. Coates was standing less than twenty feet away. "Actually, I was gonna ask for some overtime."

Toya chuckled. "Good luck."

"He let you work overtime when your car was in the shop."

"Yeah, and you know why," Toya said, referring to one of the darker secrets at the pharmacy.

Dr. Coates was a good man, in most aspects of life, but he had a glaring flaw. Nisha didn't know if he was a sex addict or simply a horn-dog, but their boss was often unfaithful to his wife.

Nisha knew of a few customers Dr. Coates dated, and she knew that he'd slept with Toya a few times. They never flirted openly. Toya told her their boss would wait until the two of them were alone before he made any advances.

Nisha lost a lot of respect for Dr. Coates when she first learned of his exploits, but she decided it was none of her business. Rumor had it his wife was a frigid bitch who knew about and even condoned the affairs, so she wouldn't have to sleep with the pharmacist herself.

As far as Toya's assertion that Dr. Coates slept with her in exchange for overtime, Nisha didn't know what to think about that. She couldn't take Toya's word for it, because Toya was a known whore herself. Nisha was pretty sure Toya would've called a lawyer long ago, if she had such a clear case of sexual harassment.

"If that's the only way I can get some overtime," Nisha muttered, "I guess I'm not getting it then."

"Why you need overtime anyway?" Toya wondered. "Lonzo's in the papers all the time. What's wrong, he won't share none of that money with his *wifey*?"

This was another example of why it was hard to believe what Toya said about Dr. Coates: Nisha's co-worker was unfailingly messy. Plus Toya had a crush on Lonzo. She was constantly looking for a dent in Nisha's relationship, so she could swoop in and possibly score with The Champ.

Before Lonzo proposed to her, Toya would say things like, "How come you and Lonzo ain't getting married?" and "You had his baby, but he still won't marry you?" or "Are you sure Lonzo's not gon' leave you when he makes it big?"

Nisha thought the hateful remarks would stop now that she and Lonzo were properly engaged, but no such luck.

"Lonzo takes care of me just fine," she replied. "I wanna work overtime so he can cut back on his work hours and train more."

"I know it's hard for him," Toya said. "I bet Lonzo wishes he was single sometimes, so he could focus more on his boxing."

Nisha's face grew warm and her nostrils flared. "I bet you better keep my man's name out your mouth."

"Calm down," Toya said without looking over at her. "I'm just saying..."

"Yeah, and I told you to watch your mouth," Nisha growled. "We gotta go through this every day? Why don't you get it through your head? Lonzo don't like you. You'll never have him. So just stop."

Toya smacked her lips. "Girl, please. Don't nobody want your man."

"Then act like you don't," Nisha advised her. She fumed for a few minutes before the stress dissipated. There was no point in worrying about Dr. Coates' infidelities or Toya's petty comments. Boys will be boys and hoes will be hoes. That's just the way the world works.

Nisha waited until Dr. Coates went into his office, before she approached him about the overtime. He looked up from a stack of papers when she entered.

"Hey, Nisha. What took you so long?"

"Huh? What are you talking about?"

"You want to ask me about working overtime, right?"

Nisha knitted her eyebrows, but she wasn't surprised. The pharmacy was small, and Dr. Coates was a notorious eavesdropper. She wondered what else he'd heard.

"You and Toya still not getting along?" he asked.

"Umm..." That question sounded loaded.

"Close the door," the pharmacist suggested.

Nisha did so.

"Have a seat."

Nisha did that too. Dr. Coates' office was cramped. There were papers and folders and medical journals covering every inch of available space. Nisha sat with her hands in her lap. The doctor leaned back and crossed his legs.

"Is it the same thing?" he asked. "You still think she's after your boyfriend?"

Nisha had been at the pharmacy for over a year, and this issue had been going on for almost that long.

"It's not a problem," she said. "She just says the wrong thing sometimes."

Dr. Coates nodded. "How are things going with you and Lonzo anyway?"

"Things are great." She looked down at her engagement ring and smiled. "Except his work schedule," she added. "That's what I wanted to talk to you about. I wanted to know if I could work on my off days for the next few weeks, so he can take a couple of days off his job and do more training."

Dr. Coates listened politely and then asked, "How's his boxing career going? I don't keep up with his fights as much as I'd like to."

"He's still undefeated." Nisha beamed. "He's been working 40 hours a week the whole time. It's not always easy, but we manage. Except now that he's getting his name out there, the competition's getting better. He needs to train more. More than he usually does."

Her boss nodded. "You're a good woman, Lanisha. You remind me of what my wife was like, in the early days. She made a lot of sacrifices when I couldn't work because of school."

And you repay her by boning Toya, Nisha thought, but of course did not say.

"You know..." Dr. Coates sighed. "You know CVS is kicking my ass. Walgreens too."

Nisha figured that was the case.

"We're in a recession," Dr. Coates reminded her. "Mom and Pop operations like this are going under right and left. Do you know the only thing saving us?"

Nisha didn't.

"No direct competition," Dr. Coates said. "The closest CVS is sixteen miles away. A lot of people in this neighborhood don't have the transportation to go there. Most of the ones who do have cars, don't want to waste the gas money."

Nisha nodded.

"But all of that's about to change," Dr. Coates went on. "Did you see they're breaking ground on Riverside and Berry?"

Nisha nodded. She had seen the construction site.

"Guess what's going to be there," Dr. Coates said.

Nisha didn't have to guess.

"A goddamned CVS," the pharmacist grunted. "It'll be open in six months – two miles away from us."

Nisha opened her mouth to say something, but he wasn't done talking.

"And what do you think is gonna happen to us?" the doctor asked. "I'll tell you what. We're going belly up, like the rest of the small-timers. We're barely making it as it is. There's no way we can compete with CVS, especially when all of these nappy-headed niggers go over there and see they sell *menthol cigarettes* and candy and chips and magazines with the *big booty hoes* on the cover. We can't compete with that.

"Hell, I'll probably end up going over there to fill out an application my damn self. And then *I'll* work for the white man. He already has everything else. He might as well have my ass too."

Nisha had to fight to keep her jaw from dropping. Dr. Coates was a bigot, that much was obvious, but most people didn't know he was equally prejudiced against his own people. He hated poor, uneducated blacks. He sided with the police whenever they murdered a crackhead or a gang banger.

Nisha started to rise from her seat, but Dr. Coates surprised her with his next comment.

"But I'm going to let you work overtime."

Her eyes widened. "Really?"

"Yes, Lanisha. You can come in on both of your days off, if you want."

She grinned broadly. "Thank you, Dr. Coates! I really appreciate that."

"It's alright," the pharmacist said. "I'm doing this because I like you, Nisha."

Her smile slipped a little.

"You remind me of what my wife was like," he repeated, "in the early days. Young and vibrant... And perky." His eyes descended to her breasts and lingered there for a moment.

Or maybe Nisha imagined it. What she knew for sure was that her overtime had been approved, and there was no need to talk to this hateful man anymore.

Maybe it was a good thing CVS was going to run them out of business. Lonzo should be getting some real money by then. Even if he wasn't, it was time for Nisha to find another job anyway. This pharmacy was saturated with enough innuendos to get somebody pregnant.

"Thank you," she said and quickly left the office.

At lunchtime Dr. Coates went to run errands, leaving Nisha and Toya in charge until he got back. The girls had their problems, but they didn't argue all the time; not at all when they weren't discussing Lonzo.

After lunch the UPS man came by with a delivery. Toya flirted with him, as was her custom, and once again he didn't give her any play.

"He prolly gay," she said when he left.

"If he don't want Toya, he *must* be gay," Nisha teased.

The delivery man left them a stack of envelopes as well as a dozen or more boxes, ranging from small to medium size. The ladies got started on stocking the products.

"I'm not saying every man who don't want me is gay," Toya said. "I'm saying *that* man is gay."

"*Or*," Nisha offered, "maybe he thinks it would be unprofessional to carry on with somebody he has to see at work all the time."

"You trying to be funny?"

"Why you say that?"

"You talking about me and Dr. Coates, ain't you?"

Nisha rolled her eyes. "I wasn't event thinking about him. You must be feeling guilty."

"I don't feel guilty. What should I feel guilty for?"

Nisha shrugged. "I didn't say nothing. Do your thing."

"He didn't say nothing slick to you when you asked for that overtime?" Toya wanted to know. She grabbed one of the boxes and sliced the tape with scissors.

Nisha shook her head. "He said I reminded him of his wife, back in the day."

Toya frowned. "What that mean?"

"He said she was a hard worker," Nisha explained. "She took care of him when he was in school and he couldn't work."

"That's it?" Toya asked.

Nisha shrugged. "Yeah. That's it."

"He must be scared of Lonzo," Toya guessed. "Or he woulda made a move by now."

Nisha braced herself for an inappropriate comment about her man, but it didn't come this time.

"You wouldn't sleep with him?" Toya asked.

"Hell no!"

"What if he offered to give you some money?"

"That's nasty!"

"You ain't gotta say it like that."

"Would, would you do that?"

Toya looked her in the eyes. "Ain't nothing wrong with getting your bills paid."

Nisha was confused. "Wait, are you saying you *would* do that, or you *have* done that, with Dr. Coates?"

"I don't sleep with nobody for free," Toya said. She turned to place a few pill bottles on the shelf.

"Are you talking like, cash money, or he let you work overtime?" Nisha wondered.

Toya turned back to her and put a hand on her hip. "Let me put it like this: I got a Visa card in my purse right now that he gave me last year. It's pre-paid. There was $500 on it when he first gave it to me. I spent it, but he told me not to throw it away.

"The next time we did something, three hundred more popped up on it. Every time we get down, some money show up on that card. I don't ask him for shit, and he don't put no money in my hand, like I'm some ho or something."

Nisha had to walk away from her. She could keep her mouth closed, but her eyes were yelling loudly: *You nasty bitch!*

Nisha read the label on one of the larger boxes the UPS guy left for them.

"What's this?" she asked Toya.

"That big one? I don't know. What it say?"

"*Drug Storage*," Nisha read. "It's from California."

"Oh, that's the new safe, to lock up some of the narcotics. Is it heavy? You prolly should leave that for Dr. Coates."

The box was only two feet by a foot and a half. Nisha nudged it with her foot, and it slid across the floor easily.

"It's not heavy," she said, but when she lifted the safe, a searing pain flashed in her wrist and shot up her arm like a bolt of lightning.

"*OWW!*"

Toya rushed to help her.

"What's wrong?"

Nisha only had the box three feet off the ground. It slipped from her fingers and impacted the floor with a loud *THUNK!*

"Girl, what's wrong?!" Toya stood with a panicked expression while Nisha softly caressed her arm.

"I don't know! Something, something popped in my wrist!"

"Did you break it?"

"*I don't know!*" Nisha squealed, near tears. "I don't know what's wrong. *It hurts!*"

"Let me see." Toya reached for her hand, and Nisha snatched her arm away roughly.

"*No! Don't touch it!*"

"I told you to leave that for Dr. Coates," Toya said, her eyebrows knitting.

"It wasn't that heavy," Nisha said, crying now. She looked down at the box and saw the corner that hit the floor was smooshed all the way in. "Aw hell," she moaned. "Did I break it?"

"You don't even need to worry about that," Toya said, and then they heard a short chime as someone entered the front door.

Nisha's face was a mess. She didn't want to turn to see who it was. Toya looked over her shoulder.

"He back," she said without emotion.

Nisha's body stiffened. A chill rolled down her spine like it might be the boogeyman behind her. "Who, who is it?"

Rather than respond to her, Toya said, "Hey, Dr. Coates."

CHAPTER FIVE
THE PREMIUM

Nisha's second meeting in her boss' office was a lot less cheery than the one they had earlier that day. Dr. Coates sat her down and knelt before her, so he could get a look at her arm. Nisha didn't like the closeness of the encounter. She didn't like his cologne. She didn't like the gleam of his bald head or the way his eyes got beady when he concentrated. Most of all she didn't like the physical contact.

"Stop," she told him and pulled her arm away.

"Hold on, I'm just—"

"No. Just, stop."

He regarded her oddly.

"I appreciate your help," she said, "but I need to go see a doctor. There's nothing you can do for me here."

The pharmacist stood with a sigh and went around to his side of the desk. He took a seat and sighed again. "Well, it's not broken."

Nisha knew that much. The pain was already receding, and the swelling wasn't that bad.

"Probably a sprain," he said. "But I can't figure how it happened. That box only weighs twenty pounds. Your son has got to weigh at least that much, and you pick him up every day..."

Nisha nodded, cradling her arm in her lap. "Yeah, he's about that much."

"So, you may not have injured yourself at work," Dr. Coates said. "Maybe this happened elsewhere, and you just aggravated it here..."

Nisha frowned. This was starting to sound like a conversation she needed a lawyer for. "I don't see what difference that makes. All I know is I need to go to the hospital, right now."

"I'm not keeping you. I just..."

She stood to leave.

"Wait," the pharmacist said and sighed again.

What's all this freaking sighing for?

"What is it?" Nisha asked. "I gotta go. My arm hurts."

"I can give you something for the pain."

"I don't want nothing for the pain," she said, no longer hiding her frustration. "Why are you holding me up?"

The pharmacist shook his head. He brought a hand to his face and rubbed his lips.

"You don't have insurance," he muttered.

Her head cocked slowly to the side. "Excuse me?"

Dr. Coates looked her in the eyes. "I haven't been keeping up with the premiums."

Nisha couldn't believe it. "I just had my baby in February. And I've been taking him for his checkups."

"This happened recently," Dr. Coates revealed. "This month. I – I can pay it, tomorrow. It'll, it'll probably be a few days before your card is good again."

Nisha was still confused. "What are you, what are you talking about? I'm paying for insurance. You take money out of my check every week."

"Only forty dollars."

"I don't care if it's only *five dollars*!" she snapped. "You take money out of my check *every week*. I better have some insurance!"

"Calm down. I'm going to pay the premium."

"That don't help me today. And what if something happens to my son?"

"Why don't we worry about what's going on right now," Dr. Coates suggested.

Nisha was fuming. "What do you mean *we*? You're the one who didn't pay your bills! You're the one who's been taking my money! You think I'm stupid, but I know that's against the law. If I don't have insurance, then you have to pay my doctor bill yourself," she demanded.

"Nisha, sit down, please."

"I don't want to."

"Please, just for a second."

She took her seat, only because her head was staring to spin. She couldn't remember the last time she was this upset.

"Okay," Dr. Coates said. "Here's what we can do: Make an appointment with your doctor and tell him you need a referral to—"

"I'm not calling my doctor," Nisha nearly shouted. "I'm going to the *emergency room.*"

The pharmacist scratched his bald dome and grimaced. "Alright. Go to the emergency room. You can bring the bill to me, and I'll pay it. I'll pay your insurance premium tomorrow, and you'll be covered again by next week."

"Fine." She started to get up, but he wasn't done.

"But I'll be honest with you, Lanisha: This pharmacy isn't doing well financially. We've been in the red all year. If you need to take some time off, I have to pay you for it, but I can only do that for, maybe a week, tops."

She shook her head. Dr. Coates definitely had a few screws loose, if he thought he could dictate how long her injury should last.

"If you want to get a lawyer," he said, possibly reading her mind, "that's your choice. But I'm going to tell him the same thing I'm telling you: I don't have any money. If you sue me, I'll file for bankruptcy. I'll board this place up, and nobody will have a job. Think about how many people will be affected. Years will go by before you get any money out of this."

She fixed a cold, hard look on her boss. "What are you saying?"

Dr. Coates clasped his hands together in a praying or possibly a begging gesture. "I'm saying you should accept what I'm offering you. I'll pay your doctor bill and give you a week off, with pay."

"You can't offer me that," she growled. "That's what I'm supposed to have already. What if I'm not ready to come back in a week?"

"Let's, let's just hope you are."

She got up and left without another word. She was disgusted. Even worse, she felt betrayed. She took this job because she wanted to make a difference in the community. But she should've remembered something her father told her when she was in middle school: Your own people are more likely to hurt you than any other race.

Walter learned that lesson from the murder of Malcolm X, but there were countless more examples that never made the front-page news.

Nisha went to Jackson Memorial and felt like a fool when they gave her paperwork to fill out, and she had to check the box that said, "No, I do not have insurance." She took a seat in a waiting room filled with dozens more uninsured people. She was still there two hours later.

She called her father, but she didn't want him to come because he'd have to bring the baby with him. She didn't call Lonzo, because she knew he wouldn't take the news well. Plus there was no sense in both of them missing half a day's wages.

This would've been a good time to call her mom, but Carol had been dead for twenty-one years. She was killed during a robbery attempt when Nisha was five. Walter didn't talk about the incident much, so Nisha researched it herself when she got older. Her mother's killer got a life sentence rather than the death penalty, but he ended up getting killed anyway during a prison riot.

Karma.

A nurse finally called her name at 4:30 pm, but that was only to take her vitals and send her to a smaller waiting room. At ten minutes after five, a tech took her for X-rays. Afterwards, she finally made it to an exam room. Nisha didn't see a doctor until four hours after she entered the hospital. He told her the X-rays didn't show a fracture, and she probably had a sprain. He put her arm in a splint and said he'd write her a prescription for pain medication.

"How long do I have to wear this?" she asked.

"Three weeks," Dr. Collins said. He was a slight man with red hair and thick glasses.

Nisha almost left it at that. Three weeks in a splint wasn't bad. But when the nurse brought her discharge orders, she had a change of heart.

"Can, can I talk to the doctor again?"

"What's wrong?" the nurse asked. She was a big girl who wheezed after every sentence.

"I don't think my arm is sprained," Nisha said, thinking about what Dr. Coates said. "I didn't fall or bend my wrist any weird kind of way."

"It prolly ain't sprained," the nurse said. She stepped closer and lowered her voice. "Dr. Collins be trying to get patients out of here as fast as he can. He don't be examining them good enough. I see the same patients when they come back. Sometimes it be something wrong with them that's totally *different* than what Dr. Collins told them."

Nisha wasn't surprised to hear that. Everyone knows life sucks for people who don't have health insurance.

"What should I do?"

"I'll tell him you want to talk to him again," the nurse conspired. "When he comes in, tell him you want him to do some more tests to make sure there's nothing else wrong with your wrist. If he don't wanna do it, tell him you want a second opinion. He won't like that, because if he refers you to another doctor, and they find something different, it'll come back on him."

"Alright," Nisha said. "Is it going to take a long time before he comes back?"

"It won't be that long. But he'll have an attitude when you see him again. Don't let him intimidate you. You deserve just as good service as anybody else."

Nisha thanked her nurse and settled in for what she expected to be another hour long wait. But Dr. Collins returned in less than ten minutes. And the nurse was right; he looked upset.

"Yes, Ms. Elder? What is it?"

"I, um, I was wondering if you can do more tests on my arm. I don't think my wrist is sprained."

The doctor looked down his nose at her. "What makes you think I don't know what I'm talking about?"

Nisha stood, because this man wasn't her father or her superior. "I didn't fall or bend my arm any kind of way that would've sprained it," she said when they were eye to eye.

"You don't have to fall or bend your wrist to sprain it," the doctor informed her patiently.

"But I've been having pain in my wrist for six months."

"You didn't say anything about that."

"Yes I did. I wrote it on that paper when I was in the waiting room. You didn't ask me about it when you came in here. You just said it was sprained, and I had to wear a splint. You didn't ask me nothing."

The doctor stared at her for a few seconds.

"Alright. I'll schedule an MRI for tomorrow morning. Can you be here at nine?"

"Yes." She couldn't believe that worked.

"Okay," Dr. Collins said. "I'll send the nurse back with the paperwork in a few minutes."

He left without an apology or even a "Have a nice day," but Nisha didn't need him to be cordial. She just needed him to do his job.

Not until she exited the hospital did she consider an MRI would probably cost as much as the ER visit. Dr. Coates wouldn't like the bill she presented him.

Oh well, she said to herself. What's the worst he could do?

She picked up her son at seven and made it home twenty minutes later. She got started on dinner right away, but Lonzo walked through the front door before she was done. He wasn't an overbearing, *Woman, where my food?* type of guy, but he was tired and hungry, and she could see the disappointment in his eyes.

"You just got home?" He stood in the hallway with his gym bag in hand. His shoulders were slumped, his expression downcast. Nisha didn't want to give him any bad news, but he saw it for himself when she turned to give him a hug.

"What happened to your arm?"

"I hurt myself. It'll be alright." She wrapped her arms around his neck and kissed him on the lips. This was the best part of her day, but Lonzo backed away too quickly.

"You hurt yourself at work?" He dropped his bag and carefully inspected her splint. She couldn't remember him ever touching her so gently.

"It don't even hurt no more."

"How'd you hurt it?"

"I was picking up a box." She went to the oven and removed a baking sheet with six breaded fish fillets cooked to perfection. The mashed potatoes and broccoli were already done. It wasn't easy to prepare the meal with her dominant hand immobilized, but she'd managed.

"What are you picking up boxes for?" Lonzo asked. He was getting irritated, already on a fault-finding mission. Nisha knew he would keep going until he found someone to blame.

"I always pick up boxes at work," she said with a smile. "That's part of my job, Lonzo. It only weighed twenty pounds."

"Where was your boss at?"

"He was out of the store. But I don't think that one box was the problem. I think whatever's been wrong with my wrist finally, I don't know, snapped..."

"What the doctor say?"

"He said it looks sprained, but they're gonna do an MRI in the morning."

"You took off work?"

"Yeah, I got the whole week off."

"Your boss ain't giving you no trouble?" Lonzo asked. "He cool with you going to the doctor and stuff?"

Nisha's heart skipped a beat. "What can he say? I got insurance," she lied.

"Yeah, but ain't it just you and one other girl that works in that store? What if you got to be off for two or three weeks? How they gon' manage?"

"It doesn't hurt that bad," Nisha said. "I can still go to work with this thing on my hand. See. I can wiggle my fingers." She demonstrated and then winced from the pain.

Lonzo shook his head. "You ain't going to work until your hand feels *all the way* better." He turned and walked out of the kitchen. "That man got to pay you for every day you stay at home, too," he called from the bedroom. "Even if it's a month."

Nisha frowned and chewed on her thumbnail. How long could she keep the lie going? Dr. Coates said he could only pay for her to stay home for a week, so when that time was up, regardless of how her arm really felt, she had to convince Lonzo she was ready to return to work.

On the other hand, Nisha wondered why she should protect Dr. Coates. He was a liar and a cheat, and he broke the law by taking her money and not paying the insurance premium.

Uh uhn, she said to herself and turned back to the stove. No way could she tell Lonzo that. Not only was beating up people the thing her man did best, but he wasn't too far removed from the streets. He cleaned up his act when their child was born, but all it took was some mess like this to bring back the *old* Lonzo.

No. She had to get better in one week. That was the only viable solution.

After dinner Lonzo took a shower and then stretched out on the carpet in the living room. He played with his son for a while, letting the baby crawl over him in a beastly wrestling match that didn't have a clear victor.

Lonzo fed the baby his last bottle for the day and put him to bed at nine o'clock. When he returned to the living room, he carried a DVD case.

"What's that?" Nisha asked.

"Some of Veston's fights," he said, referring to his next opponent. "Fats wants me to watch them as much as I can."

"Oh," Nisha said. "I thought you had a new freaky movie you wanted to watch."

He grinned at her. "Sorry. Not this time, baby." He put a disc in the player and sat on the couch next to her.

"Sit on the floor," Nisha instructed.

"What for?"

"I wanna give you a massage."

"I ain't never had no one-handed massage," he said with a smirk. He moved to the floor and positioned himself between her legs.

"I already forgot I had this thing on," Nisha said. "I think I can still do it. Take your shirt off."

Lonzo took off his tee, and she gave him the best massage she could while they watched the fight. She felt like she was half-assing it with only one hand, but the muscles in Lonzo's neck and traps were tense. He sighed and moaned in appreciation.

Michael Veston was 6'2, 228 pounds. He wasn't an overtly muscular guy, but he wasn't fat either. He was solid and burly. These were the kinds of guys Lonzo usually had a field day with, but midway through the first fight, Nisha knew Veston was like no one Lonzo had ever faced before.

The first thing she noticed was Veston's speed and defensive prowess. He had quick eyes. He slipped most of the punches thrown at him by rotating his body slightly so that the fist flew harmlessly past his ears and cheeks. And Nisha had never seen a heavyweight use his gloves to block so many punches. At one point it looked like Veston was playing patty-cake, while his opponent swung for the fences, growing more and more frustrated.

The other thing Nisha took note of was how dirty a boxer Veston was. He used the clinch to punch his opponent in the face and stomach, while the ref stood on the opposite side, unable to see what was going on.

In the tenth round, Veston's opponent didn't look like he wanted to get off his stool. He did, but there was no gas left in his tank. He had trouble keeping his gloves above chest level. This is when Veston finally went on the offensive. He charged forward with jabs and combos no one in the audience had seen up to that point in the fight.

Veston dropped his opponent with three vicious uppercuts to the midsection. The guy got up in time, but that was the only knock down in the fight. Veston won by unanimous decision.

"Man, that was crazy," Nisha said as the ref raised Veston's glove in victory. "I thought he was gonna lose that fight."

Lonzo didn't respond.

"Baby." She looked and saw that his head was down. "Baby, you sleep?"

He looked up with a start. "Naw." He looked around. "I'm woke."

"Did you see the fight?"

"I missed the last part," Lonzo admitted. "You can rewind it."

She placed her hand on his cheek and caressed lovingly. "No, that's okay, baby. We can watch it again tomorrow."

She turned off the television and followed her man down the cramped hallway to the bedroom. When they crawled under the sheets, Lonzo rolled to his side and Nisha jumped on the opportunity to spoon with him. She kissed him on the back of his neck, loving the scent of his aftershave.

She closed her eyes, but sleep was elusive. She thought about her shiesty boss and wondered what problems the MRI would reveal in the morning. She also felt guilty about lying to her fiancée. Dr. Coates was dead wrong for messing up her insurance, and this was a problem that affected their whole family. Regardless of how Lonzo reacted, he had a right to know.

"Baby, you sleep?"

She waited five seconds for him to respond, but The Champ was already in dreamland.

CHAPTER SIX
ORTHOPEDICS

The next morning Lonzo was well rested and in a better mood than the previous two days. Nisha made him a healthy breakfast of grapefruit, toast and oatmeal, and he wolfed it down.

"I wish you would've stayed up and watched that fight with me," she told him.

"I got damned near three months till I fight that fool," Lonzo replied. "I don't know why you and Fats think I'ma lose my cool with ol' boy. I been up against some defensive fighters before."

"I don't think you'll lose your cool."

"Yeah you do. I can see it in your eyes. You worried about your man."

"I worry about you every fight," she said with a grin. "I don't want my baby coming home with no bubble lip."

"You'll still kiss me though," Lonzo guessed.

"You know I will. Even if you got two black eyes *and* a bubble lip."

Lonzo laughed. "Hey, don't be wishing no bad luck on me."

"Oh, but it's cool if you do it to me?"

"I ain't never wished no bad luck on you."

"Yes, you did. Don't you remember? Yesterday when I said I wanted to work some overtime, you said, '*Ain't your arm still hurting? Your arm could fall off any minute.*'"

Lonzo shook his head, chuckling. "I was just playing."

"Yeah, but look at me now." Nisha held up her splint.

"Awww…" Lonzo got up and went to her side of the table. He knelt and reached for her injured hand. He softly kissed each one of her fingers and then her wrist and forearm.

His warm lips sent a pleasant shiver up Nisha's arm. "Dang, baby. You got candy kisses."

"You feel better?"

"Yeah, I do."

"Cool." He kissed her on the lips and pecked his son on the forehead. "I gotta go. I'll see y'all later."

"Bye, baby. Say bye to your daddy," she told Baby Lonzo.

The child gurgled something that didn't seem to be on topic.

"What he say?" Lonzo asked. *"See you later, Champ?"*

Nisha shook her head. "Uh, I don't think that's what he said."

"Yeah it is. He said, '*See you later, Champ.*' He know his daddy a champ."

"Alright," Nisha said and walked him to the door. Lonzo gave her another kiss and her booty a nice squeeze before he exited.

"Bye-bye," Baby Lonzo said and waved at him.

Lonzo turned back with a huge grin. "You gon' tell me he didn't say that either?"

"No, I heard him," Nisha said.

"Yeah, you better recognize," Lonzo said and headed down the stairs leading to the parking lot.

When she closed the door, Nisha knew she missed another opportunity to tell him about the trouble with Dr. Coates, but she didn't regret it this time. It was good to see a smile on Lonzo's face. She wouldn't rain on his parade unless she absolutely had to.

Shonda's bootleg daycare was back in business that morning, so Nisha dropped her son off before she went to the hospital.

"How was Blue?" Nisha had a few minutes to spare, so she sat on the couch and cuddled her nephew.

"Blue was *real* nice," Shonda said. She was a slim girl with no booty but enough breasts to make up for it.

"I can't believe you took a day off work to sleep with some man."

"It was worth it," Shonda replied. "If I need some money later, I'll just sell some food stamps. Anyway, what about your arm? I can't believe you're letting your boss do you like that."

"I'm not letting him do anything. I'm taking him the bill as soon as I leave the hospital."

"Yeah, but he could be paying a lot more. He cancelled your insurance, even while you was paying for it. That's a lawsuit right there. And then you got injured on the job. Hmph. Girl, I woulda been done called me a lawyer. I'd be in rehab by now."

Shonda had been the plaintiff in a slip and fall lawsuit and a car accident claim, so she knew what she was talking about.

"He said he'll file for bankruptcy if I sue."

"So? That won't stop you from getting paid. When he lose the case, he got to come up with some money from somewhere."

"He said he'll close the pharmacy."

"That's fine," Shonda said. "If he do, you can open it right back up with your name on the front. Or you can take his car or his house. Don't you know those lawyers don't get paid until they get your money? They not gon' let some slick nigga beat them."

Nisha frowned. That sounded pretty far-fetched. Even if Shonda knew what she was talking about, Nisha didn't know if she wanted to go after her boss like that. In any event, "That sounds like it would take some *years*. Lonzo will be making good money by then."

"So you just gon' let him manhandle you?"

Nisha chuckled. "Shonda, ain't nobody manhandling me."

"You said he'll pay for you to be off for *one week*. He can't tell you how long you're hurt."

"I know he wrong for that," Nisha conceded. "But sometimes you gotta do what you gotta do, you know? I'm not trying to stay at that pharmacy until I retire. I just need to make sure my paychecks keep coming for the next few months." She checked her watch. "Anyway, I gotta go. I'll give you a call when I'm on my way back over here."

Nisha got up and returned her nephew to his mother. She scooped Baby Lonzo up and gave him a snuggle. "See you later."

"Let me know if you change your mind about that lawyer," Shonda said. "I got his number around here somewhere."

"Okay, I'll let you know when I get back," Nisha said, though she was pretty sure she wouldn't take her sister's advice.

She arrived at Jackson Memorial at a quarter till nine. She had ample time to park and find the MRI waiting room, which, thankfully, was a lot less crowded than the ER was yesterday. There were only three patients ahead of her. She filled out more paperwork, and a tech called her back.

After the MRI, they sent her to a lounge area to await the results. At a quarter till noon a secretary summoned her to the last stop on this trip. Nisha barely had time to take a seat in the exam room before a tall, black man entered.

"How are you doing, Ms. Elder. I'm Dr. Moresby." He offered his left hand to shake out of deference for her condition. "I'm an orthopedic surgeon."

"Hi." Nisha shook his hand and noticed her palm was moist. Come to think of it, she felt perspiration on her forehead too, even though the room was cool.

"Could you take a seat up here?"

He helped her onto an exam table and then removed her splint. He examined her wrist, much like the other doctor did yesterday.

Nisha tried to be patient, but it was hard. The sterile atmosphere reminded her of death. "Did, did they find anything?"

"I did." The doctor let go of her arm and stepped to a portable computer. After reviewing her chart, he said, "It's not good," and Nisha's whole body stiffened. Her heart thumped, even though she knew it couldn't be *that* bad.

"I believe you have *Kienbock's disease*," the physician said. "It's a disorder of the wrist, named after the doctor who discovered it."

Dr. Moresby turned and pointed at a poster, a diagram of the circulatory system. "You have blood vessels that travel to the wrist bones to make sure they have enough oxygen and nutrients to do their job. For some reason, one of your blood vessels stopped supplying blood to your lunate bone, which is one of your wrist bones, and your lunate has begun to deteriorate. This is what's causing the pain in your wrist."

Nisha understood that, barely. This didn't sound anywhere near as simple as a sprain.

"So, what do I gotta do?"

"Well, if you wear the splint for three weeks and keep your wrist immobilized, it will start to feel better. But your wrist will never be one hundred percent unless you have surgery. We have to determine why the blood vessel isn't supplying blood to your wrist like it should, and we have to repair your lunate bone, or replace it with an artificial one."

Nisha's jaw dropped. "How, how much does that cost?" She imagined a Mercedes would be less expensive.

"You'll have to get those details from the billing office, but I can tell you, it's rather costly," the doctor confirmed. "The problem is Kienbock's is such a rare disorder, Medicaid doesn't cover this type of surgery. If you had insurance, you would probably have to pay between eight and ten thousand out of pocket. Without insurance, the surgery could cost up to fifty thousand dollars."

Nisha brought a hand to her mouth and closed her eyes. She felt a sensation of weightlessness, like the exam table disappeared from beneath her, and she was sliding down a dark abyss. She thought she was passing out, but when she opened her eyes, the doctor was still standing there.

"Are you okay?"

"No," she said softly. "Not really."

"Do you have any questions?"

She shook her head.

"I'm really sorry."

Nisha looked into his eyes, and she believed him. "Thank you." Now if only she could use his apology to pay for her surgery, she'd be in business.

She didn't see Dr. Coates' car when she pulled into the pharmacy's parking lot. This wasn't out of the norm. The pharmacist usually chose the lunch hour to do his running around for the day. Nisha wouldn't be surprised to learn he was taking women out to eat, or maybe stopping at a motel for a midday quickie.

Inside the store, Toya was alone, texting or more likely *sexting* one of her admirers. Nisha didn't think her co-worker was all that attractive, but red bones with big lips were always in demand. Plus Toya had a butt so big her lab coat couldn't hide it.

Toya's eyes widened when she saw Nisha.

"Damn, girl! Where you been?"

She came around the counter to look at her arm.

"So, what happened? Is it broke?"

"No."

"Is it sprained? Did you go to the doctor?"

"I went yesterday, and I had to go back this morning. Did Dr. Coates say when he was coming back?"

"You know he don't never say. You want me to call him?"

Nisha nodded. "Yeah."

"So what'd the doctor say?" Toya asked as she accessed her phone contacts. "Is it sprained? When are you coming back to work?"

"I have to have surgery," Nisha said. "But I want to talk to Dr. Coates about it myself."

Toya brought the phone to her ear and held up a finger for quiet. She went around the counter and kept her back to Nisha.

"Hey," Toya said into the phone. "Nisha's here... She said she got to have surgery... Okay." She disconnected and turned back to her coworker. "He on his way back."

Nisha was shaking her head. "Didn't you just hear me say I wanted to talk to him myself?"

"Oh, uh uhn. Sorry." She crossed her arms and leaned back with a smile. "So, what Lonzo say about yo arm?"

"What you mean?"

"I know you said you wanted to work some overtime to help him out. Is he mad at you now?"

"No, he's not mad." Nisha's irritation was unveiled. "He loves me, and he's worried about me. Why would he get mad? That's stupid."

"I'm just saying..." Toya bit her bottom lip. "He be working all hard *and* training for his fights, and you can't bring enough money home to help him out."

Nisha's blood started to boil, but she knew it was her own fault for giving this heifer the ammunition. She should've known Toya would seize any opportunity to make her feel inadequate.

"Why don't you let me worry about my man," Nisha snarled, "and you can worry about whatever trifling nigga you screwing this week."

Toya's smile fell. "Why you always getting a damn attitude?"

"Why you always saying shit about Lonzo when I told you to stop?"

"I just be talking to you about stuff. You the one getting all defensive; popping off like you some bad bitch or something."

"I'm bad enough to yank that weave out your hair, if you keep talking noise about me and Lonzo."

Toya's eyes narrowed. "Bitch, I wish you would."

Nisha was half a second from jumping over the counter when she remembered her hand was in a sling – her dominant hand. She figured the adrenaline would mask the pain during the fight, and she could whoop Toya despite the injury. But that was what her father called "niggerish" behavior.

Walter told her if someone had enough power to make you physically attack them, just because you don't like their *words*, then they've already won the fight. Besides that, Nisha already had one wrist bone that was defective. Did she want to risk more damage over this floozy?

"You lucky I got this thing on my arm," she said coldly.

"Yeah, any excuse will do," Toya quipped. She picked up her phone and returned to her text message.

Nisha took a seat on the bench provided for customers and fumed for fourteen minutes until Dr. Coates walked through the door.

The pharmacist read the papers Nisha gave him in great detail. He then turned to his computer and did his own research. He didn't speak for a while. Nisha crossed and uncrossed her legs. She repositioned her purse several times and sighed. Finally she cleared her throat loudly, and Dr. Coates looked up at her.

"I'm sorry. This is a lot to process."

Nisha figured as much. The five minutes of quiet time was a dead giveaway.

The pharmacist stacked all the papers together neatly and set them down again. He clasped his hands and looked into her eyes. "Let me, let me ask you something. What do *you* think I should do with this?"

Nisha didn't expect that. "Uh, I don't know. You said you wanted me to bring you my doctor bill."

"I did," Dr. Coates said. He shuffled through the papers again. "This bill. This is the one from your ER visit. But this other one..." He found the document in question. "I don't think I asked for this one."

Nisha was prepared for this. "It's part of the same visit, like a follow-up. My insurance would've covered it if I still *had* insurance."

"They would've covered some of it," Dr. Coates agreed. "But not all of it, I don't believe..."

Nisha shook her head in exasperation. She didn't feel like arguing, especially after the incident with Toya. "So, what are you saying, you only want to pay for some of it?"

Dr. Coates rubbed his forehead and frowned. "This whole *Kienbock's disease* is interesting. I'm not an ortho doc, but from what I just read, this doesn't sound like something that happened when you picked up that box yesterday. It sounds like a condition that's been going on for quite some time..."

Nisha knew he would say that. "Look, Dr. Coates, I'm not trying to sue you or blame you for anything. You said you would pay this bill and give me a little time off. That's all I want."

"But I thought you needed surgery?"

"I do," Nisha said. "But I don't have to do that *today*. I can wait until you get our insurance back."

"And then you'll have to take some more time off," Dr. Coates guessed, "after your surgery. So you want paid time off now and paid time off later. And in the meantime, who's to say you can perform your regular duties here? What if you hurt yourself again?" He shook his head. "I don't know. This sounds like a big liability."

Nisha couldn't believe this. "What? No it doesn't. You're taking it a little too far."

He shrugged. "I, I don't know what to say, Lanisha. I want to do the right thing for you, but I have to think about this pharmacy too. I mean, honestly, you probably shouldn't come back to work until *after* you have surgery. And who knows how long that's going to be? I can't pay for that many days off."

"I didn't ask you to. I can come back in a week, like we already said."

"But what if—"

"I'll be fine in a week," she insisted.

"You'll be a liability," Dr. Coates repeated. "I..." He shook his head. "I mean, I don't know if you're worth the risk."

Nisha's mouth fell open.

"You're a good worker," the pharmacist said. "But if I let you come to work knowing you need surgery, then you probably *could* sue me when you get hurt again."

"I wouldn't do that, Dr. Coates. I need this job."

"If this happened to Toya," her boss went on, "I could probably trust that she wouldn't do anything to get me in trouble. Because, I know Toya better. But, Nisha, I don't know you like I know Toya. I mean, I would like to. I've been trying to get to know you better. But you haven't been open to me like Toya has. If you want me to take this chance with you, then I have to get to know you better."

Nisha's whole body grew cold even while her heart rate increased. She knew exactly what the bastard was asking for, but she wanted to hear it in plain English; so he couldn't take it back later.

"I've been here for a year." She spoke slowly and deliberately, choosing her words carefully. "I don't understand why you're saying you don't know me."

"You know I don't know you as well as I know Toya," Dr. Coates said. He was choosing his words carefully too, Nisha noticed.

"How much better do you have to know me for me to keep my job?" she asked.

"I never said I was firing you. I simply said I don't know you well enough to take a risk like this; like allowing you to work here while you're clearly injured."

Nisha was sick of beating around the bush, but he hadn't incriminated himself enough. "You still didn't say how much better you need to know me..."

"If you want to play games, then you're not ready," Dr. Coates decided. His gaze fell to her breasts and remained there. There was no mistaking it this time. "I'm sure you know what I'm talking about."

Nisha's stomach flipped, and she tasted vomit in the back of her throat. She stood abruptly and felt lightheaded. She steadied herself with a hand on the back of the chair.

"I gotta go."

Dr. Coates stood too. "Don't misinterpret me, Nisha. I merely said I don't know you well enough. I know there's a lot of ways to interpret that, but I assure you, I meant it only on a professional level."

Nisha didn't stop walking. And she didn't respond when Toya asked, "What's wrong with you," as she exited the pharmacy.

She ran to her car, but she sat behind the wheel for a few minutes after she started it. Her breaths were hot and hard. Her eyes were wide and unbelieving. A million thoughts ran through her mind; the most prevalent being she no longer had a job. Whether she was getting fired or quitting was undetermined, but she knew she would never set foot in that pharmacy again.

She wondered if it was still possible to sue her boss. It didn't sound like her injury was work related, and Dr. Coates was smart enough to make his sexual advances ambiguous.

She didn't even want to think about how Lonzo would respond to all of this.

She threw her car in DRIVE and headed to her sister's house. Shonda wasn't the brightest apple in the bunch, but she knew how to get paid. Nisha regretted not taking her advice earlier that day.

CHAPTER SEVEN
RAGE

Around the same time Nisha decided not to jump over the counter and yank the weave off Toya's head, Alonzo "The Champ" Ingram was getting the business from some of his homies at the refrigerated warehouse in Blue Mound.

The issue of the day was Lonzo's decision to buy a microwavable hot dog from the vending machine, rather than purchase a hot meal from the food truck that magically showed up in the parking lot every afternoon.

"Quit being so cheap," Chester told him. "You know that hotdog tastes like pure-dee-*shit*. My old lady told me they put all kinds of mess in those wieners, like cow noses, chicken feet and pig dicks..."

That brought a hearty round of laughter from everyone.

"What you doing with all the money you make in those fights?" Jesse wanted to know. "Burying it in the backyard?"

"Don't you know Lonzo got *twelve kids*," Mike Johnson joked. "Child support's kicking that ass, ain't it, Champ?"

They all cracked up.

Lonzo shook his head in dismissal. "Shit ain't funny."

The break room was half full with hungry men who had worked the short half of their shift but had five hours to go before they could clock out for the day. They all wore coveralls to ward off chilly temperatures in the warehouse.

They weren't all happy with their jobs, but Lonzo and his co-workers were what America is all about. They got up every morning, kissed the wife goodbye and went to work. They endured back breaking labor day in and day out with hopes of one day getting promoted to a better paying position as a manager or supervisor. Even if they never got promoted, they did their job to the best of their ability, because that's what real men do. They bring home the bacon.

"Hey, Chester," Mike Johnson said, "how's about after work me and you go to Lonzo's house with some shovels; see if we can find his buried treasure."

"I bet not see neither one of you in my backyard," Lonzo said as he put his chili dog in the microwave. "Best believe I'll release the hounds on yo' ass."

His friends laughed. Only a couple of them knew Lonzo didn't have a house, a back yard or a pack of bloodthirsty dogs to sic on anyone.

"Naw, but for real, you want me to get you something?" Chester asked.

"Naw," Lonzo said. "I can't be eating off that food truck. I'll end up with salmonella or some shit."

"You sure don't be worried about salmonella on payday," Mike Johnson noted.

Lonzo had to chuckle because he was right about that.

"Man, get your ass out of here and go smoke your cancer sticks," Lonzo said.

"Come on y'all," Jesse said. "Don't make him angry. You wouldn't like him when he's angry!"

The guys with money in their pocket headed out into the bright sunlight. Lonzo took his lunch out of the microwave and peeled off the plastic wrapper. He had a chili dog, a bag of Doritos and a can of Mountain Dew. That was a nice meal. As a matter of fact, when he was a kid, he would've killed for a meal like this.

He didn't feel bad about the chicken feet and pig dicks that may or may not be in his processed meat. He knew one day his two worlds of fame and fortune would collide, and hundred-dollar bills would rain down on him like a snow flurry.

That wasn't a pipe dream. It was his destiny. Unlike his fiancée, Lonzo believed his life story was already foretold. All he had to do was step in the footprints God laid out for him.

After work he stopped by the gym. The place was packed with pugilists and weightlifters, trainers and bystanders. Everyone treated Lonzo like a king. No one in the history of Overbrook Meadows started off a boxing career with as many wins as him. No one possessed the superstar qualities that made crowds pack the venues and cheer for The Champ, like they would a politician or a pop star.

After wading through a crowd of friends and well-wishers, Lonzo found his trainer at the speed bags; working with an up-and-coming prizefighter named Tommy Pelts.

"Yo, Champ!" Fats was sweating profusely, though the temperature at the gym hovered at a cool 71 degrees.

"Hey," Lonzo told him. "What you got going on over here?"

"Same old, same old," Fats said, grinning brightly. "Did you watch the videos I gave you?"

Damn. Lonzo knew that would be the first thing Fats asked him. "I watched the first one. Me and my girl gon' check out the other one tonight."

Fats' smile fell. "Come on, Champ. We got less than three months before you have to get in the ring with that cat."

"I know. I'm gonna watch 'em both tonight. I promise."

"I thought you said you watched the first one..."

"I kinda fell asleep in the middle," Lonzo admitted.

That made the last flicker of light fade from Fats' eyes. "Gimme another fifteen minutes on this," he told his new fighter. "And then head to the weight room. I'll meet you there."

"Okay, boss," Tommy said.

"Let's talk," Fats told Lonzo, and the two of them walked away. "So, what's the deal?" he asked when they had a little privacy.

"Ain't nothing," Lonzo said with a snicker. "You know you pull this shit every time, Fats."

"What shit?"

"Every guy I fight is the best you've ever seen," Lonzo recounted. "Every one of them is the one I need to watch out for."

"I don't say that every time."

Lonzo laughed. "Yeah, you do, Fats. You have me scared to death every time I get in the ring."

"That's good. It's good to be scared. That's what keeps you on your toes."

"I know. But you keep telling me *this* nigga gon' kick my ass, and then it's *that* nigga or this next nigga. When it comes time for the fight, don't none of them come close to whooping me."

"You think I'm just saying that to psyche you out? That's why you're not taking Veston seriously?"

"I am taking him seriously. But we got three months till the fight–"

"Less than three months."

"We got plenty of time to prepare."

"Alright," Fats said, nodding. He pawed the sweat from his face and wiped it on his shirt. "Why don't you take off and watch those tapes I gave you? I would set you up in the media room, but every time I park you in front of the TV, you fall asleep."

I fall asleep at home too, Lonzo thought. "So, I'm off for the day?" he asked with a grin. "I can go home? That's it?"

"No, that's not it," Fats said. "I want you to watch those fights, Champ. I got six of his fight tapes. The two I gave you are the best. I want you to see how he uses his defense to tire his opponents out. You gotta get it in your head. I want you to memorize every frame, so when he does it to you, you'll see it coming a mile away. You might have to go on the defensive with this guy and let him come to you. Stuff like that will confuse him."

Lonzo narrowed his eyes. He never backed up in any fight.

"That's what I'm talking about," Fats said, reading his expression. "This fight will be different from all the others, Champ. You have to change your game plan, or you won't beat him."

"Alright," Lonzo said. "I'll watch the tapes when I get home. But after I whoop this clown, I want you to stop telling me everybody can beat my ass."

"I promise," Fats said. "I won't never say nothing like that again – until your next fight."

Lonzo shook his head.

Fats laughed at his own joke, and then he became serious. "You know, I got a lot riding on this fight..."

Lonzo did know that. Fats used a middleman to bet on all of his fights. He'd be ahead by now if he left it at that, but Fats also bet on other fighters as well as basketball and football games. Lonzo was his only *sure thing*, so Fats was known to bet more than half his savings on The Champ.

"It's not just the bets," Fats went on. "I got my whole life tied up in this, in *you* Lonzo. I've invested all my money, all my time. My wife hates me. My kids don't even know me. When I go to the bank for a loan, and they ask what's my collateral, I write your name on that line, in big, block letters. You're my whole world, Champ. When I say I got everything riding on this fight, I mean *everything*."

A lot of men couldn't handle that kind of pressure, but Lonzo had been carrying the city on his back for the last couple of years. There were at least three people in the gym who would've been homeless or in prison by now if it wasn't for Lonzo's fighting career.

"I'll watch the tapes tonight," he promised. "But you really need to lay off that gambling, man. You gon' lose your house over this shit one day."

Fats nodded and wiped his sweat again. "Just a couple more fights, and I'll be good. I promise I'll quit; just need a couple more wins..."

Lonzo was still in a good mood when he got home, but it didn't last long. Nisha had bad news from the doctor and even worse news about her employer. She stood over the stove trying to put together a spaghetti dinner using only her good hand.

Baby Lonzo crawled around the living room, babbling to no one, playing with an assortment of noisy toys. Big Lonzo loved the pitter patter of his son on most days, but at that moment, everything was irritating.

"Shonda say I can still sue him," Nisha was saying. "He can't prove I didn't hurt my arm at work – even if it happened six months ago. And him letting my insurance get cancelled, ain't no excuse for that. I called some lawyers, and they gon' call me back tomorrow."

"What about your days off?" Lonzo asked. "He not gon' pay for those?"

"I, I don't know," Nisha said. She sprinkled a little salt in the water boiling on the stove and then deposited a box of dry pasta. "He didn't say he was firing me, so I guess he's still paying for my week off."

"Why would he fire you?" Lonzo asked. Something wasn't right about the story she was telling him.

"He said I might be a liability," Nisha reported.

"What the hell that mean?"

"He said I might hurt myself again at work, and then I could sue him. He don't know if I can work before I have surgery."

"But you ain't got no insurance to pay for the surgery anyway," Lonzo said. He stood in the hallway with his arms folded under his chest. His irritation grew steadily, mainly because Nisha insisted on having this conversation with her back to him, but also because Baby Lonzo wouldn't chill with all of that noise.

"I don't have to have surgery now," Nisha said. In addition to boiling the pasta, she was browning ground beef for the spaghetti sauce. She looked back at Lonzo and then quickly returned her eyes to the stove when she saw his expression.

"What you mean you don't have to have surgery now?" Lonzo asked. "You just gon' run around with your arm jacked up?"

"Doctor said it won't hurt if I keep this splint on for three weeks."

Lonzo sighed loudly. "But you don't have no insurance to get your surgery anyway, right?"

"I don't know," Nisha said. "It don't, it don't look like it. But I can still sue Dr. Coates so he'll–"

"Yeah, you already said that," Lonzo grumbled. "Do you, do you got any idea how long it takes to sue somebody? That shit could drag on for years. You need your surgery *now*."

"No, I don't," Nisha said. She looked back at him again. "I'll be okay, Lonzo. For real."

"How the hell you gon' be okay? And how you know a lawyer will even take your case?"

"It's some more stuff going on," Nisha said and turned back to the stove.

"What other stuff is going on?" Lonzo asked. A sneer slowly twisted the left side of his mouth.

"Lonzo, it's okay. I don't, I know you be tripping. You got a bad temper, baby, and I can see you already getting mad."

He took a few steps until he was close enough to touch her. "What other kind of stuff is going on, Nisha?"

"Lonzo, it's–"

He grabbed her shoulder and spun her around. The greasy spatula flew from her hand and got wedged between the stove and refrigerator. "Look at me when I'm talking to you!" he demanded.

Nisha's eyes were wide and fearful. She held her hands up in defense or surrender. Lonzo saw her fingers were trembling. "Lonzo, please..."

She was near tears. Lonzo's heart softened, but his brain raced.

"Just tell me," he said softly.

"Some, some harassment," she said with a shudder. Her bottom lip quivered. Her chest rose and fell raggedly.

Lonzo's brown eyes became cold and threatening. "What the hell you talking about?"

"He said some stuff. He, he said some stuff to me. Like, like everything will be okay at work if I... If I..." She couldn't say it. Watching Lonzo's face transform into the monster she'd only seen in the boxing ring didn't help any.

The smell of ground beef was overpowering. Nisha turned and saw smoke rising from the skillet. She reached for it, but Lonzo grabbed the handle first. He grunted as he swung it. Nisha threw her arms over her face and ducked like she heard a gunshot. Lonzo chucked the skillet across the kitchen. It impacted the wall with a loud **THUK**! that created an inch-deep crater in the sheetrock and sent sizzling beef and hot grease flying in all directions.

Nisha screamed, though none of the grease hit her, and then she looked instinctively to her baby. Lonzo Jr. was out of view when his daddy threw the frying pan, but he crawled to the dining room to see what the noise was. He looked at his parents with an odd expression. Nisha knew he was learning a very important lesson about the way things worked in this house: There was but one Alpha Male, and when the Alpha Male was angry, shit hit the fan.

Lonzo reached for Nisha's shoulders, possibly to shake the hell out of her, but at the last moment he caught himself. He slowly lowered his hands to his sides and took a deep breath.

"Forget about the food right now and talk to me," he said. His words were nearly calm, but his face was dark. His Adam's apple bobbed as he tried to swallow his emotions.

Nisha burst into tears. Lonzo took that to mean she had done the unthinkable.

"He been messing with you?" he asked. "He touched you?"

"No!" She shook her head furiously. "He, he just said some stuff. He never touched me, Lonzo! I swear!"

"What he say?"

"He, he said I could come back to work if we, you, you know. He, he didn't come right out and say it, but he been sleeping with Toya, and he said he don't know me like he know Toya, and he wanna know me like he know her..."

She wiped her face with shaky hands. Her nose was running. She felt heat from the boiling pasta on the back of her neck. She knew the burner she was browning the meat on was glowing red. She wanted to turn it off but dared not. There was meat and grease all over the kitchen floor, but she couldn't attend to that either. The only thing that mattered at the moment were the red veins growing in the whites of Lonzo's eyes.

"Who the hell is Toya?"

"She, she the girl who work with me. She been, sleeping with Dr. Coates."

"He touched you?" Lonzo asked again.

"No, baby! I swear. He never – we never touched. Never, Lonzo! *I swear!*"

"I'ma kill him," he said definitively. His nostrils flared like a bull's.

"No, please," Nisha begged. "Nothing happened! He just said some stuff."

"That's enough right there," Lonzo growled. "That nigga can't, he came at you like that? Goddamned snake in the grass, perverted, sonofa..." He couldn't get his words together, so he balled his fists instead. His whole body trembled. "I'ma kill him."

"No!" Nisha grabbed hold of him, hoping to calm him down before he worked himself into a frenzy. She wrapped her arms around his torso and clinched her hands behind his back. She pressed her cheek against his chest and cried while she listened to his heartbeats. His body was hot, and so was the rest of the kitchen. Nisha sensed a fire would start soon, or maybe it already had.

"Lonzo, please," she pleaded. "Please, Lonzo, let it go. He gon' get his. I talked to Shonda. I called some lawyers already. I can sue him. If you go over there and start some mess, ain't nothing good gon' come from it. You'll go to jail, and we won't have nothing. We won't have nothing without you. I need you to stay here with me," she moaned. "*I need you.* The baby needs you..."

She clung to him like a baby possum on his mama's back, and gradually she felt his tension subside. He broke away from her without saying anything and went to the bedroom to change out of his work clothes. When he exited the closet, Lonzo stretched across the bed and stared up at the ceiling, while Nisha cleaned the mess in the kitchen.

She finished the spaghetti sauce with onions, garlic, bell peppers and mushrooms, but it wasn't as good without the meat. Lonzo didn't each much of his supper, and neither did she.

After dinner, he didn't want to talk about Dr. Coates anymore. He didn't want to watch the videos Fats gave him either. He went to bed early, while Nisha rocked the baby to sleep in the living room. She didn't think their apartment had ever been so quiet and lonely.

The next morning, The Champ was quiet during breakfast. Nisha didn't want to talk about Dr. Coates, but she needed to know he believed her about what happened at work.

"Are you mad at *me*, or about what's going on?"

"Just the situation," Lonzo said. "This ain't a good time to be losing no money. Got a fight coming up. I don't have time to train as it is."

"Don't we still have some money left, from your last fight?"

"We got some, but not like you thinking. I had to pay for your ring. I gave my grandmama some too..."

Nisha looked down at her engagement ring, not for the first time feeling like she wasn't worthy of such a gift. "I'm gonna talk to the lawyers," she promised.

"That ain't gon' help us today," Lonzo said. "And it ain't gon help us next week, when you supposed to get your paycheck. I already know that ho ass nigga ain't gon' pay you. And then he got the nerve to..." His jaws clenched. Nisha saw a vein bulging on the side of his head.

"You, you not gon' mess with him, are you?"

"What for?" he asked, shaking his head. "What can I do, beat him up and take his money? That shit won't help."

Nisha was glad he had sense enough to know that. "So you not going over there? You promise?" She begged with her eyes, and he shook his head again.

"He ain't gon' do nothing but call the law on me."

Nisha sighed gratefully. "I'm sorry," she said. "I wish I never woulda got hurt."

"Why you say that? So you could stay there working for Chester the Molester?" He pushed away from the table and stood abruptly. "I'm finna go."

"Baby..."

"I don't wanna talk no more," Lonzo said on his way out of the kitchen. "I ain't got shit else to say."

He made it through his shift at work without losing his cool. His co-workers knew something was wrong with him, so they didn't criticize his meal selection at lunchtime. There was a running joke about Lonzo turning into the Incredible Hulk when he became angry, but there's a bit of honesty behind every joke.

His co-workers never wanted to get on The Champ's bad side. Lonzo didn't talk to them when he was upset, and in turn they all left him alone, and everybody got to go home safe and sound.

Except Lonzo didn't go home when he left the job that day. He knew it was foolish to have any interactions with Dr. Coates, but it was equally wrong to stand idly by when a man insults your woman. In the hood, you could get killed for shit like that. Even aristocrats had the right to slap an offender with a glove and challenge him to a duel.

Lonzo pulled into the pharmacy's parking lot at 5:45, fifteen minutes before they closed for the day. He stepped boldly through the front door, and a chime went off overhead. He was greeted by a light-skinned girl with big, red lips and wide, child-bearing hips. She looked him up and down, taking in his work clothes, his bronze tint, and the wild look in his eyes. Rather than take off running, like a smart woman would, Toya smiled.

"Hey, Lonzo."

She licked her lips, and that stopped him in his tracks. His mind was ripe with fury, but her heart was filled with lust. The conflicting emotions made him wary. He suspected a trap.

"How you know me?"

"You Nisha's boyfriend," Toya said. "I seen you in the papers. You won all your fights."

He looked into her eyes and quickly recognized her as a whore. He saw the look in the groupies who came by the gym or tried to get into his training room before and after his fights.

"You looking for Dr. Coates?" Toya asked.

Lonzo nodded, not liking the vibe in the pharmacy. Nisha told him her co-worker was a whore. Maybe she was a siren, luring him to his death. Either way, he said, "Yeah."

"He in there," Toya said and pointed to a closed door behind the counter.

Lonzo expected her to summon Dr. Coates, but she simply pointed. He stepped around the register, and she didn't back away from him. He regarded her queerly.

"What the hell wrong with you?" he asked.

"Nothing," Toya said. "I like you."

This was getting stranger by the second, but Lonzo would not be swayed by this tramp. He turned away from her and approached the boss man's office. When he pulled the door open,

Dr. Coates looked up at him like he saw a ghost. And then the pharmacists' eyes narrowed, and he slowly rose from his seat.

"What can I do for you, Alonzo?" he asked calmly.

Lonzo had so much on his mind, he forgot what he wanted to say. Behind him a whore licked her lips. In front of him stood a man who had every reason to fear for his life, but he didn't look afraid at all.

"Did you come to talk about Lanisha?" the pharmacist prompted.

"Yeah," Lonzo said and walked into the cramped office. "She say you fired her 'cause she hurt her arm. Then you talking about she can still have her job if she give you some."

Dr. Coates smiled and shook his head. "I didn't say that, Alonzo. I told her I didn't know her very well. I had a feeling she would misinterpret my words, and I was right. But I assure you, I only meant that I didn't know her very well *on a professional level.*"

At that moment Lonzo knew the pharmacist was full of shit, and everything happened just as Nisha said. He also knew they would never get a dime from this slick sonofabitch. All the pain and rage from last night returned in an instant. His muscles tensed. He took another step forward.

Dr. Coates saw the change in his demeanor, but he continued to smile. "What are you thinking, Alonzo? Did you come here to talk or start some trouble?"

"You fired Nisha for nothing. She ain't never did nothing wrong."

"I didn't fire her. She's welcome back anytime she wants."

"Nigga she ain't finna come back to work for yo bitch ass!"

"That's fine," Dr. Coates said. "That's her decision. I'll accept that as her resignation."

"What about her surgery?"

"The insurance would've covered it," Dr. Coates said. "But I'm not paying for Nisha's insurance now that she doesn't work here. That, that wouldn't make sense."

The bastard had an answer for everything. Lonzo knew he'd been outsmarted once again. The sting of inadequacy was strong, because he hadn't experienced it much since high school. God made a way for him to fight his way to a better living, because his brain wasn't as quick as the smart kids'. But even as an adult, these nerds always came along to knock him down a peg. His face reddened, and he balled his fists, on purpose.

"Don't do it," Dr. Coates warned. "That would be the–"

Lonzo shut him up with a quick left hook that sent the pharmacist crashing to the floor in a twisted heap of legs and arms. The blow sounded off like a paintball gun.

POP!

Lonzo regretted the move right away. He knew he shouldn't have come here. He knew he wouldn't be able to control himself once he and Nisha's boss were face to face.

Worry washed over him like a cold shower, and he reached for the pharmacist. He wanted to help him up. Maybe there was a way they could rewind all of this and nobody had to go to jail.

But Dr. Coates was as tall as Lonzo and nearly as big. He sprang to his feet with a slight wobble, and rather than back away from his assailant, he stood his ground, grinning now. Blood spilled from his split lip and stained his teeth, but the bastard was still grinning.

"You did it now," he said, nodding ferociously, like a mad man. "That is *assault*! And you are a *boxer*! That makes it assault with a deadly weapon, asshole! Did you know that, you big dummy? Did you know that, Mr. *Alonzo*?"

The pharmacist sounded like a white man now, and that freaked Lonzo out more than his actual words. White people knew how to use the judges and police to put blacks away for decades at a time. A nigga would've thrown caution to the wind and hit Lonzo back, but white people like to fight with their brain. They like to run and tell it.

Lonzo took a step back, and Dr. Coates laughed.

"Yeah, got your attention now, don't I?" the pharmacist said. "That's 'cause you're a *nigger*, Alonzo. And the one thing all niggers are afraid of is *jail*."

Dr. Coates even said the word *nigger* like a white man. Lonzo didn't know what to make of it. His confusion was obvious, and Dr. Coates loved it.

"Yeah, I'm finally getting through your thick head, now, ain't I, boy?"

The condescending tone made the sneer return to Lonzo's lips, but Dr. Coates wasn't afraid.

"Do it!" he shouted. "Come on, man! You wanna kick my ass? Do it! But smile for the camera first!"

Blood and spittle flew from the pharmacist's mouth, and Lonzo hesitated again. He looked up and saw the camera in the corner to the right, pointing right at him. It was a trap. He knew it all along.

"No?" Dr. Coates said. "You through assaulting me? Okay. Now that you've had your way, let me tell you how this is gonna go: You're gonna walk out of here, and I never want to see you or your nappy-headed girlfriend *ever again*. I'm gonna take pictures of this nice little wound you gave me and get the tape from that camera.

"But I'm not gonna call the police on you. No. I'm not going to do that. What I'm gonna do is put my evidence in a manila envelope and tape it closed. I'm gonna give it to my lawyer, and if you or Lanisha ever even *think* about suing me for anything, *that's* when my folder's going to the police.

"Sure, you might get me for some workman's comp, but I'll ruin your career, you ignorant thug. By the time you get out of jail, you'll have to do all of your fighting in a nursing home. You'll be *done*, son! Do you understand what I'm telling you? Do you see how this shit's gonna go?"

Lonzo did see how this shit was gonna go. He understood perfectly. And though he was pretty sure Dr. Coates couldn't get him locked up until he was old enough to go to a nursing home, any arrest at this point in his life could derail his boxing career.

Lonzo thought about the promises he made to his woman and all the people in his camp. He thought about the desperate look in Fats' eyes and the confused look in his son's eyes when Baby Lonzo crawled into the kitchen and saw their dinner splattered on the kitchen wall.

It took every bit of his will power, but he found the strength to turn around and walk out of the pharmacy.

CHAPTER EIGHT
THE DANGEROUS MR. BROWN

The drive home was slow and tedious. Lonzo felt like he was a child again, expecting a whooping when he got home for something bad he did at school that day. His grandmother whooped him a lot when he was young, but he loved her dearly. His biological mother never laid a hand on him, and he hated her guts.

Lonzo hated his biological father too, though he never met him. Rumor had it his father was a marine who *supposedly* died overseas when Lonzo was in grade school. If that was true, Lonzo's grandmother said he should get money from the government. But he never got a dime of his dead dad's money, so he figured Larry was never a marine. He was probably a john, or maybe a crackhead like Lonzo's mom.

He checked the rearview mirror frequently as he drove home, thinking the police would pull behind him at any moment, even though Dr. Coates said he wouldn't call them unless Nisha tried to sue.

"Dammit!" Lonzo cursed himself and banged his fist on the steering wheel. Nisha was a beautiful woman. She was a good woman. She deserved a man who would make better decisions for their family. Instead she gambled on a dumb boxer who had made a lot more bad moves in his life than good ones.

When he pulled into his apartments, Lonzo remained in the car for a few minutes and collected his thoughts. What he was really looking for was a distraction. He found one when he saw Reggie step out onto his breezeway and head down the stairs.

Reginald was Nisha's big brother by a year and a half. Once upon a time he was a contender like his father. Reggie dropped out of high school and gave boxing his all for a few years, but after starting his career with a record of 1-8, Walter pulled him aside and told him, "Hey, son, boxing ain't for you."

Reggie toyed around with a few other dreams as he grew into an adult, but he was never any good at anything legal. Finally he decided if he couldn't beat the devil, he might as well join him. He became the first career criminal in Nisha's immediate family. Five years later, he was still going strong.

Lonzo got out of his car and met him with a handshake and a quick embrace.

"What's up, homeboy."

"Oh, shit! It's The Champ!" Reggie's smile was broad and genuine. "What it do, Lonzo? Sorry I missed your last fight. Heard you tried to knock that boy's head *clean off*!"

Reggie was a skinny guy, 6'1, no more than 170 pounds. He sported a baby afro. He was dark-skinned with a big nose like his father and big, bushy eyebrows that didn't seem right for his face.

Overall Lonzo thought Nisha's brother was unattractive, but Reggie always had plenty women because he was well paid, and his reputation in the streets was solid. He sported a thick gold bracelet, a more expensive chain and real diamonds in each ear.

"You know I try to knock a head off *every* fight," Lonzo said. "Ain't got one of 'em to fly off yet, though."

Reggie laughed. "You keep trying, man."

"You know I will," Lonzo said. "What's been up with you?"

"Just came to holler at Nisha, see if my nephew's learning to walk yet."

"He almost got it," Lonzo said. "He gon' be something else, watch."

"Most definitely," Reggie agreed. He pulled out his keychain and pushed the alarm button.

Lonzo heard a chirp behind him. He turned and his mouth fell open when he saw Reggie's ride. Nisha's big brother had a new Chrysler 300 sitting on 22-inch rims. His two-tone paint job shined like a new quarter.

"*Daaamn!*" Lonzo exclaimed. "Man, I didn't know you was rolling like *that*."

"Yeah, this my baby," Reggie said with a grin. He checked out Lonzo's old Buick and quickly looked away. "So, how's it been going with you? You still waiting for the big one?"

"I'm getting close," Lonzo said, but his shoulders drooped in defeat.

"How you and Nee Nee doing?" Reggie asked. "I see she got that cast on her arm. Look like she gon' be out of work for a minute."

"It was only gonna be for a week," Lonzo revealed. "But I went down to her job and got into it with her boss. Now she straight up fired. I haven't told her yet." He looked up at his apartment. "I ain't in no rush to talk to her."

"Aww, it'll be alright," Reggie said. "You know Nee Nee down for you – no matter what. Y'all been through some hard times before. She always got your back."

"I know," Lonzo said. "But it feel different now. Ain't no dirty money to fall back on. It's like, whatever I make at my job and the little cash I get from fighting – that's it. That's all we got to live on."

Reggie pursed his lips and scratched his nose. "You know, if you ever need something–"

"Naw, we cool," Lonzo said right away. Reggie should've known The Champ wouldn't take money from him.

"I know you don't wanna come back to work for Mr. Brown..."

That was a touchy subject. Lonzo looked into his eyes, and Reggie looked down at his sneakers.

Back when Lonzo first started dating Nisha, he palled around with her brother a lot, and Reggie introduced him to Overbrook Meadows' most notorious kingpin. Mr. Brown took Lonzo under his wing and paid him handsomely for an assortment of illegalities. When Nisha got pregnant with Baby Lonzo, The Champ decided he'd had enough. Lonzo was one of few men to leave Mr. Brown's employment with no repercussions.

"Nah, you don't want that," Reggie said and kicked a stray pebble. "I'm just saying, you know he'll take you back. If you need some ends to get over this little hump, until your boxing money gets better…"

The thought of seeing Mr. Brown again made Lonzo's heart race. He sighed and wiped his brow, which was unexpectedly moist. He looked up at his apartment, and this time he saw Nisha standing on the breezeway, looking down at them. She had the baby in her arms.

Lonzo couldn't see her expression from his vantage point, but he knew she was not pleased. Nisha loved Reggie as much as any sister loves her brother, but she thought Reggie and Lonzo together was a bad combination. Considering what happened three years ago, Lonzo figured she was right.

But there was nothing wrong with testing the waters a little bit, was there?

"When you gon' see Mr. Brown again?" he asked, returning his gaze to Reggie.

"I'm headed that way now," Reggie said. "Why? You want me to tell him something?"

"I don't know." Lonzo stuffed his hands in his pockets. "I might wanna see what he talking about; see what's popping over there."

"You know it's all good," Reggie said. He reached into his pocket and produced a huge fold of bills that made Lonzo lick his lips. "Everybody on Mr. Brown's team gets paid. But you know Nee Nee don't want you over there." Reggie looked back at their apartment and saw Nisha himself. "Say, man, you know she watching us?"

"Yeah, I seen her."

"I'm finna bounce, before she starts tripping. You want me to tell Mr. Brown something, or what?"

"I kinda wanna talk to him myself," Lonzo said. "Can I roll over there with you?"

Reggie grinned. "Yeah, man. You know you can roll." He looked back at his sister. "She gon' start hating me again, though…"

"I'm a grown man. She can't hate you for nothing I do."

Reggie laughed. "Yeah right."

Lonzo chuckled too, but his was a nervous laughter.

They climbed into Reggie's car, and Lonzo fell in love with the leather and wood grain interior. He looked up at his breezeway again as he fastened the seatbelt. Nisha was no longer in sight. Two seconds later his cellphone rang. He gave Reggie a look as he dug it from his pocket.

"Hey, what's up, baby?"

"What are you doing?" Nisha asked.

"Nothing," Lonzo said. "Chilling."

"Why you get in the car with Reggie?"

"We finna roll for a second. I'll be right back."

"Where you going?"

"I said I'll be right back."

"I know you didn't forget what happened. Reggie ain't got nothing going on that involves you. You need to get out of that car."

Lonzo knew his woman was right. After the fiasco at the pharmacy a few minutes ago, he understood his way of thinking was flawed. But he was already in Reggie's car. He'd look like a bitch, if Nisha made him come inside.

"I'll be back in a minute," he said and hung up on her.

Reggie watched him for a few seconds and then asked, "You still wanna go?"

"Yeah," Lonzo said and leaned back in his seat. "What you waiting for?"

Reggie shrugged. He started the car, and Lonzo was hit with bass from all the factory speakers as well as two sub woofers in the trunk. The Tupac song was one of his favorites.

"Damn. It's like that?"

Reggie had to turn the volume down to hear him. "What's up?"

"I say, '*It's like that*?'" Lonzo repeated. "That shit sound clean as hell!"

"Oh, *yeah*." Reggie grinned. "The more bass you got, the quicker them hoes panties fall off. Check this out..." He pushed a few buttons on the radio, and a tune that was dear to Lonzo began to play.

"Turn that shit up!" Lonzo said, and he and Reggie bobbed their head to Slick's song as they exited the apartment complex.

"Here come The Champ!"

Mr. Brown was Overbrook Meadows' Teflon Don. It was common knowledge he was involved in all types of iniquities, from guns and drugs to gambling and prostitution. The district attorney attempted to prosecute him a dozen times, but the crime lord had more lawyers than OJ, and so far no witness had been willing to testify against him.

Mr. Brown was known to order a hit on a dopefiend or a police officer with the same nonchalance. He once killed a man's wife and their autistic child over a $10,000 gambling debt. The city would never forget the time his henchmen took out an eight-grader who was selling weed on the corner.

Lonzo didn't fear any man, but Mr. Brown wasn't on the level of normal men. He was more of a phenomenon, an act of nature. He was the personification of evil, yet people flocked to him, because money is the root of all evil. Lonzo hadn't seen him in three years. He wondered if Mr. Brown remained fond of him after all that time.

Reggie drove north to a neighborhood called Fossil Creek. This part of town featured upscale homes that cost half a million or better. Lonzo felt out of place as they navigated smooth streets that had never seen a pothole. Reggie finally pulled into the circular driveway of a three-story home that looked like a miniature castle.

"He still living large," Lonzo noticed.

"This ain't even where he stay," Reggie informed him. "He bought this house for his baby-mama. Don't nobody know where he really lives."

One day, Lonzo told himself as he stared out of the passenger window like a tourist. He could imagine the look on Nisha's face when he brought her to a house like this and gave her a set of keys. *It's yours, baby. All yours.*

Lonzo's fascination continued when they got inside. He felt like he was in a museum, or on the set of an episode of Cribs. Mr. Brown's pad was spacious, decorated with an African motif.

There were paintings and sculptures artfully arranged to catch the eye.

In the foyer, Lonzo and Reggie encountered two men, one of whom Lonzo knew. Bumpy was tall and dark like the bottom of a grave. He was a hulk of a man stuffed in an Armani suit. His cohort was equally massive and just as dapper. They gave Reggie an approving nod, and Bumpy stared at Lonzo with a serious, yet almost bored expression.

"How's it going, Champ?" Bumpy was Mr. Brown's personal assistant. He didn't crack a smile or exhibit any show of emotion.

"What's up," Lonzo told him.

"Hold your hands out," the other goon said.

Lonzo frowned, but he complied. The bodyguard frisked him and then nodded to Bumpy when he didn't find anything.

"Follow me," Bumpy said.

He took them to a living room that was so exquisite, Lonzo didn't want to sit down in his dirty work clothes.

"Wait here," Bumpy told them and continued down a long corridor.

Lonzo didn't like the stuffy atmosphere, but somewhere around the corner he heard music playing and men laughing boisterously. He wished he could wait with those guys, but more than that he wished he had gone home to his woman instead of getting in Reggie's car.

Bumpy returned after a few moments and told The Champ, "Come on."

Lonzo gave Reggie a look before he followed the bear down the hallway. His sixth sense was blaring: *Danger! Danger!* But Lonzo kept his cool, because he knew he didn't owe Mr. Brown any money. This was simply a meeting. There would be no obligations unless Lonzo agreed to them.

Bumpy stopped at a large door and pushed it open. He stepped aside, motioning for The Champ to enter ahead of him.

Lonzo wasn't surprised by how plush the room was. Your attention was immediately drawn to an 85-inch plasma television mounted on the wall like a movie screen. That was nothing compared to the Parnian desk made from six different kinds of exotic wood. It had to cost over a hundred thousand.

Behind the desk sat the man himself. Mr. Brown was tall and stout, no less than 260 pounds. He had thick lips and a flat nose, short hair that was always trimmed to perfection. The kingpin didn't wear a beard or moustache. His hands were large and calloused from the hard work he put in before he became the richest thug in the city.

Mr. Brown's suit was black. His shirt was lime green. His skin was dark with a hint of red, like a shot of cognac. He smiled, revealing larger than normal teeth that were a constant reminder that he was Overbrook Meadows' deadliest predator. He stood and reached to shake Lonzo's hand.

"Well, ain't you a sight for sore eyes." Mr. Brown's voice was deep and gravelly. He wore one ring on each hand. Both were diamond clustered. He even smelled expensive, though Lonzo couldn't place the fragrance. "How's the world treating you, Champ?"

Their handshake lasted longer than normal, but Lonzo was used to this. Ever since he became locally famous, everyone wanted to shake his hand. Few people let go in a timely manner.

"I'm good," Lonzo said. "I see you still on top of your game."

"I'm just a hardworking man like you," Mr. Brown said, grinning broadly. "Have a seat. Take a load off."

Mr. Brown sat in an executive chair that was big enough to be a throne. Lonzo took a seat across from him in a smaller leather chair that was almost as nice.

"What brings you to this neck of the woods?" Mr. Brown asked. "I couldn't believe it when Reggie said you wanted to see me."

"I know. It's been a while," Lonzo said. "I just, you know, came to say what's up." He shrugged and looked around the office. "I like your digs, man. You got this place decked out like the white folks."

Mr. Brown nodded. His eyes narrowed, but his smile remained. "What about you, Champ? You got that warehouse uniform on. I always admired that about you: A lot of people hustle because they too lazy to go to work every morning, but you handle your business."

"Got to," Lonzo said. "Got mouths to feed."

"You still with the same gal?"

"We getting married," Lonzo confirmed.

"That's good," Mr. Brown said with a nod of his massive head. "That's real good, Champ."

Lonzo shrugged. "It's good, but it ain't easy."

"I know it ain't. What about your boxing? They ain't paying you like they should?"

"I do alright. In a couple more fights, I'll be making some real money. But for now, you know, just some local shit."

"That's a damned shame," Mr. Brown said. "Good fighter like you, strong, family man... Gotta work for the man every day, even though you the best heavyweight out there."

"I gotta beat the best to be the best," Lonzo corrected him. "But I'm getting there. About three more fights, and I'll be at Madison Square Garden."

"I believe it. You the best, Champ. Everybody know it. Ain't no reason you should be fighting for chump change. Fats still managing you?"

Lonzo nodded and braced himself for the criticism he knew was coming.

Mr. Brown's smile fell for the first time. He twisted his jowls in disgust.

"You know that fat bastard ain't worth a shit. With anybody else, you'd be making fifty thou' a fight by now. How Fats gon' represent you, when he can't represent his damn self? He can't walk in a room without sweating. His clothes ugly, and they don't fit right. Nigga prolly ain't never met a tailor his whole life."

"Me and Fats never lost a fight."

"That ain't got nothing to do with him managing your money. I can't say if the man is a good trainer or not. My guess would be *no*, because he never had a fighter that was worth a shit, except you. You ever think about that, Champ? You the only one. You know what that tells me?"

Lonzo had an idea, but he didn't say anything.

"It tells me Fats ain't the reason you winning. You winning 'cause you a bad motherfucker. Fats is just riding on your coattails. Why don't you let me take over as your manager and promoter? I'll make it so you get paid *every* fight. Not in two years. Not when you get to be champion. I'm talking about *right now*.

"Matter of fact, I'll give you fifty thou' today, as an advance for your next fight. You can call your boss in the morning and tell him you ain't never coming back to that warehouse. Leave that kind of work for the Mexicans."

Lonzo's heart skipped a beat. Mr. Brown certainly had the capital to invest in him, but that fifty thousand wouldn't come without a price. If Lonzo won his next fight, everything would be cool.

But if something unexpected happened, say Lonzo got into a freak accident and couldn't fight, things would go very badly very quickly. Besides that, he didn't want to be mixed up with a known gangster when he made it to the top.

He shook his head, thinking about how Mike Tyson ended up going broke, while Don King got richer and richer. "I don't want no money for something I haven't did yet. Fats is a sloppy ass nigga, but I got love for him. I respect him."

That wasn't the answer Mr. Brown was hoping for, and he couldn't hide his disappointment. If this wasn't about money, it was a waste of time.

"So what you come here for, Lonzo? I know you don't wanna go back to work for me, not after that shit that went down with HB."

Lonzo's stomach churned again. He hadn't thought about HB much since the incident. "I been thinking about it," he said. "Some shit went down today. My girl lost her job, and she injured. Gotta have surgery. The next couple of months gon' be hard."

Mr. Brown watched his eyes. "So you just want some temporary work? Like a summer job?"

"Yeah," Lonzo said, though it was early November. "I'm not a hundred percent positive I wanna do this," he added. "I just came to, you know, talk to you, see if you would even take me back."

Mr. Brown gave it some thought. He would much rather take over as the boxer's manager, but he could use another enforcer on the payroll – especially someone who was well known around the city. Mr. Brown imagined the fear he would incite by uttering the words, *Don't make me send The Champ over there...*

"Alright," he said. "If you wanna come back to work, I got a job for you. How long before you make up your mind?"

"Gimme a couple of weeks," Lonzo said. "I need to, you know, make sure there ain't no other way to make this shit work."

"Why I always got to be your last resort?" Mr. Brown wanted to know.

Lonzo didn't answer. No one makes a deal with the devil unless it's their last resort. Surely the mastermind knew that.

"Alright," Lonzo said and stood stiffly. "I'll get in touch with you."

Mr. Brown stood too, and they shook hands again. Their handshake was a lot less warm and fuzzy this time.

"Take it easy, Champ. And good luck with your situation. Hope you get things squared away. Even if you don't need the work, you don't have to wait till you're in a bind before you come see me. You're always welcome around here."

"Thanks," Lonzo said. "I appreciate that, man. For real."

When he got back to the living room, there was a small crowd that hadn't been there a minute ago. Most of them were men, but Lonzo saw a few females among them. The girls were dressed like they were headed for their jobs at a strip club. Lonzo knew they all worked for Mr. Brown.

The men recognized The Champ and wanted to strike up a conversation, but Lonzo wanted to go home. He looked around for Reggie and saw someone else he knew.

"Slick! What up, boy!"

The rapper was surprised to see him. "Lonzo! Yo, what up!" He crossed the room and gave him some dap. "What you doing over here?"

"I was gon' ask you the same question. I'm looking for Reggie, to see if he can give me a ride home."

"I'll give you a ride," Slick said. He smiled brightly, his gold grill gleaming. He looked back and told someone, "Say, I'll be right back. Gotta give my nigga a ride to the crib. Come on," he told Lonzo.

"So, what you doing here?" Slick asked again when they were outside. "I thought you didn't mess with Mr. Brown no more."

"Nisha lost her job. I might need some ends pretty soon."

"What about your boxing?" Slick asked. "Man, if I was you, I'd just roll with that. Ain't nothing over here but trouble. You doing good, Lonzo. You don't need to be getting back in this kinda shit. It ain't your thing."

Slick disabled his alarm and Lonzo got into another ride that was worth more than his and Nisha's cars combined.

"You still ain't told me what *you* doing over here," Lonzo said as he fastened his seat belt. "I thought your rap shit was taking off."

"It is," Slick said, "slowly but surely. Mr. Brown is my manager. He pay for all my studio time and for my mixtapes. He lines up my shows too. All I got to do is show up and rock the house."

"He paying you good?"

"I do alright. But on the real, most of my ends come from *other* stuff I do for Mr. Brown."

Lonzo already had an idea, but he asked, "Like what?"

"I drop off a few packs every now and then," Slick said. "Some safe shit. I only deal with regulars. I move about half a ki, maybe a ki a week. Sometimes a couple of weeks go by, and I don't have to do nothing. I can come over here anytime I want. Get high. Mess with them gals. It's all good."

It sounded nice, but driving around with a half or a whole kilogram of coke in your car is a huge risk. If Slick got caught, he'd be charged as a major distributor. He'd have to do a minimum of ten years in the penitentiary.

"Be careful," Lonzo told him. "Don't forget, I need you to lead me to the ring when we get to Austin."

"Nigga, don't you forget that shit yourself," Slick replied. "You hang around Mr. Brown too much, and yo ass won't make it to Austin."

Lonzo knew he was showing concern, but Slick's comment sounded like a bad omen. And there was no wood around for Lonzo to knock on to chase away the premonition.

CHAPTER NINE
BLEED OUT

Nisha was waiting on Lonzo when he got home. She hadn't called again since he left with Reggie, and that was one of the things he loved about her. She cared for him dearly, and she could nag with the best of them, but she always seemed to know when she had to let her man be a man.

She also knew when it was time to lay out all of the cards and hopefully refocus her man's errant thinking.

She fixed low, curious eyes on Lonzo when he walked through the front door. He gave her a look that said, *I know what you're gonna say, and I'm sorry*, so she didn't follow him when he went to the bedroom to change out of his work clothes.

When she heard the shower turn on, she warmed his dinner and waited for him to come eat with her. He emerged from the bedroom wearing a white tee and a pair of boxers. He looked exhausted. Nisha knew he would fall asleep within minutes when he lie down for the night.

"Where'd you go?" she asked when he sat on the couch next to her.

"I went to see Mr. Brown," Lonzo replied. There was no point in lying. Reggie would probably keep the secret if Lonzo asked him to, but Nisha was a smart girl. She would've figured it out on her own.

"Why you go over there?"

"You know why I went over there." He watched the television instead of his woman's eyes. She turned it off, and he slowly met her gaze.

"You ain't gotta do nothing like that," Nisha said. "I talked to a lawyer. He said I can sue and make Dr. Coates pay for my surgery. He said I can sue him for firing me, and if I can get Toya to testify against him, I can sue him for that other stuff too. If we can get Toya to give a statement, he'll front us some money, until the case is settled. We won't have to wait a whole year to get paid."

Lonzo was shaking his head.

"Why not?" Nisha asked. "What's wrong? What, you didn't go over there, to the pharmacy, did you?"

He didn't say anything.

"You said you weren't going over there..."

"You shouldn't have told me about it," Lonzo argued. "You knew what I would do."

Nisha brought a hand to her mouth and shook her head.

"What'd you – tell me what happened."

"We had an argument," Lonzo explained. "He started talking shit, and I popped him."

Nisha's eyes grew large. "Lonzo, it's cameras in there..."

"You couldn't have told me that before?"

"That's common sense. How could, why would you think there wasn't no cameras?"

"So, what you saying? I'm stupid?"

Nisha was upset, but she was rational enough to recognize the dangerous buzzword. Lonzo believed his intellect was his only short-coming. The majority of his childhood fights were against people who were foolish enough to call him *dumb* or *retarded* or *stupid*.

"I'm not saying you're stupid. It's just, forget it. What happened? Did he, did he call the police?" Nisha's brow was furrowed, her eyes desperate.

"He said he will if you try to sue him," Lonzo reported. "He said he's gonna keep the video and take some pictures of his lip. He don't want to hear nothing else about you getting fired or needing surgery. If we leave him alone, he won't call the police."

Nisha knew Dr. Coates was smart, but she never thought he was this much of a conniver. Even still, she thought Dr. Coates's actions were a lot worse than what Lonzo did.

"He's bluffing. I'll call the lawyer back tomorrow."

"He ain't bluffing," Lonzo said. "He got the whole thing on tape."

"Even if he does report it, it's just a simple assault. You won't go to jail for that. You can probably get it dropped or get probation."

"You coming with these *probably's* and *if's*," Lonzo noticed. "But this is my life you talking about. What if I get a year? Everybody knows I ain't no choir boy. What if they give me two years? Them judges like to send a nigga up the river."

"That's not gonna happen."

"And then he can sue me when I get out," Lonzo said. "I seen that shit on TV. When Rick Ross and them beat up that DJ, he sued them for three hundred thousand. They had to pay it, too."

Nisha knew that he was right about a civil suit.

"So you sue him, then he sue me right back," Lonzo deduced. "How that's gon' help?"

"What are you saying? You just wanna forget about it?"

"I'm saying maybe you can get him, but he can get me too. So, yeah, forget it. It's squashed."

"Alright, but what about Mr. Brown? What he got to do with this?"

"He ain't got nothing to do with this," Lonzo said. He leaned back and closed his eyes. "I just went to holler at him."

"You're not going back to work for him, are you?"

Lonzo didn't respond.

"I know you haven't forgot what happened..."

He sighed.

"You should be locked up *right now*," Nisha reminded him. "The only reason you free is 'cause you got away from them people."

"I'm not back with them," Lonzo muttered. "I just went to holler at the man."

"About what?"

"Damn, woman. Get out my business." He got up and staggered to the bedroom.

Nisha remained in the living room and watched the blank television screen. She couldn't believe he would risk twenty years to life just so he could *talk* to a man. How could he care so little about his family? How could he be so selfish?

Nisha also resented her brother for his role in this foolishness. Reggie was at risk for the same prison time. He chose to continue working for Mr. Brown, and that was his bone-headed choice, but he had no right to drag Lonzo back into it. Nisha's man was on the straight and narrow now.

She sighed and pushed herself off the couch. She put away their uneaten meal and turned the lights off in the kitchen and front room. In the bedroom, Lonzo lie on his side with no sheet covering him. Baby Lonzo lie in front of him in a similar position. Lonzo Sr. was already snoring.

Nisha scooped up the child and deposited him in the crib they kept in the room. She crawled into bed with her fiancée and pulled the sheets over both of them. She inched closer, so she could spoon with him. Lonzo didn't stir. She kissed him on the back of his neck and closed her eyes, hoping she could find the Sandman as easily. The sooner she got this horrible day over with, the better. Surely things would turn around tomorrow.

Lonzo dozed off quickly, but he woke up when Nisha kissed him on the back of the neck. He opened his eyes and stared straight ahead, careful not to make any movements that would reveal his awareness.

If she knew he was awake, she'd want to talk more about Mr. Brown. He knew everything she had to say was on point, and those are the worst kinds of lectures to listen to. You can't do anything but nod and say, *"Yeah, baby. You right, baby. I know, baby. I'm sorry, baby."*

He closed his eyes again, but this time sleep was elusive. Now that Nisha planted the seed of dread in his heart, it wouldn't stop growing until thick branches of worry filled his whole chest. Inwardly he cursed her for bringing up the past, but it wasn't her fault. He was the one who did the deed. He had to live with the guilt and stress and the long stretch in prison if he ever got found out.

He wondered if Reggie suffered the same mental turmoil, or if his conscious was nonexistent after so many years of lawlessness. He wondered what HB was up to these days. He used to blame HB for the incident, but Lonzo understood he was just as culpable, even though he didn't pull the trigger.

That's the way the judge would see it, if they ever got prosecuted.

The night of *the incident* started like any other. Back then Lonzo's boxing career was off to a good start, and Baby Lonzo had not yet been conceived. Lonzo had never held down a steady job, and he was pleased with his role as Mr. Brown's enforcer/intimidator.

Mr. Brown sent him to handle sensitive matters that had not escalated to gunplay but were past the stage of a friendly phone call. Nisha's brother was one of Lonzo's ride-or-dies in those days. They participated in all sorts of mischief together, most of which Nisha never found out about.

Like Slick's dope-running, Lonzo didn't have to do a job for Mr. Brown every day, but he did enough to maintain his employment. Mr. Brown paid Lonzo two thousand a week, which was more than enough to pay all the bills, while Nisha went to school and figured out what she wanted to do with her life.

The night of December 23rd changed all of that.

It was seasonably chilly in Overbrook Meadows that day, with temperatures below freezing. The wind chill dipped even further after 11 pm. Lonzo stepped out of Mr. Brown's compound on the east side of town and stuffed his hands in the pockets of a leather trench coat. He shivered uncontrollably, blowing a soft plume of foggy vapor.

"Man it's colder than a polar bear's *toenails*!" Reggie exclaimed as he slid behind the wheel of a fully restored Cutlass Supreme.

"Hurry up and turn the heat on," Lonzo said. He opened the passenger door and took a seat next to Nisha's brother. "Why we can't do this in the morning?"

But Reggie had turned the ignition, filling the car with the tunes of a Marvin Gaye CD he was listening to at the time. He turned the music down and said, "Huh?"

"Never mind," Lonzo said. He fastened his seatbelt and put his hands back in his pockets. His breaths were still visible inside the car. The old Cutlass wouldn't put out any significant heat until they got on the freeway.

Reggie rubbed his paws together and put his ride in gear. He saw something out of the corner of his eye before he backed out.

"Look at this shit."

Lonzo saw a tall, muscular brother with a bald head like a Milk Dud exiting Mr. Brown's home. The man waved for them to stop as he took hurried steps towards the car.

"Who's that?" Lonzo asked.

"That's HB."

"What he want?"

"I don't know. I hope that nigga don't ask for a ride."

"Why?"

"That fool talk too much shit," Reggie said. "And he can back it up. That's two things you don't never want at the same time."

The Champ nodded, but he didn't know if that was such a bad thing. He talked plenty shit too, and everyone knew he had the fighting skills to back it up.

He rolled down his window, but HB pulled the passenger door open when he reached the car.

"Y'all going by Las Vegas Trail?" he asked.

"We going to Bryant Irving," Reggie said. "Not all the way to Las Vegas Trail."

"Nigga, that's the same way. You can drop me off when you get through with your job. Let me in, cuz," he said, pulling on Lonzo's seat.

Lonzo didn't like this thug forcing his way into Reggie's car, and he certainly didn't like being ordered around. "Nigga, who is you talking to?"

HB's bald dome shone under the bright moonlight. He wore no hair on his face other than bushy eyebrows that were perfect for the look of disapproval he fixed on The Champ.

"Yo name Lonzo, right? You supposed to be a boxer?"

"Yeah, fool. Now who is you?"

"I'm HB. I work for Mr. Brown too. Tell him I'm cool, Reggie."

Reggie didn't look like he wanted to vouch for him, but he said, "He cool, man."

"Whatever," Lonzo said. "That ain't got nothing to do with you running up on this car, telling me to move and shit."

HB stared down at him. For a moment, Lonzo thought he might have to get out and administer a beat-down. But the bald man's features softened, and he smiled.

"Alright. My bad. I don't know you, and I shouldn't have came at you like that. I would like a ride to the west side. Can I ride with y'all?" he asked in a voice that was prim and proper.

Lonzo couldn't help but laugh. "Cuz, you sound like a white boy." He pulled the seat release and leaned forward to allow HB entry.

"I'll talk like *Driving Miss Daisy* to get out this cold," HB said as he squeezed in the back.

Everyone laughed. HB pulled a blunt from his coat pocket to further lighten the mood.

"Y'all wanna smoke?"

"Do a fat girl like Little Debbie's?" Reggie said as he backed out of the driveway.

"What Mr. Brown got y'all doing?" HB asked.

"Finna go holler at a dude named Lou," Lonzo said. "He owe Mr. Brown twenty G's."

"Damn, that's a grip," HB said. "I wonder why he ain't sent no shooters over there yet."

"They related somehow," Lonzo informed him. "Like a distant cousin or something."

"I guess if *you* going to see him, they ain't related enough for Lou not to get his ass whooped," HB deduced.

"Naw, they ain't that close," Lonzo agreed.

Lou Alston lived in a one-story home in the Ridglea Hills neighborhood. It turned out, he was married to a favorite niece of the notorious Mr. Brown. But their marriage was on the rocks, and the bride moved out three months prior to Lonzo's visit.

Lou worked as a delivery driver for FedEx. He made good money, but he had always been the type who liked to live above his means. When he married Mr. Brown's niece, he wanted to offer her all the finer things she hadn't experienced up to that point.

This thinking caused Lou to borrow money from his bank for home improvement projects that were never completed. There was a huge hole in the backyard where he planned to build a coy pond, the skeleton of a deck on the back porch and a few walls torn down inside his home.

When Lou defaulted on his loan, the bank threatened foreclosure on his love nest, and he ran to the only person in the city who would give him twenty thousand cash with no credit check or even an application. Lou used the money to pay off the bank, but when the time came to pay Mr. Brown, he defaulted again, hoping his marital status would curtail the kingpin's tactics, which he'd heard about but never witnessed firsthand.

His assumption was correct, but the departure of his spouse changed everything. Even though Lou wasn't formally divorced, with his wife gone, he was no longer a fringe relative of Mr. Brown. He could no longer hide under the umbrella of safety that came with such a relationship.

Lonzo approached the front door, because he had no reason to believe Lou might flee the scene. Reggie stood near the back door just in case. HB walked along the side of the house, to make sure no rats sneaked out of the bedroom window. Lonzo didn't want HB's help with this, but the three hoodlums had become cordial on the way to Lou's house, and HB didn't want to miss the action.

Lonzo knocked on the door at 11:28 pm. After a few moments, a disheveled gentleman answered wearing a tee shirt and boxers. Lou was fair-skinned and handsome, in his late twenties. He had fuzzy dreadlocks and a potbelly that was out of place with the rest of his frame. His eyes were red, nearly bloodshot. Lonzo could smell a heavy stench of alcohol, even before Lou opened his mouth to speak.

"Can I help you?"

"Move out the way," Lonzo said. "I come to see about Mr. Brown's money."

Lou's eyes brightened, but he was too drunk to respond in a speedy manner.

"Boy, I said move!" Lonzo shoved the door open, knocking him to the ground in the process.

"*Ow!*"

The debtor rolled to his stomach and slowly scrambled to his feet. His boxers were too small, and both of his balls dangled from the shorts for a moment before he righted himself and faced Lonzo again.

"Hey, man! What the, what the hell, man? *Why?*"

Lonzo was so high, he found the rambling amusing. "Shut your bitch ass up! Go open the back door."

Lou looked over his shoulder, and his eyes widened.

Lonzo looked back and saw that HB had entered the home as well. HB closed the front door and locked it and folded his massive arms over his chest. Lonzo wasn't impressed, but he couldn't deny he was an imposing figure. The look in HB's eyes could make the average lame piss his pants.

"Hey, man, *please...*" Lou held his hands up, as if they were pointing guns. Each one of his fingers was shaking. "I'ma, I'ma, I'ma pay Mr. Brown. Juh, Juh, Jocelyn's coming back. We, we just split up for a min–"

SPLACK!

Lonzo slapped him hard across the cheek. He was so fast, even HB didn't see it coming. It was an open-handed blow, but Lonzo put a good deal of force behind it, and Lou already had equilibrium problems because of the liquor he'd been consuming. The debtor hit the floor again, landing hard on his side with a hearty BOOMP! that shook the whole house.

"*Aw, man, please! Don't hit me, man! Don't hit me!*" He cowered on the floor in a fetal position, shielding his face with his forearms. "*Please, man! Please! I'ma pay Mr. Brown! I'ma pay him!*"

Lonzo delivered a kick to the anus to get him moving again. "I said open the back door." He spoke coolly, but the sneer on his face was worse than HB's.

"*Okay!*" Lou cried. "Okay, man! *Please don't hit me no more!*" He lowered his arms and reluctantly looked up at his attacker. The left side of his face was candy apple red. Lonzo's blow left him with a split lip and bloody nose.

The sight of blood incited a primal urge to pummel him further, but Lonzo took a step back. Mr. Brown made it clear he didn't want Lou hurt too badly. Lonzo never wanted to find out what would happen if he defied his boss.

"Get up!" he barked.

"*Okay, man!* Okay!" Lou's eyes leaked tears, in addition to the blood dripping from his rapidly swelling face. He made it to his feet hesitantly, expecting the intruder to strike him again.

"*Me and Jocelyn gon' get back together*," he squealed. "*I swear, man!* She, she love me."

"This ain't got nothing to do with her," Lonzo said. He followed the weasel down the hall, making sure he didn't try to run into any of the rooms or grab a weapon of some sort.

"Aw, man, what you gon' do to me?" Lou wailed. "Y'all gon' kill me? *Please don't kill me!*"

Lonzo didn't respond because the fear of death is one of the best bargaining chips known to man. Even the most pathetic derelict wants to hold on to the tatters of his miserable existence for as long as possible.

"*I'ma pay that man*," Lou cried. "I'ma pay him. *I swear to God, man.* I ain't, I ain't never did nothing to nobody..."

Lou flipped the light in the kitchen, revealing a disgusting scene that was no doubt getting worse every day he lived without a woman in the home. The sink was filled with soiled dishes and food wrappers. Half eaten meals and liquid stains on the floor filled the room with an overpowering stink that curled the hairs in Lonzo's nostrils.

"*Please*," Lou cried. He reached for the back door, and that's when things went wrong.

Lonzo was high, but he saw the mark unlock the back door with his left hand. With his right hand, Lou made the mistake of reaching for an object on the stovetop. He was most likely going for a butcher's knife that was stained with a white, crusty substance, but there was no way he'd make it in time. Lonzo reached back to deliver what was sure to be a skull-shattering blow to the back of his head. Before he swung, something exploded behind him.

BLAK!

Lonzo ducked, immediately recognizing the sound as gunfire. With his heart high in his chest, he spun and saw HB holding a chrome handgun that looked big enough to drop a bull moose. A curl of smoke wafted from the barrel. His eyes wide, Lonzo looked back to the mark, who was crumpled on the floor again. Lou had both hands wrapped around a new hole in his thigh. Lonzo had never heard anyone scream so loudly.

"*OW! MAN, YOU SHOT ME! WHAT THE HELL – YOU SHOT ME! YOU DONE KILLED ME, MAN! WHY YOU KILL ME?*"

Reggie pulled the back door open cautiously. He peered inside, took in the look on Lonzo's face and the bleeding man on the floor, and his mouth and eyes stretched open at almost the same pace.

"What y'all do?"

Lonzo was at a loss for words. Blood squirted between Lou's fingers like he was trying to block a shower nozzle.

HB returned his gun to an inner coat pocket and told Reggie, "Get in here, nigga. Close the door." He spoke calmly.

Lonzo realized for the first time that he was in the presence of a stone-cold killer. He knew Mr. Brown was surrounded by men like this, but Lonzo never witnessed one in action before.

Reggie stepped over Lou and closed the door softly. His eyes were glued to the bleeding man. Lou's dreadlocks were wrapped over his face, like he was being attacked by a mop. His teeth were bared, his eyes were clenched shut. He wasn't applying enough pressure to his injury. The puddle of blood beneath him grew at a deathly pace. His boxers were already drenched.

Lonzo finally gathered his wits and asked, "What the hell you do?"

"He was reaching for that knife," HB said.

"I saw him, nigga! I was finna get him," Lonzo spat.

"How the hell I know you saw him?" HB said. "I ain't taking no chances with this shit. I was trying to save *your* life."

Lonzo shook his head and turned back to the victim. He had never seen anyone get shot, up close and personal. His heart raced. The puddle of blood was already reaching his sneakers, even though he was standing three feet away.

"*Why you shoot me, man? I didn't do nothing! Why y'all shoot me?*"

Reggie thought that was a damned good question. "Why you shoot him?"

"*He killed me,*" Lou gasped.

"Why you do that, man?" Reggie whined.

"Look, nigga, y'all need to calm down," HB said. "We can't go back in time, so quit worrying about that old shit."

Lonzo couldn't believe his ears. *Old shit?* "Mr. Brown say I wasn't supposed to hurt him too bad. You done shot this nigga in the leg."

"*Call the amberlamps,*" Lou begged. He looked up at Lonzo with his swollen lips slurring his speech. "He done killed me, man..."

Lonzo hoped that wasn't the case, but Lou's face was turning gray, and the blood was steadily pumping.

"Wha, what we gon' do?" Reggie wondered.

Lonzo shook his head.

"We gon' take him to the doctor?" Reggie asked.

"Hell naw," HB said. "He'll have all our asses locked up."

"I won't tell," Lou promised. "Please, I won't tell nobody." He was strangely coherent, though his voice was growing faint.

"He is gon' die," Lonzo said numbly.

"He ain't gon' die," HB countered. "I shot him in the leg, fool. I aimed right for his leg. I coulda shot him in the chest, if I wanted to."

"It don't matter," Lonzo said, shaking his head. "You shot him in the, uh, that, that, uh..." he didn't have a good memory when it came to scientific terms. "It's a, uh, a, uh, a *vein*, that go through the leg."

"His artery," Reggie offered. "You hit him in the femur artery."

"That's *his* fault," HB said coldly. "He was reaching for a knife."

"*No I wasn't,*" Lou lied.

"We can't let this man bleed to death on the floor," Lonzo said.

"Well *you* call the police," HB said. "While you at it, you might as well stay here and wait for them, 'cause your ass is going to jail."

Lonzo shook his head. His life flashed before his eyes. "Naw, man. Mr. Brown don't want this man hurt. He wouldn't want us to let him die."

"I'ma call and ask him." Reggie reached for his phone, but HB stopped him.

"Fool, put that shit up! You can't call from this house."

"It's a *cellphone*," Reggie argued. "They can't trace this."

"Hell if they can't," HB said. "You got cellphone towers all over the city. If that signal goes to a tower around the corner from here, you just put yourself in this house. Y'all act like y'all ain't never killed nobody before."

Neither Reggie nor Lonzo had, but they didn't bother mentioning it.

"So what we gon' do?" Lonzo muttered. "Just stand here and let 'em die?"

"You can go wait in the living room," HB said nonchalantly. "Ain't nobody said you had to watch."

Lonzo stared into HB's eyes and knew he was in the presence of evil. The color drained from his face, and his mouth filled with saliva. He suddenly had to vomit. "Move." He pushed past HB on the way to the living room.

"Don't throw up in this house!" HB warned. "And don't touch *shit*. I ain't going to jail 'cause y'all niggas scary."

True to his word, HB stood over his gunshot victim and watched him die.

Except Lou didn't die. Five minutes later he was still breathing, barely, and Lonzo heard sirens in the distance. Reggie thought it was imperative they flee the scene, and everyone agreed. HB wanted to finish Lou off, but Lonzo was vehemently against it. It was bad enough the man was bleeding to death on his filthy kitchen floor. Another gunshot would've vaulted them over the point of no return.

So the trio made their getaway and explained themselves as best they could to Mr. Brown when they returned to the compound. Mr. Brown would almost always rather have the money, but he wasn't too upset about the drama that unfolded with his niece's husband.

"Some people too stupid to live," he said and paid the three-man crew twenty-five hundred a piece, promising more if Lou succumbed to his wound.

Later that night, they heard he was clinging to life at Jackson Memorial. He barely had a discernible pulse when the paramedics found him. They gave him twelve bags of blood during surgery, and the sonofabitch survived.

Lonzo feared he would be arrested for aggravated assault, or even worse *attempted murder*, but Mr. Brown assured him Lou wouldn't cooperate with the detectives investigating the shooting. Mr. Brown had spoken with his in-law directly. Lou understood pieces of his body would turn up in every waterway in the city if he implicated the men responsible for his injuries. In return for keeping his mouth closed, Mr. Brown was gracious enough to forgive his twenty-thousand-dollar debt.

Lonzo did a few more solo projects for Mr. Brown, but when Nisha got pregnant, he decided it was time to quit. Mr. Brown grudgingly accepted his resignation.

"I understand," the kingpin said. "It takes a real man to get comfortable with this line of work."

Lonzo knew what Mr. Brown was trying to do, and he didn't take the bait. He walked out of the gangster's office with hopes of never looking back. In the dark recesses of his mind, he would always fear getting arrested for what happened to Lou, but as weeks became months and then years, Lonzo tried to forget the incident altogether.

The next morning, he woke up refreshed and surprisingly at peace. He told Nisha he was sorry for visiting Mr. Brown last night.

"We need the money, but I can't put myself in a position like that no more. Every time I see your brother, I think about that man bleeding on the floor."

Nisha sat across from him at the kitchen table. She subconsciously fiddled with her wrist splint as she spoke. "You want me to ask my daddy for some money, till your next fight?"

"Naw," Lonzo said with a frown. "I'll work some overtime at the warehouse. We'll be alright."

"What about your training?"

"We'll be alright," he assured her. "Ain't no way in hell Veston can beat me. As hungry as I am right now, I'm liable to kill that boy in the ring."

Nisha didn't wish for brutality on that level, but she always hoped her man would be victorious. "I'll try to get a job in a couple of weeks," she said, "when they take this splint off."

Lonzo rose from his seat shaking his head. "You don't need to be looking for a job until after you have surgery. You ain't gon' do nothing but make it worse."

Nisha stood too. She walked with him and gave him a kiss before he left for work.

"I love you, baby."

"I love you too," Lonzo said. "Don't worry. We gon' make it, just like we always do."

CHAPTER TEN
WHAT A MAN

November didn't get off to a good start, but the rest of the month wasn't bad. The temperature in Overbrook Meadows mellowed out to a beautiful 65 degrees on most days, offering respite from the horrible hundred-degree days of summer. On Thanksgiving, Nisha realized she had a lot to be thankful for.

The trouble with Dr. Coates irritated her when she thought about it, but even that travesty had blessings. Nisha knew the pharmacy was not the right place for her. Getting away from the perverted pharmacist was a good thing. Not having to interact with Toya on a daily basis was also a stress reliever.

Nisha returned to the hospital three weeks after her MRI, and they removed the cumbersome splint. Her arm felt weak for the first few days, but gradually she began to use it more and was able to gauge her limitations. After a week without the splint, she told Lonzo she was ready to find a new job, but he poked his chest out and reiterated his stance that she shouldn't work until after she had surgery.

"Lonzo, we got two months before your next fight," she argued. "You won't make enough that night to pay for my surgery. The doctor said it would cost fifty thousand without insurance."

"I'm putting you and Baby Lonzo on my insurance. You said the surgery was ten thousand with insurance."

"Yeah," Nisha said, "but you'd have to spend your whole purse on me. We can't afford to do that."

"Yes, we can. Stop worrying."

"Baby, I wouldn't even feel right about that," Nisha argued. "You're the one training and fighting for that money. I don't want you to blow it all in one day."

He grinned. "You think paying for your surgery is *blowing money*? What if you had a hunchback? You wouldn't want to get that fixed either?"

Nisha smiled too. "I don't have a hunchback."

"What if you had a club foot *and* a hunch back?"

"I guess I'd be limping around with a hump in my back. I still wouldn't want you to spend your whole boxing check to get it fixed."

"You'd pay for me to have surgery, if I had a hunchback," Lonzo guessed.

"Yeah, I would. I can't be walking around with some Igor-looking dude."

"Aw, that's wrong. You supposed to love me no matter what I look like. I still woulda hollered at you if you had a club foot. I'd even give you a foot massage. And I'd whoop on anybody that tried to crack jokes; talking about, *"Why her toes pointed that way?"*

Nisha laughed. "You would?"

"For sho."

"I'd still be with you if you had a hunchback," she conceded. "I'd give you a back rub every night, even if your hump felt weird and squishy."

With her new insurance card, Nisha went to the doctor in January, to make sure everything they told her at the county hospital was true. Her new doctor confirmed the Kienbock's disease. Lonzo's insurance would cover 90% of the surgery costs, which left $5,000 they had to come up with out of pocket. That was better than the $10,000 she expected, but it was still a lot of money. Lonzo said he didn't have a problem paying for it, but Nisha didn't think she could let him do that.

On January 12th the devil tried to break them down again by putting Lonzo's 2002 Buick out of commission. This wasn't a big surprise, because Lonzo had been talking about his transmission problems for months. But the timing couldn't have been worse.

"Don't you have some money left over from your last fight?" Nisha asked him.

"I got fourteen hundred," Lonzo said with a slow shake of his head. "The shop said they need twelve hundred to fix it."

"Are you gonna get it fixed? Your car's pretty old."

"What choice I got?"

"If you wait till after your fight, you can buy another car," Nisha suggested.

"I told you I'm using that money for your surgery."

"But I don't have to have—"

"Kill that noise. Your arm's worth more than this car or any other car."

Nisha didn't argue with him, and Lonzo bit the bullet and withdrew twelve hundred from the bank.

"I swear this car ain't even worth that much," he told the owner of a blossoming chain of repair shops called TC's Automotive.

"Why don't you get a new car?" the stranger asked. He was a handsome, fair-skinned gentleman with a nametag that said, "Tyrone."

"I want to," Lonzo said. He stuffed his hands in his pockets and grimaced. "But I can't afford it right now."

"Ain't you a boxer?" the man with the Tyrone nametag asked. "I swear I saw you in the papers before..."

"Yeah," Lonzo said with a sigh. He expected Tyrone to make fun of his financial woes, but the mechanic gave him sound advice instead.

"I know how it is, man. I think everybody got potential to do something good with their lives, but most people can't stick it out through the hard times. We get lazy and end up going to the joint behind some get-rich-quick scheme. Usually selling crack is our downfall. I know that's how it was for me..."

"You been to prison?" Lonzo asked him.

Tyrone nodded. "I did six years flat. Lost everything I had. But I got out and worked my ass off. Now I own this shop and five more."

Lonzo couldn't believe it. "Damn, man. You did your thing, for real."

"It was hard," the shop owner said. "But being in prison was hard too. We all got a choice, and we already know what will happen if we choose wrong. You'll be alright, man. You got a light in you the whole world wants to see. Give it some time. You gon' be rich one day."

"Thanks," Lonzo said. He returned to the waiting room wondering if God put this entrepreneur in his path to steer him away from the evil he'd been contemplating. Each day he fought the temptation to call Mr. Brown and make a few thousand the easy way. His talk with Tyrone helped him subdue these urges.

On January 30th Lonzo was one week away from his 18th fight against Michael Veston. Nisha was surprised they made it that far without hard times giving way to bad decisions. It was times like this that brought out the true character of a relationship. Nisha didn't think she'd ever been more in love with her man.

Lonzo always promised to take care of her and their child, and he hadn't let them down. Even with her injury and the loss of her job, he buckled down and picked up the slack. He worked overtime at the warehouse and continued to train hard every night. He watched all of Veston's fight videos, some three or four times, and he wasn't worried about the rope-a-dope technique he knew his opponent would try.

In the weeks preceding his fight, his workout regimen became more rigorous. But he never complained, even when the alarm clock was like Satan's laughter every morning, and he was so exhausted, he could barely lift his fork to eat at dinner.

The final few weeks of training was also the time when Nisha had sexual fits on a daily basis. Lonzo didn't let her down in that department either. He saw the way she watched him when he did his push-ups and sit-ups before he went to bed. He peeped the gleam in her eyes when he stepped out of the shower with his torso cut up like a He-Man action figure. Nisha couldn't stop from molesting him one Friday morning. Lonzo didn't hold it against her.

"Dang, baby. You hot as a firecracker, ain't you?" he teased.

She sat on the corner of the bed and pulled him between her legs. She kissed his well-toned stomach and twirled her hot tongue in his belly button. She groped his chest and sucked his nipples ravenously.

"I'm sorry, baby," she breathed. "You look too good. Like a big ass Sugar Daddy." She ran her tongue the full length of his stomach, loving each ripple in his six-pack. His body was wet from the shower. She thought he tasted like caramel.

He touched her face gently, and then his hands moved to the back of her head. He ran his fingers through her hair and sighed. This was his favorite position for fellatio.

"*Damn baby*," he moaned. "I know you going through it, but why you wanna put me through it too?"

She felt bad about her seduction, but she looked up and saw he was smiling. Beneath her chin, she noticed the bulge growing under his towel. She wanted to toss the fabric to the floor and feast on his manhood like never before, but she restrained. It was bad enough she was exciting him when she knew he was abstaining from sex.

"I'm sorry, baby." She gave his stomach one last kiss and scooted back on the mattress.

"I'm sorry too," he said. "I know it's getting hard."

"You getting hard too," she kidded. She lie back and rubbed the lump under his towel with her bare foot. "I'm sorry, baby. I'm trying to stop. Why don't you go put some clothes on?"

He took hold of her ankle and then lifted her other foot. He stared between her legs and hummed quietly. Nisha wore only a tee shirt and a pair of panties. He slid his hands up her thighs and hooked her underwear. He pulled them off with minimal assistance. He spread her knees apart and shook his head in wonderment. Nisha chewed on her fingernail, not sure where he was going with this.

"Alright, baby, I'm sorry," she said. "I know I was wrong, but you don't have to get me back like this."

"What you talking about? How am I getting you back?"

"Why you take my panties off? You know what you doing to me."

"You getting wet?"

"What you think?"

He dropped to his knees and placed both hands on her thighs. He caressed her, and then one hand slipped between her legs. He inserted two fingers effortlessly.

"*Hot-damn*!" Lonzo said. "You ain't never been this wet."

She gasped, unable to respond right away. "I'm sorry. I didn't mean to..."

"What you apologizing for?"

"Baby, I know you can't have sex. I ain't trying to – Lonzo, what is you doing?"

His fingers slid in and out of her juice box rhythmically. Nisha squirmed, her ass sliding on the mattress.

"I'ma hook you up," he explained. "Just 'cause I can't have none, don't mean we both gotta suffer."

"You don't...." She was about to tell him he didn't have to do that for her, but he removed his fingers and inched his face closer. He gave her kitty a playful lick that sent a chill down her extremities. He sucked her labia one at a time. He parted them with his tongue and quickly found her clitoris. He caressed it with his lips and tongue.

Nisha's heart knocked so hard, she thought she might pass out. She reached for his head cautiously. Lonzo backed away when she reached with her other hand.

"What'd you say?"

She looked down at him, her stomach quivering. His lips glistened, his eyes low and sexy.

"Nuh, nothing," she whispered.

"You was fixing to say I don't have to do *something*," Lonzo prompted.

"You don't."

"So I can just get up and–"

He tried to move, but she grabbed hold of his ears.

He laughed. "Damn, baby. You strong!"

Nisha was wound up too tightly to laugh. She caught herself being greedy and let go of his head. "I'm, I'm sorry, baby. You don't have to."

"I ain't no tease," he said with a grin. He leaned forward and lapped her juices pleasantly. "But I gotta leave in twenty minutes. You think you'll be done by then?"

He spoke directly into her mound. Nisha was going wild with the blended sensations of his breath and taste buds. She threw her head back and closed her eyes. Moons and quasars exploded in her mind.

Lonzo sucked and licked for a few moments more and then asked, "You hear me, baby?"

"I'm..." She swallowed. "I'm good," she breathed.

"What you mean?" Lonzo asked and noticed her leg was trembling. "Damn, girl? Already?"

She nodded weakly. It had been over a month since she had an orgasm. Her body felt weightless.

"Shit, if it's that easy, I can give you another one," he said and continued to stimulate her with increased vigor.

He brought her to the verge a few more times, but he didn't induce her second explosion until eight long minutes had passed, and the muscles in her legs were numb. She didn't think Lonzo had ever pleased her so thoroughly with just his mouth.

She wanted to get up and make him a steak and baked potato to take to work with him, but when he finally rose to his feet, she could barely move. She rolled to her side and took slow breaths as her body recuperated. Her mind slipped into something like a catatonic state. She had an urge to suck her thumb, although she never had that problem as a child.

By the time she found the energy to get out of bed, Lonzo had dressed and left for work. She sent him a text message:

Baby, that felt sooooo good. Thank you. I love you so much!

He responded a few minutes later:

I didn't wash my face. I still smell you.

You a freak, she texted.

You a bigger one, he countered.

Nisha's day got a little boring when her man was at work. She knew she was never meant to be a stay at home mom. Baby Lonzo didn't require as much attention as he did six months ago. She read to him and lie on the floor so she could play with his toys on his level, but when he took his nap, she longed for the company of an adult.

She got dressed at lunchtime and bundled the baby up in his winter coat. She picked up a few dollar burgers from McDonalds and went to visit her sister on the south side of town.

What she failed to take into account was her sister's home-daycare business was bustling, and a lot of the kids Shonda took care of were old enough to talk. As soon as Nisha walked in, she was bombarded by toddlers who spent way too much time at fast food restaurants.

"*McDonalds*!"

"She got McDonalds!"

"*I want some*!"

"Aw hell!" Shonda called from the kitchen. She was boiling water for what was going to be a simple Ramen Noodle meal. "What the hell you done did?" she asked Nisha.

"I am *so* sorry," Nisha said. She held her McDonalds bag at chest level, to keep the rug rats from snatching it from her. "Calm down!" she told the tallest boy. "Stop jumping!"

"I know you didn't bring enough food for everybody," Shonda said. She came to the living room wiping her hands on her shirt.

"I only got three cheeseburgers," Nisha said. "I don't know how I forgot about all these kids." She did a quick head count. Only five of them were old enough to tackle solid foods. "You can give these to them," she offered. "But they'll have to split them."

"I don't wanna split mine!" the oldest boy said with a frown.

"Well, you ain't gotta eat *nothing*!" Shonda snapped at him. "Everybody's getting half a burger and some *goddamned noodles*. Now go sit your ugly ass over there and be quiet!"

Nisha's mouth fell open. She followed her sister to the kitchen and asked, "Why you talk to him like that?"

"Cause he *bad*," Shonda informed her. "He don't listen to nothing, unless you yell at him."

"What if he tell his mama?" Nisha wondered.

"Hell, she talk to him way worse than I do."

"I bet not never hear you talking to my baby like that," Nisha warned her.

"I wouldn't talk to my nephew like that. Baby Lonzo can't even talk, so he can't piss me off that bad."

"Have you ever thought about doing something else for a living?" Nisha wondered.

"Why I wanna do something else?" Shonda asked. "I'm a good baby sitter. Half these bitches bring they kids over here, then go back home and go to sleep. They don't wanna put up with they bad ass, so they can't say shit about the way I do it!"

The ladies got the hamburgers divided up and fed the little ones. The youngest two were still on the bottle. Shonda fed one while Nisha changed the other's diaper and tried to rock her back to sleep.

"What you so happy about?" Shonda asked. She flipped channels on the remote until she found a cartoon.

"What you mean?" Nisha asked.

"You damned near floating in the clouds," Shonda said. "Ain't you supposed to be going through some rough times? I know you ain't happy about not going to work, is you?"

"No, I'm not happy about that," Nisha replied. "I wish I had a job."

"What is it then?" Shonda asked. "Lonzo ain't giving you none, so that can't be it either."

Nisha wasn't generally one to kiss and tell, but she couldn't help but brag about what a good man Lonzo was.

"We can't have sex till after the fight," she confirmed, "but he hooked me up this morning before he left."

"Hooked you up?"

Nisha sighed and hummed pleasantly. "Yeah, girl. He *hooked me up...*"

"What he do?" Shonda asked, her grin devilish. "Don't tell me – he used his mouth?..."

"You asking too many questions."

"Alright, but am I right or wrong?"

"Well, you ain't wrong."

Shonda laughed. "Ha ha! It must've been the *bomb*!"

"You can't really tell by looking at me, can you?"

"I knew something was up as soon as you walked through the door. I figured you either got some money, or you got some *good good*."

Nisha smiled warmly. "It's been a month since we made love. But this morning..." She shuddered. "It was so good, I think I passed out for a minute."

"Damn," Shonda said and squirmed in her seat. "You a lucky girl."

"I know."

"Your man is fine, and he can fight, and he pleasing you like *that*... You better hold on to him."

"I ain't going nowhere."

"I know a lot of bitches be coming at him," Shonda said.

"He ain't going nowhere either. You know what he told me?"

"What?"

"He said he wants to pay for my surgery with his fight money next week. It cost half his purse."

Shonda shook her head. "That's love right there. I woulda took your ass out back and shot you like Old Yeller."

Nisha laughed.

"So he's paying all the bills," Shonda surmised. "He gon' pay for your surgery, *and* he put a big ass ring on your finger?..."

"He handles his business in the bedroom too."

"So... What's wrong with him?" Shonda wondered.

"Who said something got to be wrong with him?"

"It's got to be something wrong with him. Either he's boning somebody else, or he's hitting you, or he's selling drugs; about to go to the pen or *something*."

Nisha thought about it for a second. She couldn't fathom Lonzo sleeping with another woman. The thought of it made her stomach hurt. None of her sister's other guesses were right either.

"The only thing Lonzo does that I don't like is when he hangs with our brother and Mr. Brown and them."

"Mmm hmm. I knew it was something."

Nisha realized her sister was looking for drama in her relationship.

"Lonzo's not going back to work for Mr. Brown. After he wins his fight next week, he got one more match in Overbrook Meadows, and then we're going to Austin. The Austin fight will be on TV, and he'll get paid three hundred thousand. When he win that one, they have to let him fight for the championship. That fight will be for some millions."

"And you just gon' roll right into a mansion," Shonda said sarcastically. "From hoodrat to millionaire."

Nisha cut her eyes at her. "You starting to piss me off. You hating or what?"

"I am," Shonda said right away. "I'm sorry."

Nisha laughed. Shonda did too.

"You think if I go to the gym, I can find a man like yours?" Shonda wondered.

"You can go," Nisha said, "but you'll *never* find a man like Lonzo."

Shonda frowned. "See, bitch. You *trying* to make me jealous."

"I'm just getting you back."

"Will you buy me a daycare center when y'all get rich?" Shonda queried.

Nisha imagined her sister cursing at children on a mass scale, and she cracked up.

"I can already see the banner," she mused. "*Welcome to Shonda's Daycare, where we'll beat the hell out of your bad ass kids!*"

"I'ma get all the parents to sign a release," Shonda agreed, "so they can't try to sue me later."

CHAPTER ELEVEN
PERFECT RECORD

Nisha woke up early on Sunday, February 7th. She felt electricity in the air the moment she opened her eyes. She rolled over to kiss her man, but Lonzo was already up and out of bed. She found him in the living room facing the largest wall that had no pictures hanging or any other decorations.

Lonzo had the shade removed from a lamp, strategically positioned behind him. Nisha used to think shadow boxing was an antiquated form of training, when you considered all the technology available. But whenever she saw her man doing it, she realized the basic exercise was essential.

It was 7:30 am, and The Champ had already worked up a sweat. He was topless and barefoot, wearing a pair of boxing trunks. His feet were quick on the soft carpet. His fists were even faster. He bobbed and weaved and threw a barrage of combos that would topple any man.

The muscles in his upper body flexed and contracted. The stretching of each sinewy tendon was like a work of art. His cat-like reflexes were remarkable. Baby Lonzo sat up on the couch and watched his father with wide, unblinking eyes. Nisha leaned on the doorframe in the hallway and did the same. The theme music from Rocky forced its way into her mind.

Eye of the tiger!
Dun dun dun
Dun dun dun

She giggled. Lonzo stopped punching. He looked back at her and grinned.

"What's up?"

"Nothing," she said. "How long you been up?"

"About an hour." Sweat trickled down his face and glistened on his chest and stomach.

"The baby woke you? You could've told me to get him."

"Maybe I want to have him to myself sometimes," Lonzo said. He went to the couch and lifted his son. "I be teaching him stuff. He little, but he's smart. You see the way he watches me? He wants to learn how to fight."

"I watch you like that too," Nisha said. She stepped to her man and hugged him tenderly. "You nervous?"

"Nope. But I know you are..."

"I'm always nervous. I know you're gonna win, but I don't like seeing you get hit *at all*. I wanna jump in the ring sometimes and help you."

He laughed. "How you gon' help me?"

"I can jump on your opponent's back," Nisha offered. "Or kick 'em in the nuts."

"*Damn*! You a little violent, ain't you?"

Baby Lonzo laughed and said, "*Damn!*"

His parents looked at him in surprise.

"How did I know his first curse word would come from you?" Nisha said.

"Hey, don't say that," Lonzo chided his son. "You need to say 'Dang' or 'Darn.' Can you say 'darn?' *Daaarrrn...*"

The boy narrowed his eyes in confusion.

"What about '*Dang*?'" Lonzo said. "I know you can say that: *Dang.*"

"Dane," the baby said.

Nisha grinned.

"That's my boy," Lonzo told him. "Remember, you need to do *better* than your daddy. You gotta talk better than me, and you gotta be smarter than me."

Nisha pecked her son on the cheek and kissed her fiancée on the lips.

"I love you," she whispered.

"I love you too."

"*Damn!*" the baby shouted, and they all laughed.

Lonzo's fight days were always stressful for Nisha. Each time she tried to go about it differently, but things always played out the same: She'd wake up early and have more than twelve hours to think about all the things that could happen in the ring. Lonzo would eat a small breakfast and go to the gym to talk to Fats and watch more of his opponent's fight videos.

He told Nisha he didn't do any real training on the day of his fights, but she wouldn't see him again until she arrived at the arena later that night. She didn't know what he did with the bulk of his day, but she doubted if he spent most of his time worrying like she did.

By noon he had been gone for three hours, and Nisha felt like the walls of their apartment were closing in on her. She sat. She stood. She went outside and admired the weather from her balcony. She made a salad for lunch but couldn't eat more than half of it.

At one-thirty she called her dad and told him she didn't feel good.

"What took you so long?" Walter asked. "You usually call before twelve."

"Can I come over?"

"Of course," he said with a chuckle. "I got rocks in my gut too."

Nisha saw smoke drifting from her father's backyard when she pulled into the driveway. She walked around the house and found him at his barbecue pit. The smell made her mouth water, even though she wasn't hungry thirty minutes ago.

"What you cooking?"

He looked up at her with a smile. "Baby girl!" He gave her a hug and plucked the child from her arms. The baby clucked pleasantly.

"Got some deer meat on the grill," Walter told her.

"Ugh." Nisha frowned.

"Whatever. Don't get all saddity on me."

"I ain't never had no *deer meat*. But it do look good," she admitted.

"Yes, you have had deer meat," Walter said. "Rabbit too. Don't you remember?"

She shook her head.

"I had a friend named Don who used to hunt with his greyhounds," Walter recalled. "He'd bring us a couple of rabbits every now and then, and I'd fry them. Reggie was the first person at his school with a *real* rabbit's foot. I don't know why I gave it to him; it was the ugliest thing. You don't remember that?"

"I do now," Nisha said. "That thing was nasty. I remember he used to try to touch me with it, and I'd run and jump in your bed. It came from a real rabbit?"

"Sure did," Walter said. "I cut it off myself. And it wasn't one of those cute bunny rabbits either. It was an ugly jack rabbit foot with scratches and stuff, dirt under the toenails."

Nisha shook her head, giggling.

"You wanna try some of this when it's ready?" Walter asked. "Maybe it'll bring back more memories."

"Okay." Nisha's mind was already filled with recollections from the good old days. She wondered if she could get her dad to tell her a story about her mom while they ate. She knew he didn't like to talk about Carol, but it had been a while since she asked.

The meat was better than she expected. As Nisha chewed her first succulent bite, the taste registered with her memory bank. Walter retrieved one of his photo albums and flipped through it until he found a picture.

"Ah. Check this out."

Nisha took it and saw herself at the age of four. She was cheesing at a picnic table, with a forkful of Bambi. With the album in hand, she seized the opportunity to wander down memory lane. She found a picture of her mom and asked Walter to tell her something she didn't know about his fondest love. His disposition changed, but then he smiled and complied.

He told her about the day Shonda was born, which coincided with one of the worst floods Overbrook Meadows had ever seen. On the way to the hospital, Walter's car got stuck in water that was as high as the tires. He and Carol argued because he wanted to get out and push the vehicle to safety, but she wanted him to save her first.

"She told me, *'I'll never forgive you, if you don't get me out of this car right now!'*" Walter recalled. "And I told her, *'Woman, if you let me push this car ten feet, it'll start right up tomorrow. If I leave it here, it'll be totaled!'*"

Nisha laughed, listening intently.

"She was so mad, she refused to turn the wheel while I pushed," Walter said. "Finally I gave up and went and got her out the car. Needless to say, that Plymouth was totaled."

"A *Plymouth*, Daddy?" she shook her head. "You cared more about a Plymouth than Mama?"

"Now you sound just like her."

When they finished eating, he told her another story about how much Carol fretted when he fought Larry Holmes for the heavyweight title and about the time she happened upon a raccoon family in the shed of their new home.

Nisha felt blessed when her father was done spinning yarns. She noticed his eyes were glossy when he excused himself.

"I'm gonna pack up some of that meat for one of my friends."

"Okay," Nisha told him. She curled up on the couch with Baby Lonzo, and they quickly fell asleep.

At 6:30, her phone woke her from what she thought was a pleasant dream, but she couldn't remember what it was about.

"Mmm. Hello?"

"What you doing?" It was her sister Shonda.

"I'm over Daddy's house. I must've fell asleep."

"Asleep? How the hell can you sleep at a time like this?"

Nisha's heart started to race, but she checked the clock and saw they had plenty of time. "The first fight doesn't start till nine."

"Are you gonna pick me up?"

"Yeah. I'll be there in about thirty minutes…"

Shonda's house was filled with people when Nisha arrived. Her boyfriend Blue was there with a couple of his homeboys. Both of them had a girlfriend tagging along. Everyone was dressed fly with their jewelry blinging and their smell-good spritzed on their chests and necks. They were loud and excited, like they were on their way to a party.

"Why you need a ride from me?" Nisha asked her sister when she found her in the bedroom. "All these people going to the fight?"

"Yeah." Shonda leaned towards a mirror and put on her earrings. "Some of them never seen Lonzo fight before. Me and Blue riding with you. You excited?"

"That's one way to put it," Nisha said. She put a hand over her lower belly and grimaced from what felt like menstrual cramps.

"Girl, don't even trip," Shonda said. "Everything gon' be fine. Lonzo gon' have more people supporting him tonight than he ever had."

It turned out, Shonda was right about that. It took them a while to find a parking spot when they arrived at the arena. Fighting their way inside was like arriving late to a graduation.

When they entered the auditorium, Nisha's heart danced as she surveyed the scene. There was nearly two thousand in attendance, dwarfing the crowd at Lonzo's last fight.

"I told you!" Shonda yelled. She had to speak close to Nisha's ear, because the building was rumbling with excited energy. People were laughing, drinking beer from plastic cups, munching nachos and popcorn. Everyone looked happy and eager and just a little blood thirsty. Nisha's smile was ear to ear.

"I'll be back!" She handed Baby Lonzo to her sister.

"You going to see Lonzo?"

"Yeah. You see Daddy?" She scanned the seats and pointed when she saw the back of Walter's head. "He down there, on the third row. Those empty chairs next to him are ours."

"Alright," Shonda said and dragged her boyfriend in that direction.

In the underbelly of the coliseum, Nisha encountered the same crowd of trainers and security personnel that always congregated there. This time she made it all the way to Lonzo's training room before her progress was impeded by two burly brothers wearing all black. She didn't bother trying to reason with the security team. She looked around and was lucky to spot Lonzo's cut man Gillespie heading in her direction.

"Gillespie!" she called and waved at him.

"Come on," he shouted. "Hey, she's alright," he told the guards. "This Lonzo's woman."

The men parted. Gillespie threw a string necklace over Nisha's head when she was closer. Dangling from the string was a laminated card that read VIP. Nisha noticed he wore an identical card around his neck.

"When'd y'all get these?"

"We have to use them from now on," he informed her. "Lonzo's getting big. Too many people hassling him."

The cut man pushed the training room door open, and Nisha was hit with the familiar smell of adhesive tape, Vaseline and a distinct mixture of sweat and adrenaline that made her heart skip a beat. She spotted her man in an instant.

Lonzo stood before Fats, who sat on the corner of a desk, taping up The Champ's hands. There were a dozen people in the small room. The Champ looked up at her and grinned slightly. He was dressed for the ring in shiny, blue trunks and black boots with white laces.

He waited until Fats cut the last strand of tape before he broke away and approached his woman. His hands felt good on Nisha's body when they embraced.

"What it look like up there?" he asked.

"It's packed. Gotta be sold out. Wait till you see."

Lonzo smiled. He kissed her, and she hugged him again. She laid her head on his chest, oblivious to the people watching them.

"What's wrong?" he asked when she backed away.

"I don't know," Nisha said, as a tear came to her eye. It spilled and rolled down her cheek. Lonzo wiped it away with his thumb. "It's crazy," she said, "to watch your dream come true."

"It's not my dream. It's *our* dream. Don't ever forget that, baby."

"I won't." She kissed him again, and Lonzo laughed.

"Baby, you messing up my vibe with all this emotional stuff. I'm trying to have the heart of a warrior. You making me feel like a teddy bear."

Nisha giggled. "You got three people fighting before you. You got time to get your warrior's heart back. But I'm finna go. I'm sure somebody's trying to take my seat."

"Bet nobody *won't* take your seat," Lonzo said with a frown, and she saw his fighting spirit was as strong as ever.

"I'll see you later," she said and reluctantly left the room.

On the way back to her family, she ran across a group of beautiful women. One of them carried a sign that read "MARRY ME CHAMP!"

Nisha grinned and kept moving. She was happy the strangers took time out of their day to enhance her man's superstar status. Some folks had to pay for promotions like that.

No one had taken Nisha's seat, but her row was completely full. She had to squeeze by a lot of people to get to her father. In addition to Shonda's crew, Lonzo's brother Leo was there with a Hispanic fellow, and Lonzo's sister Shay brought a tall, handsome brother Nisha had never met before.

"How's he doing?" Walter asked when she took her child from him.

"Same as always," Nisha said. Inside the ring, the announcer introduced the first two fighters. "I don't think he ever gets nervous."

"That's okay," Walter said. "You do enough worrying for the both of you."

"I'm okay," Nisha said, "now that I saw him."

"Really?" He gave her a doubtful look and held his bucket of popcorn under her nose. "Want some?"

Nisha's stomach churned, and she shook her head roughly. "Uh uhn!"

Her father laughed.

The first fight featured two featherweights who made up for their lack of brawn with blistering speed. At one point during the third round, they stood toe to toe and threw haymakers relentlessly, like they were tethered at the waist. That match ended with a decision, but no one was upset about the lack of a knockout.

The next fight featured a middle weight named Timmy "Iron Jaw" Peoples, who Walter had been following for over a year. It was a good thing he had such a strong chin, because he took some of the most gruesome punches Nisha had ever seen in a local match. Thankfully his fight was only scheduled for three rounds. He lost by unanimous decision. Nisha gave her father a cynical look as the ref raised the winner's glove.

"Gee, Dad, you sure know how to pick 'em."

Two heavyweights duked it out in the third fight on the card. It was the best fight up to that point. Neither of the sluggers had a defensive game plan, which left them both susceptible to countless uppercuts, hooks and jab after brutal jab. They both hit the canvas twice during the bout. An ugly fellow named "Pee Wee" Johnson was the only one to get up both times.

After Pee Wee and his team left the ring, the lights dimmed, and everyone knew it was time for the main event. People started clapping and stomping their feet, creating an awesome rumble that made Nisha's heart drum.

Chants of "**WE WANT THE CHAMP!**" erupted from several groups scattered across the arena, and within seconds nearly everyone was on one accord. The populous rose from their seats and screamed so loudly, Nisha couldn't hear anything the announcer said as Lonzo's opponent made his way to the ring.

When Slick's familiar tune began to play on the loud speakers, hundreds of people threw their hands in the air and sang the rapper's catchy song.

Nisha's pulse raced at the same rate as the applause, and she knew she wouldn't make it this time. All of the stress from today and the weeks leading up to this fight had finally caught up with her. She thought she might pass out, so she sat down, even though she couldn't see past the people standing in front of her.

Her dad leaned down and shouted, "Are you alright?"

"I'm fine," Nisha said and offered a weak smile.

"It'll be over soon," he said, but Walter was wrong about that, just as he was wrong about Timmy's iron jaw leading him to victory that night.

The fight started in typical Lonzo fashion. The Champ was the early aggressor, but Lonzo didn't make any of the mistakes Fats warned him about. Everyone expected his opponent to backpedal and wage war with defense. Veston followed that plan to a T.

Lonzo was used to ending things in the first round. Nisha worried he would exhaust himself with combos that didn't land effectively. But he stuck to his training regimen. He chased Veston around enough to show dominance, but he didn't take the bait when Veston covered up and invited The Champ to give him his best shots.

Round two was much like the first, except both fighters seemed to adapt to their opponent's style. Veston began to time Lonzo's jabs better, and Nisha thought he blocked or dodged more than half of them. Lonzo, in turn, found a gap in Veston's defenses, and he delivered a good number of shots to the ribs and gut. But by the end of the round, Veston started blocking those too. Once again Lonzo did enough to win the round, but it wasn't with his usual breathtaking flair.

Nisha didn't start to worry until the warriors got off the bench for the third round. This was uncharted territory for Lonzo, and this was when he started to show signs of stress. Each punch Lonzo threw zapped a little more of his strength, whether it landed or not. And the fact that he wasn't landing well aggravated The Champ.

With his eyebrows furrowed, he slipped into the mind state of a street fighter and decided to try harder. He backed Veston against the ropes and threw a series of speedy combos that brought the crowd to their feet again, but Nisha saw only three out of twenty blows landed flush on Veston's melon.

"Slow down," Nisha muttered under her breath. She couldn't stop her knee from bouncing. Something like a freight train rumbled between her ears. At the end of the round, Walter told her it was okay; Lonzo was still winning. But Nisha didn't take comfort in that. They had five rounds to go, and it appeared The Champ was succumbing to Veston's strategy.

"Slow down, baby. Please, slow down..."

Fats must've delivered the same message between rounds, because Lonzo altered his style again in round four. He reverted to the cautious manner he used in round one, and some of the folks in the crowd began to call for more action.

"*Idiots*!" Walter grumbled. "Do they want him to lose?"

Nisha didn't say anything, because the possibility of losing was never an option in any of Lonzo's previous fights. But now that Walter had uttered the ugly word, it hung in the air like the stench of death.

Lonzo won each of the first four rounds, but his frustration spiked again in round five. Veston's defense was uncanny. He easily blocked or dodged up to eighty percent of Lonzo's punches. In addition to his formidable protection, Veston started to mix in a little offense, and Lonzo was caught off guard. He ate three stiff jabs and winced when Veston went downstairs for a looping hook to the liver.

Lonzo fired back with what appeared to be his whole arsenal. He landed a few power shots to the head, but Veston was unfazed. The Champ went back to his corner at the end of the round with his shoulders slumped, while his opponent retreated with his head held high. Nisha's eyes filled with tears, but they didn't spill until the unthinkable happened midway through the sixth.

Lonzo was almost out of gas by then. Veston still looked strong and sure. He'd been backing up so much throughout the fight, Nisha thought his legs only moved in that direction. But when Lonzo started throwing sloppy haymakers that wouldn't have hurt even if they did connect, Veston took the fight to his opponent – much like he did in each of the fight videos Fats had urged Lonzo to watch.

The Champ couldn't keep up with Veston's speedy combo to the head, and he got rocked with an unexpected uppercut that landed flush on the chin and caused an arena filled with two thousand bloodthirsty fans to gasp in unison. Lonzo retreated until his back hit the ropes, and Veston charged forward.

With one minute left in the round, Veston connected with two jabs to the nose and an uppercut to the jaw. Blood spilled from Lonzo's face for the first time in a professional bout. Nisha was on her feet, bawling and screaming instructions that Lonzo couldn't hear because of the ringing in his ears.

In a last-ditch effort to turn the fight around, Lonzo lunged forward with his signature punch. Veston dodged the left uppercut and countered with a liver shot that slammed into Lonzo's flesh like a nuclear bomb. All the air vacated Lonzo's lungs as a surprised "*OOF!*" ejected his mouthpiece like a loogie.

The Champ reached reflexively to his side, and his body descended to the canvas in slow motion. But when he impacted, there was a huge *THUD!* that echoed two thousand times as two thousand unbelieving hearts sank in two thousand sunken chests.

The referee counted slowly. Lonzo fought valiantly to make it to his feet in time, but he could not get enough oxygen to his exhausted muscles. The Champ was only able to make it to one knee before the ref waved his hands in the air, proclaiming Michael Veston the winner by knock out.

CHAPTER TWELVE
THE MORNING AFTER

"Damn, I can't believe he lost like that."

"Nigga got murked."

"I had some money on this fight too."

"Me too, cuz. Who didn't?"

"And he got *knocked out*! That's the worst thing."

"I seen De La Hoya get dropped with a body shot like that, by Bernard Hopkins."

"Fool, you wasn't there! You saw the highlights on ESPN."

"So. I still saw it."

"I'ma go ask The Champ for a hundred dollars to pay this bet I lost. Can't believe he let that sorry ass nigga jack up his perfect record."

"Bet you won't ask him for it. He can still whoop yo ass."

"No he can't! I know his weak spot now. I'll just punch him in the side."

The two men laughed as they made their way down the aisle. The arena was clearing slowly. There were few smiling faces. Most had their heads down and their mouths closed, like they were following JFK's funeral procession. Nisha thought *everyone* should show the same reverence. She wanted to turn around and curse out the men cracking jokes behind her, but she knew she looked terrible, and she wouldn't be able to get her words straight.

It was Walter who snapped her out of it. He called her name a few times and then touched her shoulder when she didn't respond. Nisha looked up at him. Her eyes floated in a pool of misery that also ran down her cheeks like rain on a window pane.

"You want me to take the baby?" he asked again.

Nisha shook her head. What was the point in that? It wasn't like she and Lonzo had a party to go to. Celebrations were cancelled that night.

She looked back to the ring where everything came crashing down. The announcer and referee were talking. There were a few reporters and trainers hanging around. Lonzo and Veston were in their locker rooms. Nisha figured the folks in Veston's room were laughing and popping bottles.

"Baby girl..."

She returned her gaze to her father who appeared to be on the verge of tears himself. But she had never seen him cry.

"You got to pull it together," Walter told his daughter. "That man is hurting. When he gets out here, he gotta look everybody in the eyes. He don't need to see you crying like this. If you wanna be with a fighter, you gotta be his rock. When he's at his lowest, he got to be able to lean on you. You got to be strong enough to hold him up."

That was good advice. Walter lost nine fights during his career, so he had to know something about what it took to recover mentally and physically.

Nisha wiped her face and told her brain to tell her eyes to stop the waterworks. It took a few minutes, but her cheeks were dry when Lonzo emerged from the tunnel with his entourage. Nisha thought his whole team looked sick. Lonzo approached his family and well-wishers with his head down, but he found the strength to show his face.

Nisha's throat tightened. She choked off a wail when she saw the damage Veston had inflicted.

Lonzo only got hit in the head twenty or so times, but half of them were power shots. His right eye was partially closed, mainly due to the swelling under his eyebrow. The Champ had a cut on his bottom lip, an abrasion on his cheek and a couple of small contusions on the side of his head.

This was the worst condition Nisha had ever seen him in. At that moment her admiration for Lonzo quadrupled: He could've slipped out one of the back doors, but he came to face his people like a man.

"I guess I didn't win that one," he said. His eyes were red and wet, but he wasn't crying. The same couldn't be said for his family members.

His brother Leo brought a hand to his mouth and let the tears fall freely. Lonzo's sister also sobbed openly. She gave her brother a hug. Nisha stood back while everyone offered their sympathy.

"It's alright, brother."

"You'll get 'em next time. This ain't your last fight."

"You still the best, Champ. He got lucky, that's all."

After everyone had their say, Lonzo looked around and said, "Y'all can still go to Pappadeaux if you want, but me and Nisha going home." He looked at his woman. She was glad to offer him dry eyes. "You ready, baby."

She nodded and reached for his hand.

The couple walked away and left the crew to decide what they wanted to do with the rest of their evening. The way everyone looked at each other when Lonzo was gone made it clear they would all go their separate ways and mourn in the privacy of their homes.

Lonzo didn't talk much on the way to the apartment. There was only one thing he wanted to ask Nisha, which, coincidentally, was the one thing she didn't want to talk about: "Do I look bad?"

"No," she said without looking away from the road. She kept both hands on the steering wheel at ten and two, as if Lonzo was a driving instructor.

"Don't lie to me. My eye damned near closed up." He watched her profile, looking for any sign she was deceiving him.

"It don't look that good," Nisha conceded. "But it'll heal."

He looked away after a couple of seconds, and Nisha had to dig deep down into a well of courage she didn't know she possessed to keep from crying again.

It was after midnight when they got home. The baby was fast asleep. Nisha took him to his crib, and Lonzo stopped in the front room and turned on the television. He searched for a late-night news channel that might have a segment for local sports, but thankfully he didn't find one.

When Nisha returned to the living room, Lonzo was sitting on the couch. The television was off. It was dark in there, and that was good. Lonzo sniffled, and she stood uneasily in the doorway. She'd never seen him cry before. She didn't know if Lonzo wanted her to see.

She stepped to him hesitantly. He didn't say anything, so she sat with him on the couch. She leaned towards him slowly and laid her head on his shoulder. Lonzo put a comforting arm around her. Nisha wrapped both arms around him and held tightly.

"What I do wrong?" he asked after a while.

Nisha sighed but didn't say anything. She hoped he was talking to himself, but he waited a few heartbeats and asked again.

"Baby, what I do wrong?"

"I don't know." She spoke softly. "You should, I'm not your trainer. I don't know that much."

"Yes, you do. You grew up in boxing."

"Wait till Fats get the video," she suggested. "Then y'all can watch it together."

"What did you see?" Lonzo pressed. "Don't bullshit me."

Nisha squeezed her eyes closed and shuddered. "You didn't stick to the game plan," she offered. "You had him beat, but then you started fighting his fight."

"I got tired," Lonzo admitted. He sniffled and reached up to wipe his face. "I knew I wasn't gon' make it, so I tried to end the fight, while I still had some strength left."

Nisha already knew that. She didn't say anything.

"Now it's all messed up," Lonzo said.

"No, it's not, baby. It's just one fight."

"You don't understand," Lonzo bawled. "They'll knock me down in the rankings, 'cause I ain't undefeated no more. They gon' say I ain't got what it takes to go the distance. I don't even got enough money for your surgery now."

Nisha knew Lonzo would get a reduced purse if he lost, but, "Baby, it's not a big deal. Don't worry about that."

"How you figure it ain't a big deal? I said I was gon' get your surgery done. Now I can't do it."

"I can get a thousand from my Dad."

"You need more than that," Lonzo said. "I told Fats I'd give him half my check."

Nisha's eyes flashed open, but she didn't move. "*Why*?"

"He lost some bets," Lonzo said, "'cause of me. I told him I'd help him pay."

Nisha didn't know much about the business side of boxing, but she knew a manager/promoter shouldn't bet on his own fighter or ask the boxer to help pay the debts if he lost. "Baby, that's not your fault. That man has a problem with gambling. He needs some help. He don't need to be taking money from you."

"I let him down," Lonzo said. "I let everybody down."

Nisha sat up and looked him in the eyes. His tears hurt her more than anything else she saw that night.

"You only need to worry about yourself," she urged.

"I let you down too."

"No, you didn't. I love you. You could never let me down."

"My perfect record is *gone*," Lonzo cried. "I can't never have it back."

"Nobody has a perfect record," Nisha argued.

As soon as she said it, she remembered Rocky Marciano and Floyd Mayweather Jr. retired undefeated. But Lonzo didn't call her on it.

They sat on the couch and held each other for a long time. Neither of them had anything else to say, but their silence and their tears and their closeness spoke volumes.

Nisha hoped things would be better tomorrow when the sun ushered in a bright new day, but deep down she knew that wouldn't be the case. The only thing sunlight would do was expose Lonzo's wounds and give the people more time to talk and criticize and condemn.

Nisha didn't realize she'd fallen asleep until Lonzo woke her at three a.m. and walked her to the bedroom.

For the first time in nearly five years, they didn't make love after one of Lonzo's fights.

The next morning, Nisha thought she'd get first dibs on adjusting Lonzo's personality for the day, but no such luck. She sat up in bed at seven a.m. and found herself alone. She checked the crib and saw Baby Lonzo snoring pleasantly.

She crawled out of bed and headed for the front room, not sure why she was on pins and needles. She found The Champ sitting on the living room floor. The television was tuned in to the Channel Six News. Thankfully the report was about the recession rather than boxing.

She walked around the couch, and he glanced up at her. Surprisingly, he looked a lot better than he did last night. His eye was swollen, but it wasn't half closed anymore. The contusions on the side of his head didn't look that bad either.

Nisha was about to comment on his miraculous recovery when she saw a newspaper spread on the floor between Lonzo's legs. He finally made the front page of the sport's section. The headline read: THE CHAMP FALLS. There was a huge picture of Lonzo sprawled on the canvas, his face stretched in a scowl that would forever immortalize the pain of his shot to the liver.

He watched Nisha's eyes as she looked from the damning headline and back to him. He didn't look angry, but her heart began to thud, as if she had something to do with the article. She knew he expected her to say something, but she didn't have the right words.

"Where, where'd you get the paper?" she asked as a distraction.

"I stole it," Lonzo said, "from the lady downstairs."

Nisha stared at him, not sure how to respond to that. Lonzo used to have a bad habit of stealing their neighbor's newspaper from her doorstep. Mrs. Jeffries caught him red-handed one day, and he promised to take his lazy self to the corner store the next time he wanted a newspaper. Nisha was embarrassed to hear he'd reverted to his thieving ways.

"I made the front page," he said, holding up the paper.

She started to tell him it was only the front page of the *local* sport's section. Big papers that mattered probably wouldn't mention him at all. But she sensed placating wasn't what he needed. Depression must be met head on – not danced around.

"You knew you were gonna be in the paper," she said. "That shouldn't surprise you."

"Yeah, but they got me on my back," Lonzo said. "They got a picture of me on my back. In *color*."

"Baby…" She sat on the couch and wrapped her legs around him. "I know you wanted to go undefeated. Everybody wants that. But this ain't the end of the world. You young. You got a lot of fights ahead of you. This is gonna make you stronger and smarter. You'll see. You're still the best."

He looked into her eyes and then back at the paper.

Nisha checked the clock and pursed her lips before she asked, "You not going to work today?"

He shook his head.

She placed a hand on his cheek and caressed tenderly.

The baby started to cry, and Nisha moved to get up. But Channel Six's star reporter Chad Collins graced the viewers with his presence at the same moment.

"Welcome back, folks. Alright, before the break, I told you we had bad news in the world of *boxing*. Our sports anchor, Wally Mitchell, is going to fill you in on that now. Wally…"

Nisha hesitated. The baby's cries continued.

"Thanks, Chad," Wally said. He was a handsome man with a strong, rugged voice. "Last night Will Rogers Coliseum hosted an awesome night of fighting, featuring our local favorite, Alonzo "The Champ" Ingram. It was a great show, but no one expected things to end like they did…"

Baby Lonzo's wails intensified. His father gave Nisha a look.

"Ain't you gon' get him?"

Nisha rose to her feet. She looked back at the screen a couple of times before she disappeared down the hallway. She gathered the baby from his crib and rushed back to the living room, but the child wasn't comforted. He continued to cry mightily. Lonzo Sr. threw up a hand and waved her back.

"*Shhht!*" he spat, his eyes glued to the screen. "I'm trying to hear this."

Nisha backed away and rocked the baby in the hallway. "Come on, now. Shhh. Shhh. It's alright, boy..."

From her vantage point, she could still see the TV, which was showing highlights from yesterday's fights. Lonzo leaned closer to the screen. The shot cut back to the sports reporter. Wally said something somber and shook his head, and then they showed a little of the action from Lonzo's fight.

Nisha's eyes were wide and fretful. She took a step into the living room, but the baby was still kicking up a racket. She felt his diaper. It was bloated and stinky. Lonzo shot her an angry glare and grumbled something she couldn't make out.

Nisha shook her head and went back to the bedroom. She couldn't believe he wanted her to miss his segment on the news. But it wasn't a huge deal. She was sure she'd see that infamous fight more times than she wanted to before it was all said and done. She changed Baby Lonzo, and he quieted down right away.

She returned to the living room, but she was too late. Lonzo was on his feet, heading in her direction. He passed her in the hallway without a word. He went to the bedroom and lie face down.

Nisha started to go after him, but he told her, "I don't wanna talk right now," so she went to the kitchen instead and got started on breakfast.

The couple tried to live a life of seclusion for the rest of the day, but Alexander Graham Bell ruined that. Their phones started ringing at eight o'clock, and they were a constant annoyance from that moment on.

Most people called to give their condolences, as if there was a death in the family. Fats called to say he had Lonzo's winnings, minus the portion The Champ promised to loan him.

Someone called from Lonzo's job, and he went to the bedroom to take that one.

Every time his cellphone rang, Nisha felt like someone was picking at an old wound. She couldn't tell if Lonzo felt the same way. He took each call graciously and stayed on the phone however long the other person wanted to talk. Nisha heard him saying things like, "Yeah, I know," "It's all good," and "I ain't worried about it," but he sounded less sure of himself each time.

At noon Nisha made chicken fried steak for lunch. It was one of Lonzo's favorites. He ate heartily, and they made love afterwards. The intimacy was wonderful, but it was shrouded with grief. Nisha offered her body as a sponge to soak up all of the pain and negativity in her man.

She thought he looked better afterwards, but the phone calls continued.

And then Lonzo began to make calls of his own.

At five o'clock he came to the bedroom and woke Nisha from a nap.

"We need to talk," he said, and then headed for the living room.

Nisha looked around in confusion. In her dream she was at the arena again. Only this time she was in the ring with Lonzo, warning him about Veston's tricky rope-a-dope. As her mind came back to reality, she realized the fight was over. Her hopes of altering the outcome were quickly dashed.

In the front room, she found Lonzo standing in front of the television with his arms crossed over his chest. He told her to, "Sit down," furthering her perceptions that this was not going to be a good conversation.

She sat on the couch obediently. She knew he wanted to make changes in the wake of his first lost, but she had no idea.

"I'm going to work for Mr. Brown."

Nisha eyes widened. She stared at him like he grew a horn in the middle of his forehead. "Excuse me?"

"I'm going to work for Mr. Brown," Lonzo said again. "Don't try to talk me out of it, 'cause I already made up my mind."

His face was stern and emotionless. Nisha sensed she was about to argue with a brick wall, but if a brick wall says something ludicrous to you, even an intelligent person is apt to say something back.

"Why you feel like you gotta do that?"

"'Cause we need the money. I can't lose no more fights, so that means I have to train harder than I did last time. I can't be working overtime no more. Matter of fact, I'm dropping to part-time at the warehouse."

Nisha was glad he had thought it out so well. That meant he was still rational. Maybe there was hope.

"Lonzo, you don't have to work for Mr. Brown. You can cut down to part time, and we'll still be alright. I can get a job. We can move in with my daddy. He got plenty of space. I know he won't mind."

"You can't get a job until after you have surgery," he reminded her. "And I'm not taking my family to your dad's house, like I can't afford to take care of y'all. I can take care of y'all just fine."

"My dad knows you can take care of us. You don't have anything to prove."

"I said I ain't doing it."

"Well, you can't go work for Mr. Brown either."

"Who said I can't?"

"*I* said you can't!" Nisha caught herself getting angry. She tried to calm down. "You said you wanted to *talk*, Lonzo. That means you want to hear what I got to say. You can't make decisions like this without me having a say in it."

"What you got to say don't matter, 'cause you always saying the same thing. I'm the man of the house. So what I say goes."

Nisha was shocked by his words and his tone. She tolerated it because she knew he was hurting. She thought fast. She didn't want to use her injury as an arguing point, but Lonzo opened the door by bringing it up.

"You can't cut your hours at work, because you have to be full time to get insurance for me and Baby Lonzo."

He had a comeback for that too. "It don't matter, 'cause they already dropped you from my insurance at work. They called and told me today."

Nisha's mouth fell open. "They dropped us?"

"Naw, just you."

"*Why*?"

"'Cause we ain't married," Lonzo stated. "When I filled out that form, I said we was married. But I didn't send them no papers, so they dropped you."

Nisha brought a hand to her mouth, feeling like her life was spiraling out of control. There were so many questions. The most serious ones already had answers:

Why would you say we were married, Lonzo?

Because that's what Lonzo does. He doesn't care about the rules.

How could you go back to work for Mr. Brown?

Because that's what Lonzo does. He doesn't care about the repercussions of his actions.

"Then we'll get married," Nisha said, though at that moment, she wasn't sure if she wanted to do such a thing.

"Getting married means I gotta work full time to keep you on the insurance," Lonzo deduced. "You said so yourself."

"Stop using my surgery for an excuse!" she shouted. "You wanna go work for Mr. Brown because that's what *you* want to do! You wanna take the lazy way out and end up going to jail!"

"No, going to stay with Walter and letting him take care of us is the lazy way. I can't afford to lose no more fights, girl! I don't wanna end up like one of them bums they throw in the ring when they can't find nobody else to fight. I'm gonna make it to the top the best way I know how!"

"Mr. Brown ain't the best way!"

"Well, that's what I'm doing."

"No, you're not," Nisha said defiantly.

Lonzo cocked his head. "Girl, you can't tell me what to do." As if to illustrate this point, he snatched his keys from the coffee table and headed for the door.

"Where you going?"

"Minding my business."

Nisha got up and blocked the exit with her body. Lonzo regarded her with the sternest look of disapproval she'd ever seen.

"Don't you ever pull no shit like that," he breathed. "Get out the way. You can't hold me in here if I wanna go."

Nisha's eyes filled with tears. She squirmed, but held her ground.

"*Move!*" he barked, and she jumped out of the way.

He left the apartment without another word.

He returned a few hours later with a bottle of Dr. Pepper and a bag of Funyuns. Nisha was busy with a homemade enchilada dinner, another one of The Champ's favorite meals. She didn't think he'd eat, but he had a big appetite. He didn't talk much during dinner, but she could tell he was in a better mood. She didn't ask about Mr. Brown because, frankly, Lonzo had frightened her earlier that day.

By ten o'clock she assumed he'd had a change of heart. But when she let her guard down, he went to the bedroom and got dressed. He pulled a black tee shirt from the dresser and a pair of black Dickey workpants from the closet.

Nisha was afraid to ask where he was going, and she didn't have to. While he dressed, someone knocked on the front door. She answered it and almost vomited when she saw her brother standing there.

"Lonzo ready?"

Nisha's closed her eyes and shook her head slowly. "What are you doing here?"

Reggie was taken aback. "Damn, girl. It's good to see you too."

She remained ice cold. She didn't invite him inside. "What do you want, Reggie?"

He frowned. "Lonzo didn't tell you I was coming to get him?"

Nisha looked over her shoulder fearfully and then returned her gaze to her big brother. "Don't do it," she whispered. "He just mad right now. He don't–"

"What the hell you doing?"

She looked back again and saw Lonzo standing there this time.

"I'm, it's, nothing," she stammered. "Reggie here..."

Lonzo was fully dressed. He approached her with the angry look he wore earlier, and she cowered under his glare.

"I told you about that," The Champ said coldly.

Nisha backed away from the door, and Lonzo greeted his old friend.

"What's up, man."

"You, y'all alright?" Reggie asked, looking from his sister to the much bigger man she fell in love and made a baby with.

"We cool," Lonzo told him. "People argue. Ain't no big deal." He snatched his keys from the coffee table and softened his eyes for Nisha before he stepped outside.

"I'll be back."

She didn't respond. She locked the door behind them and stood there, in somewhat of a daze. In a few moments, she heard muffled music from the powerful stereo system in Reggie's car. She strained her ears and listened until the music faded away.

CHAPTER THIRTEEN
SEA LEGS

Reggie waited until they exited the apartment's parking lot before he turned the radio down and fixed a concerned look on his sister's fiancée. Lonzo was an imposing figure. Reggie had no doubt Lonzo could whoop him if they ever got into it, but some things are worth taking an ass whooping for. Sticking up for your baby sister happened to be one of those things.

"I ain't trying to get in your business," he said, "but Nee Nee was looking upset when we left the house. Y'all alright? I know shit's going bad right now, after what happened with your fight..."

Lonzo looked his homeboy in the eyes and nodded. Generally any problems he had at home would stay *at home*, but Reggie was Nisha's brother, and he was also a good friend.

"You know how womens is," Lonzo said. "They want everything to be plain and simple. They start tripping whenever it's a little bump in the road."

"Yeah." Reggie nodded, though he disagreed with Lonzo's assessment. Most women do want their lives to stay on the straight and narrow, but Nisha wasn't simpleminded like that. She grew up in the hood and was used to things not going her way.

"You saw my fight?" Lonzo asked.

"I seen it," Reggie said. "But you shouldn't worry about that shit. That nigga got lucky. You was better than him. He just caught you with a lucky punch..."

Lonzo sighed. "Ain't no lucky punches in boxing, man. He hit me exactly where he was aiming to hit me. Ain't nothing lucky about that."

Reggie didn't respond.

"Shit like that makes you open up your eyes," Lonzo went on. "I ain't gon' lie: I was a little arrogant about that fight. I knew he was gon' try to tire me out. I figured if I could avoid that, you know, make sure I had enough juice left for the last couple of rounds, I'd be alright.

"But it's not that easy when you get in the ring. I gotta deal with the crowd and my ego. They want me to put on a show, and I started getting mad, 'cause I couldn't do it. I wanted to knock him out so bad, but at the same time I knew I had to hold back, 'cause that's what that chump wanted me to do; swing for the fences so he could lay into me when I got tired.

"And then you got the street-nigga pressure. He was talking to me during the fight. The people in the crowd don't know about that stuff, how he's talking noise when we're in the clinch. He's telling me I ain't got nothing for him, and I can't knock him out. And me being a street nigga, that shit fed right into what I'm used to. I *know* what he's doing, but it's hard not to let it get to me."

"I feel ya," Reggie said.

"As far as your sister," Lonzo said, "man, you know I ain't never did nothing to hurt her. She get mad at me for stuff, and I get mad at her too. But I wouldn't never put my hands on her. I got too much respect for her. Matter of fact, I ain't never put my hands on *no* woman. Shit ain't in me."

Reggie nodded. That was good to hear, but he knew sometimes you don't have to hit a woman to break her down. If a she loves you enough, you can do it with just your words or the look on your face.

"Nee Nee don't want you to go back to work for Mr. Brown," he said.

"Why would she?" Lonzo replied. "We got a baby at home. She ain't got no job. If I get locked up, it'll mess up everything we got going. She care for me. She wants me to make it. I can't be mad at her for that."

Reggie nodded. "You really do got a lot going for you. I respect you, Champ. You know that. But Nisha wanted me to talk to you about this, and I feel like I'd be doing her wrong if I don't tell you; this probably ain't the right move for you. You don't wanna mess up like I did. This is the only life I can have right now. You can have something way better."

"I know that's your sister," Lonzo said, "and you gotta look out for her. But you and me, we mens. Sometimes we gotta do things our women don't want us to, so we can put food on the table.

"I'm not trying to get in this for the rest of my life. It's just something I gotta do for now. I gotta take my training more seriously. Might have to quit my job. I can't lose another fight, Reggie. I would make a deal with the devil to make sure I don't."

Reggie still thought Lonzo should find a better way to make his dreams come true, but if Nisha couldn't talk him out of it, it wasn't likely anyone else could. Even if Lonzo's thinking was flawed, his motive was pure. Nisha was lucky to have a man who loved her enough to take this type of risk.

"Alright," he said. "I'ma leave it alone. You know what you doing, man. You know exactly what you getting into."

"You ain't gotta say it like that, nigga," Lonzo joked. "Damn! You sound like when the movie's about to get scary: *You know exactly what you getting into*," he mocked in an eerie voice.

Reggie laughed. "Naw, man. You know I wouldn't do you like that. I got much love for you, Champ." The matter settled, he turned the radio back up and found half a blunt in the ashtray. He offered it to Lonzo. "Wanna smoke?"

The Champ shook his head. "Naw, man. But you go ahead. Do your thing, bruh..."

Reggie took him to a seedy south side neighborhood called Berry Hill. They pulled up to a nondescript three-bedroom home. Inside, Lonzo and Reggie were greeted by Mr. Brown's personal assistant, a bear-shaped man named Bumpy.

"Wait in there," he said and left them in the front room. "I'll let Mr. Brown know you here."

The Berry Hill clubhouse was more relaxed and sparsely decorated than the compound in Fossil Creek. The carpet was well worn and dirty. The walls were bare. The smell of cigar and marijuana smoke was nearly overwhelming. There were four people in the living room. They all regarded The Champ with varying degrees of recognition.

Reggie sat on the arm of the couch next to a female who didn't mind his presence. Lonzo was lucky enough to get the loveseat to himself.

"What's up," a wolfish man wearing a fitted cap said.

"What's up," Lonzo replied.

"Hey, ain't you–" A high-yellow heifer with long, curly hair started to say something, but the man in the cap cut her off.

"Yeah, that's him, bitch. Keep your mouth closed, and leave him the fuck alone."

The girl's mouth snapped shut. She rolled her eyes and sank back in the cushions.

The other girl in the room looked Lonzo up and down and smiled. An old Scarface CD played on the stereo. The people in the living room didn't appear to be doing anything but sitting there, and that made Lonzo nervous. He looked around for Bumpy. Thankfully the bodyguard rounded the corner at that moment.

"Mr. Brown ready for you."

Bumpy led him to the master bedroom. Lonzo was shocked to see HB exiting the room as they approached. He hadn't seen him since the fateful night when Lou got shot in his femoral artery. Lonzo had assumed the trigger-happy gangster was dead or in the penitentiary.

Seeing HB was alive and well brought all their evil deeds to the front of Lonzo's mind. He swallowed hard, hoping his face didn't show his inner turmoil.

"Oh, shit! What it do, Champ!" HB gave him a handshake and a quick hug. "I ain't seen your ass in a minute! I been keeping up with your fights, though. Sorry about that loss, man. You gon' be alright, though. Don't even sweat that shit."

"I ain't sweating it," Lonzo said. "You been alright?"

"Yeah I'm good," HB said. He scratched the back of his bald head, grinning devilishly. "I'm real good, man."

"Cool," Lonzo said.

"Alright, well, I'ma holler at you later," HB said and squeezed by him in the hallway. "The Champ is in the house!" he said to no one in particular and laughed. *The Champ is in the motherfucking house!*"

Lonzo shook his head and entered the bedroom. Inside he saw Mr. Brown sitting behind an ugly desk that looked like it came from a classroom. The desk was completely bare, except for an expensive chess set with glass figurines standing strategically on the black and white squares. Mr. Brown studied the game intently, with his elbows on the desk and his massive head resting on his fists.

The kingpin wore a white suit with a black shirt and no tie. His size alone made him an imposing figure, but it was his air of sophistication that impressed Lonzo. He looked up with dark eyes that rarely revealed what was on his mind. He gestured with a meaty paw.

"Come over here, man." Mr. Brown's speech was slow and bass-filled, like the rumbling engine of an eighteen-wheeler.

Lonzo stepped to the front of the desk, but there was no chair for him to sit in. He stood uneasily with his hands at his sides. "How you doing, Mr. Brown?"

"I'm fine, man. Didn't think I'd hear from you again. You said you might wanna come back to work three months ago and then... Nothing. No word. Then you lose your fight, and lo and behold, you call me. Coincidence?"

Lonzo frowned. "Naw, man. It ain't no coincidence."

"You change your mind about me managing you?" Mr. Brown asked. "You finally get it in your head that Fats couldn't manage his way out of an elevator?"

Lonzo shook his head. "No sir, Mr. Brown. I know Fats ain't that good, but I'm sticking with him."

Mr. Brown shook his head in disappointment. "So, what you want with me then, Champ? I already got enough fist-men, more than I know what to do with. Plus you lost your last fight. People ain't gon' be scared of you like they used to be. Matter of fact, some of 'em probably think they can whoop your ass..."

Lonzo took offense to the comments, but he knew Mr. Brown was testing him. He didn't like how Lonzo only came to him when he needed something. But the kingpin wouldn't have agreed to the meeting if he didn't plan on hiring him.

"I wish somebody would try to whoop my ass," Lonzo said. "Yeah, I lost last night, but I ain't losing no more."

"Is that right?"

"Yeah, that's right."

Mr. Brown smiled, showing off large teeth that could crack a turkey leg. "Is that right?"

Lonzo sighed angrily. "Yeah, man. That's what I said."

Mr. Brown laughed. It was a sinister bellow that made the hairs stand on Lonzo's arms. "Calm down, Champ. I'm just jiving you man, trying to see if you still got it. People lose their killer instinct, if they stay away too long."

"I'm alright," Lonzo said. "I ain't lost nothing."

"I hear you talking. But the fact remains: You been gone for a long time, Champ. In the last three years, you ain't hit nobody who didn't sign up for it. How can you go back to hitting people who're begging for you to stop? You sure you got the stomach for it?"

"Who you want me to hit?" Lonzo asked. "Point 'em out."

Mr. Brown chuckled and grinned an evil little grin. "Just like that?"

Lonzo nodded. "Yeah. Just like that."

Mr. Brown pursed his lips and thought for a second. "Okay. I got something for you. This ain't a hard job. Dude owes me two G's. But he a hot head. I want you to go to him, make it known that I will kill him over that two thou', just like I would if it was two million or two cents. I think this'll be a good one, to help get your sea legs back under you."

"Cool," Lonzo said. "Where he at?"

"Go talk to HB," Mr. Brown said. "I gave him the address. He'll give you a ride over there."

Lonzo's heart stopped beating for a few seconds. He tried not to show it. Of all people Mr. Brown could've sent him with, he picked the one person Lonzo wanted to avoid. He swallowed roughly and nodded, hoping to leave the room before the sweat blossomed on his forehead.

"Alright. That's cool."

"That's cool?" Mr. Brown asked.

"It's cool," Lonzo said and made his exit.

He slid into the passenger seat of HB's Impala and buckled his seat belt. His job for the night was to beat up and maybe tattoo (permanently scar) a club owner named Fat Pat. Lonzo didn't know the debtor, and he didn't know if the man really owed Mr. Brown. He didn't even know where to find Fat Pat, but HB had the address.

The driver waited until they got on the freeway before he tried to spark up a conversation.

"You don't like me, huh?" HB wore baggy jeans with a Dak Prescott jersey. His bald dome glistened, even though there wasn't a light source in the car. His smile was big and annoying.

"Didn't nobody say they don't like you," Lonzo said with a sneer.

"I can tell you don't like me. I can tell by the way you look at me."

"It don't matter if I like you or not. We need to get through with this shit and go on about our business."

"But I want you to like me," HB said. "Everybody else like me."

Lonzo stared sideways at him. "Man, what the hell is wrong with you?"

HB laughed. "I'm just messing with you, Champ. Why you so uptight? Yo ass don't never laugh or nothing."

"Ain't nothing to laugh about."

"Well, at least tell me what I did to you," HB said. "I only met you a couple of times. What I do to make you not like me?"

Lonzo shook his head. "You tripping."

"Naw, I'm serious. I know you ain't a hater, so it's got to be *something*. Did I kill somebody you know?"

Lonzo sighed. "Naw, man. You ain't killed nobody I know."

"I ain't never stole from you," HB said. "I ain't never messed with your woman either..."

Lonzo shook his head. "Dog, you know why I don't like you."

"I don't," HB said quickly. "That's what I'm trying to figure out, Champ."

Lonzo looked into his eyes and frowned. Either HB was a good actor, or he really had no clue. "You don't remember when you went with me and Reggie that time, to do that job?"

HB thought about it and shook his head. "What happened?"

"What you mean '*What happened*?'"

"What happened on the job?" HB asked. "What I do?"

Lonzo grunted. "You shot that man in the leg, almost killed him."

HB's eyebrows knotted in confusion. "Who I shoot, Champ?"

Lonzo's eyes widened. "You shot that fool, Lou, man! Dude had dreadlocks. He was supposed to be married to Mr. Brown's niece or something..."

"Oh!" Recognition dawned and HB smiled again. "I do remember that. You was scared than a bitch!" He laughed. "That's why you don't like me? 'Cause I shot that fool in the leg?"

Lonzo shook his head in wonderment. "How can you forget about something like that?"

"I shot a lot of people," HB said matter-of-factly. "But I ain't never shot nobody that didn't deserve it. That dread was reaching for a knife. I remember now."

Lonzo sighed. "You crazy, man."

"Naw, I just handle my business. I didn't know you was still mad at me for that. If it make you feel better, I'm sorry I shot that dude."

Lonzo didn't know what to say. It was bad enough HB was a psycho, but he was also a gentleman, willing to be the bigger man and apologize.

"So we cool?" HB asked. "No hard feelings?"

"We straight," Lonzo decided. "Just don't shoot nobody else while you around me. I ain't trying to go to jail for murder behind some dumb shit."

"Alright," HB said, but he looked as trigger-happy as ever. He pulled his visor down, and a perfectly rolled blunt fell onto his lap. He offered it to Lonzo.

"Wanna smoke?"

"I don't smoke no more. Bad for my lungs."

"You don't care if I smoke, do you?" He lit the cigar before Lonzo responded.

"Naw, I don't care," Lonzo said, though he did have a preference. A weed head is bad enough, but a weed head with a gun is intrinsically and substantially worse.

HB drove to a west side neighborhood called Como. He pulled into the parking lot of a large building that had CLUB PINKY printed on a marquee out front. The place looked like it had been closed for years, but there were a couple of cars in the parking lot. The front door swung open when Lonzo gave it a push.

Despite the size of the building, the club was no more than a hole in the wall. There was a collection of tables on one side with a mess of mismatched chairs pushed under them. On the other side was a stage big enough to fit a small band. Along the east wall, there was a simple bar. The place reeked of stale beer and tobacco. Lonzo spotted a man cleaning mugs behind the bar.

"Say, who is y'all?" the barkeep asked.

He was black like oil with big, bug eyes that made him look spooked or maybe high on cocaine.

This was Lonzo's job, so he took the initiative. "Mr. Brown sent us. I'm here to see Fat Pat."

The bartender stared at him for a second and then turned slightly to his left. "Hey, Pat! Some folks here to see you!" Spook Eyes turned back to Lonzo, and the men stared at each other forebodingly.

A moment later, a door behind the bar opened, and three men emerged. Lonzo hadn't totally forgiven HB during the ride to the club, but he was glad he had some kind of back up. All of the men looked to be heavy drinkers, in their mid-forties. One of them was sure to have a gun, or at least a knife.

Of the three guys standing before him, it wasn't hard for Lonzo to figure out who Fat Pat was. The mark was 6 feet even and well over three hundred pounds. But he looked more muscular than fat, like a nose tackle or an offensive lineman.

"You Fat Pat?" Lonzo asked.

"Yeah," the biggest man said. "And you The Champ. What you doing over here? We closed."

Fat Pat had a soft, almost polite voice that didn't match his looks. Lonzo didn't expect the mark to recognize him, but that didn't change his plans. He shortened the distance between them with four quick steps.

"Mr. Brown sent me. He say you owe him two G's. I'm here to collect."

Fat Pat's eyes narrowed. He looked from Lonzo to HB and then back at the men in his corner. He chuckled. "You playing, right? This one of those caught on camera shows, right?"

Lonzo shook his head. "You know you owe that man some money. Break bread."

Fat Pat's smile teetered. "What the hell is this? I know you, man. I mean, I don't *know* you know you, but I done seen your fights. I saw you fight *last night*, as a matter of fact. You famous, nigga. What you doing coming in my club like this?"

Lonzo didn't have to worry about his celebrity status the first time he worked for Mr. Brown. He knew things would be different now, and he was prepared to prove his legitimacy.

He stepped even closer with a no-bullshit look in his eyes. "Alright, I know this might seem strange to you, that I'm doing this kinda shit. But you need to focus on what I'm telling you: Somebody finna get they ass whooped, if I don't get two G's in my hand in the next ten seconds. And the first one to get they ass whooped is gon' be you, Fat Pat, since you the biggest."

The mark chuckled nervously, so Lonzo popped him with a quick jab to the chops. Fat Pat stumbled backwards, his eyes wide. His friends were equally caught off guard. The spook-eyed bartender reached for something under the register, and HB's hand disappeared under his shirt.

"Be easy," HB told the bartender. "This ain't got shit to do with you. This between this man, and that man…"

The bartender slowly brought his hand up.

"Man, what the hell is wrong with you?" Fat Pat wanted to know. "This some *bullshit*, man! You can't come in *my* goddamned club, hit me in the mouth like that!"

"Do something about it," Lonzo dared him. He assumed a boxing stance with his big fists balled and ready. "Come on. You a big nigga. You think you can whoop me?"

"Get his ass," Fat Pat's friend suggested.

"He ain't all that," another said.

"I saw you get your ass kicked last night," Fat Pat said. Blood leaked from his lip and stained his teeth.

"Bet *you* can't do it," Lonzo said.

Fat Pat took a step forward.

"You can take him!" His friends egged him on. "Hit him in the side."

"*Come on!*" Lonzo urged. "Bring yo ugly ass to the square!"

Fat Pat hesitated. He sneered at him. "This some bullshit."

"Pay your debts," Lonzo advised him, "and shit like this wouldn't happen to you."

Fat Pat turned to his bartender and sighed. "Give 'em the money."

The bartender twisted his lips and fixed an evil glare on Lonzo. Rather than pop open the cash register, he dug in his front pocket for the loot. Lonzo lowered his fists and watched Spook Eyes count out 20 one hundred-dollar bills.

"I ain't coming to no more of your fights!" Fat Pat said, rubbing his mouth.

Lonzo thought that was an odd thing to say, but it seemed like a perfect ending to what had been a bizarre day.

"Pay your debts, and shit like this wouldn't happen." He snatched the money from the bar, and he and HB left the building without further incident.

When they returned to the clubhouse, Mr. Brown was so pleased with Lonzo's results, he wouldn't take the money.

"Damn, I just sent you over there to holler at him. I didn't think you'd get that asshole to pay. You can keep that."

Lonzo tried to hide his elation as he stuffed the bills in his pocket. "'Preciate it."

"You wanna stay for a while?" Mr. Brown offered. "Or you got somewhere to be? I got some honeys coming over; big titties, big asses, skinny girls, whatever you like."

"Naw, I got somewhere to be."

He was anxious to get home, but when Reggie dropped him off thirty minutes later, Lonzo found the reception very chilly.

Nisha was waiting for him in the living room. He walked in with a dopey grin that faded when he saw the look in her eyes.

"What'd you do?" she asked.

"You know how it is." Lonzo shrugged. "I don't wanna talk about that stuff, baby. I got paid. That's all that matters." He reached into his pocket to show her the finances. Nisha got up and left the room.

Lonzo stared after her, and then he took a seat on the couch and grabbed the remote. He pursed his lips and shook his head. He could've been parlaying with fine women with big titties and asses (or skinny girls, whatever he liked), but he chose to come home – and this was the thanks he got.

Oh well. Nisha was overdramatic, but she wouldn't stay mad at him for long. Things would get better once she got used to their new lifestyle. If there was one thing Lonzo was sure of, it was that his woman knew how to roll with the punches.

CHAPTER FOURTEEN
MARY JANE

Nisha held on to her grudge for the next couple of weeks, but Reggie was right about his sister being accustomed to turmoil. She wanted Lonzo to do right as much as any woman wants the same for her man, but at the end of the day it all boiled down to what she was going to do about it: Tuck tail and run away, or take the good with the bad, like she always told Lonzo she would.

She and Lonzo shared a bond that was stronger than the battle of wills his reckless decisions led them to. They had a child together, and they had dreams. Of course she wanted her man to become a world champion, but she would stay with him if Lonzo decided to flip burgers or clean toilets for a living.

She gave him the silent treatment for the first few days after he went back to work for Mr. Brown, but they lived in the same apartment, and it was not possible to ignore him 100% of the time. She settled on giving him the cold shoulder instead, and she withheld sex. Lonzo took his punishment like a man. He never complained about being in the dog house.

After a month, Nisha threw in the towel and allowed him to creep back into her heart and their bed.

On Wednesday, February 24th, Nisha's dad took her out to lunch. They stopped by the gym afterwards to see what The

Champ was up to. Normally Lonzo would've been at work at that hour, but Wednesday was now his day off, thanks to his night job with Mr. Brown.

They found him in the main ring sparring with a larger heavyweight named Mookie. Sparring sessions didn't usually attract much interest, but more than a dozen boxers were watching the action, hoping to soak up as much knowledge as they could from Overbrook Meadows' brightest star.

Nisha approached the ring and looked up at him, remembering how they met at this exact spot five years ago. On that day, Lonzo got overly aggressive with his sparring partner for her benefit. Today was no different. When he spotted her and Walter, his punches became quicker and harder. He bobbed and weaved like a Jack-in-the-box and danced like Sugar Ray. After a minute of this, Mookie shook his head and backed away.

"Alright, man. That's it."

"What you mean, '*That's it*?'" Lonzo cut him off before he could climb through the ropes.

"Gone now," Mookie said. "You know you hitting too hard. You always start tripping when people watching you."

"Aw, whatever. Come on. We ain't through yet."

"*I'm* through," Mookie assured him.

"Quit acting like a broad," Lonzo suggested.

"Yeah, get back in there!" one of the onlookers shouted.

Mookie turned angrily and yelled at the spectator. "Why don't *you* get in there with him?"

The middleweight piped down and looked around warily.

"Yeah, that's what I thought," Mookie said. He climbed out of the ring, and Lonzo came and stood before Nisha and her dad. He leaned with his forearms on the ropes, catching his breath.

"Hey, what y'all doing here?"

"We were in the area," Walter said. "Thought we'd stop by, see how things were going."

"But I can see we shouldn't have," Nisha teased. "You done lost another sparring partner."

"Aww, that dude's a mark." Lonzo waved his hand in dismissal. "He was gon' quit anyway."

"Sure," Nisha said with a smirk. "You never have anything to do with it."

"Not me," Lonzo agreed. "You know I'm a teddy bear."

She laughed. "What time are you coming home?"

"I'm leaving here at five. But I got something to do tonight..."

Nisha's smile disappeared, and Walter took that as his cue to give them some privacy.

"I'll be, over, that way..." He took off towards the weight room.

"Don't start tripping," Lonzo said to his woman. He ducked under the ropes and hopped out of the ring. He managed to take his son from her, while wearing boxing gloves.

"What you gotta do tonight?" Nisha asked him.

"You know what I'm doing tonight. You can't be getting an attitude every time I gotta take care of some business. I always come home to you. It's all good."

Nisha shook her head. "You know it's not all good, Lonzo. I worry about you every time."

"I know." He kissed her softly. "It'll be over soon."

By *soon*, he meant the two more months he planned to work for Mr. Brown. His next fight was scheduled for May 29th. Despite his loss to Veston, The Champ was guaranteed $30,000 for that bout. That would be enough to provide for the family while he trained for his 20th fight in Austin. So far he'd managed to avoid legal trouble, but Nisha knew a lot could happen in the next two months.

"What you want for dinner?" she asked.

"I got a taste for fish. Not catfish though. Something nice. I left some money in the cookie jar."

Having money in the cookie jar was about the only thing Nisha liked about Lonzo's new job. They never had *whatever* money before. Now there was always up to $500 in the kitchen cupboard, available for anything she wanted to spend it on.

"Alright." She took the baby and gave him another kiss. "I'll have dinner ready by the time you get home."

"Stop worrying so much." He rubbed the worry lines between her eyebrows with his glove. "You gon' get wrinkles."

"Don't worry about my wrinkles. Just be careful while you're with my brother."

"Yes, ma'am."

He watched her walk away and then turned to face the boxers who were standing around, looking for something to do.

"Whoever ain't no pussy, get in this ring!" He waited a few beats, but no one jumped at the opportunity to prove their masculinity. "All y'all some busters," Lonzo decided. "Straight up *busters...*"

Rather than take her straight home, Nisha asked her dad if he could stop by the supermarket so she could pick up something for dinner. Walter was always eager to spend time with his youngest child. While Nisha tried to decide between red snapper, bass or mackerel, her father asked about the trouble in paradise he caught wind of while they were at the gym.

"I don't know what's wrong with him sometimes," she confided. "I love him, but I don't know where his head's at."

"What's he done now?" Walter asked with a chuckle.

"He went back to work for Mr. Brown," Nisha said, and the smile fell from her father's face.

"He did what?"

"He did it after he lost that fight. He said he couldn't afford to lose no more, and he had to cut his hours at work. With me not working, he said he didn't have a choice."

"Of course he has a choice. Y'all can come stay with me, or I could loan you however much money you need."

"I told him, but he wouldn't do it. He doesn't want you to think he can't take care of us."

"That's crazy."

"I know," Nisha said. "I told him that too."

"How are you okay with that? How can you go on about your business, like it's nothing?"

She lowered her gaze. "Daddy, I've been back and forth, up and down, and every which way I can with Lonzo about this. He won't change his mind. He promises it will only be for the next couple of months. The only thing I haven't done yet is leave him..." She waited, eager to hear his advice on that option.

Walter shook his head. "What's he doing? The same as last time?" He knew all about Lonzo's dirty deeds three years ago, including the attempted murder that never got reported by Lou Alston.

"It's the same," Nisha confirmed, and the full burden of Lonzo's decision fell on her shoulders again. "He can go to jail any day." Her eyes were wide and glossy. "He could get *killed*."

"Hey, hey…" Walter gave her a comforting hug, like only a father can. "I didn't mean to get you all worked up. I know you been through these feelings already. You got through it and somehow found a way to go on with your life without crying your eyes out. It's okay to be strong for him. I don't wanna take that from you."

"But, but you said–"

"I'm an old fool," he interrupted. "I'm the one who told you not to go out with Lonzo in the first place. Remember? I was wrong then, and I'm wrong now. You guys will get through this. Look how far you made it already…"

Nisha forced a smile. A lone tear rolled down her cheek. She brushed it away with her shoulder. "Thanks, Daddy."

"So, what are you getting?" he asked, turning back to the fish.

"I don't know. What do you think?"

"Bass is good. But they so *ugly*. Look how big they mouth is."

Nisha laughed. "Daddy, that's a *large mouth bass*!"

"They should call it the *ugly face bass*," he said, and Nisha laughed. "If you want something that looks pretty on the plate, I'd go with that red snapper."

"Alright." Nisha called the butcher over and pointed at her selection. "Can I have three of those? Can you keep Baby Lonzo tonight?" she asked her father.

"Anything for my baby girl," Walter said with a grin.

Nisha grilled the snapper and served it with wild rice, red potatoes and a cherry tomato vinaigrette. Lonzo thought he walked into a restaurant when he got home from the gym at 5:30.

"Damn, girl! You put your foot in that for real! It smells good."

"It is good," she assured him. "You ready to eat?"

"Let me take a shower first." He gave her a hug and a kiss on the side of the neck. "Is it our anniversary? Did I forget your birthday or something? Shit, did I forget *my* birthday?"

"No. I just wanted to do something nice for you."

"Where the baby?"

"At my daddy's house."

"That's perfect," Lonzo said. "'Cause I wanna do something nice for you too." He moved in for a hug. Both hands quickly dipped to grab her booty. Nisha kissed him and nibbled his bottom lip before she let go.

"Go take your shower, boy. I'll set the table."

Fifteen minutes later, Lonzo sat across from her and chowed down on what he said was Nisha's best meal *ever*. By the end of dinner, he was full and happy, satisfied with his life and his woman. He wanted to express his gratitude romantically, but she wasn't ready for him yet.

She told him, "I'm getting a headache."

Lonzo frowned. "You got a headache? Dang, girl. That's the oldest excuse in the book. If you don't want me to tap that, you can just say it."

She giggled. "I really do have a headache, baby. Why wouldn't I want to make love to you? You The Champ. Who wouldn't want you?"

"I know, right?" Lonzo said with a grin. "Who wouldn't want all this manliness?"

"Don't get carried away."

They watched a couple of sitcoms together, and at seven Lonzo went to the bedroom to take a nap.

That was perfect. Nisha couldn't have planned it better if she gave him sleeping pills.

At ten o'clock he woke up and started to get dressed for his late-night antics with Mr. Brown's crew. Nisha jumped in the shower and stepped out ten minutes later, smelling like scented body wash. Rather than get dressed, she pulled on a sexy Victoria's Secret robe that extended midway down her thighs. She put on makeup and let her hair down and spritzed perfume on her neck, chest and stomach.

When she knew she looked irresistible, she stepped out of the bathroom with her robe partly open. Lonzo's eyes nearly fell out of his head when he ran into her in the hallway.

"Damn, baby."

"What?" she said, heading for the bedroom.

Lonzo followed like a dog in heat. "You ain't, you ain't got no drawers on?" He lifted the back of her robe and hummed at the sight of her naked ass. "I say *hot damn!*"

Nisha pushed his hand away playfully. "Gone, boy." She went to the dresser and pretended to look for a bra and panties.

Lonzo caught up with her and embraced her from behind. He kissed her ear and inhaled the scent wafting from her neck. His hands slid from her stomach to her breast and then between her legs. She turned to face him, and he kissed her deeply. He gripped her hips and pulled her closer. He squeezed her ass and grunted, and Nisha picked that moment to start the psychological warfare.

"Baby, I want you so bad," she whispered.

"Shit, I feel ya," Lonzo breathed.

"I wanna suck your dick."

Lonzo shuddered. "What? I get dirty talk too? You sure I didn't miss our anniversary?"

"No. You like it when I talk dirty to you, don't you?"

"Yes, ma'am."

"You like it when I talk about sucking your dick?"

He swallowed roughly. "I, I sure do..."

"Take your pants off," she said in her sluttiest voice. "Let me see what you working with."

"I'm working with a lot," Lonzo assured her.

"Ooh, you got my mouth watering," Nisha cooed. "Come on, baby. Don't keep me waiting."

Lonzo backed away and ripped his pants open roughly enough to break the zipper.

"Wait." She put a hand on his chest. "Are you going somewhere?"

"Yeah, but not for a minute," Lonzo said. "We got time."

She shook her head and frowned. "Uh uhn."

Lonzo's pants and boxers fell around his ankles. His soldier was rock hard and ready for service. The look on his face was priceless. "What you mean 'Uh uhn?'"

"I didn't know you was going somewhere. I don't want a quickie."

"I told you I had something to do tonight."

"I forgot."

"What?" Lonzo stared at her in confusion. "So, what you saying? We ain't gon' do nothing?"

"Yeah, baby. I want to. But I don't want no quickie."

"It ain't got to be a quickie." Lonzo took her hand and pulled her towards the bed. "I can stay here for an hour if you want. I ain't in no rush."

She pulled her hand away. "I want you to stay here *all night*."

"Baby, I got something to do tonight." He was near exasperation. "Don't do me like this. Come on, now. You got me excited."

"I'm excited too. But I don't want you to leave me afterwards."

Lonzo's brow furrowed as he made the transition from confused to angry. "I got to go to work tonight," he said calmly.

"That's not your *job*," Nisha said sternly. "You don't have to do that, not tonight or any other night. We already got enough money to last till your next fight."

"No, we don't."

"Yes, we do. And my daddy said he'll loan us some more if–"

"Aw hell," Lonzo grumbled and pulled up his pants. "Now you wanna come with this shit again? I already told you I'm not taking money or nothing else from Walter. I make my own money."

"Stop saying it's about the money, Lonzo! We don't need that much money. We can get by on two thousand dollars a month, and you already have that!"

"Get by?" He frowned. "Hell you mean *get by*? You talking about eating Ramen noodles every goddamned day? That's what you mean *get by*?"

"I'd rather eat Ramen noodles than worry about you going to jail."

"I'm not just making money for our rent," Lonzo reminded her. "I'm trying to save up for your surgery too."

"I don't want you to do that!" Nisha yelled. "I don't even wanna have no surgery!"

"Well, you getting it!" Lonzo snarled. He buckled his pants and stepped into his shoes angrily. "Can't believe you get me all hard, and you don't even wanna do nothing. This some straight-up *bullshit!*"

Nisha put her hands on her hips, making sure to pull her robe fully open so he could see the full awesomeness of her nudity. "You can have me right now. *All night long.* I just want you to stay here with me. I don't want you to work for Mr. Brown."

He looked her up and down. Nisha knew he was about to give in, but the bastard said, "I'll get some when I get back," and walked out of the room.

"If it's still here when you get back!" Nisha yelled after him.

He stopped and turned in the hallway. "What that mean?"

"It means I want some *now*, Lonzo. If you leaving, I might have to take care of myself."

"What you talking about, playing with yourself?"

"If I have to." She knew Lonzo hated when she masturbated. For whatever reason, it made him feel like he wasn't fulfilling his manly duties. But even this threat couldn't loosen the hold the streets had on him.

"Do what you gotta do," he said and slammed the door on his way out of the apartment.

Nisha stayed up past midnight, unable to go to bed until her man was safe at home.

Lonzo walked through the door at 2:30 am. He had the nerve to have a smile plastered on his face. Nisha had been simmering in the discomfort of her failure for the last four hours. It would've been nice if Lonzo at least *pretended* to feel her pain.

"Hey, baby." He plopped down on the couch and leaned on her heavily. "I'm ready to pick up where we left off!" He laughed drunkenly.

Nisha backed away and wrinkled her nose in disgust. "You stink! You been drinking?"

"Naw, baby." He placed a hand in her lap and rubbed her thigh. "Come on, girl. I been thinking about this all night. Take your clothes off."

She wore a pair of his boxing shorts and a tee shirt. She didn't take care of her own sexual needs while he was gone, but Lonzo's behavior wasn't even close to romantic. "You not turning me on *at all*," she said honestly.

"What you want?" he asked. "A kiss?" He smooched her cheek playfully and laughed. "Aright, come on," he said and laughed again. "Get naked."

She pushed him away and stared into his eyes. "What the hell is wrong with you?"

"Nothing," he said giggling. "I'm trying to make you happy, baby."

His eyes were low and red. That wasn't a definite sign of inebriation, but coupled with his goofy behavior, you didn't have to be a doctor to make a diagnosis. "Lonzo, you been smoking *weed*? Is, are you high?" she asked in disbelief.

"A little bit," he admitted. He chuckled, but Nisha couldn't have been more disgusted. She jumped to her feet.

"What the hell is wrong with you? You don't even smoke weed!"

"I know I don't. I just hit a blunt like, two, three times. Ain't like I do it every day."

"Why you doing it *at all*?!" she nearly screamed. "You got a fight coming up!"

"Not for two months. Why you bugging?"

"You're the one who's bugging, Lonzo! It's bad enough you hang around those people. Now you wanna pick up their bad habits? You won't be happy 'till you mess everything up!"

"I ain't messing nothing up. I'm just having a little fun. Now is you gon' gimme some ass or not?"

"No!" She turned and stomped down the hallway.

"I been waiting for you all night!" he shouted.

"So!"

"This some bullshit. I had, like, three bitches trying to *throw* the pussy at me. But naw, I came home to you..."

Nisha stopped in her tracks. She returned to the living room with her eyes wide, her nostrils flared. "You had *what*?"

Lonzo caught himself and wisely said, "Nothing." He tried to change the subject. "Say, I'm hungry. You got some more of that red snapper?"

"No, I heard what you said!" She stood in front of him and pointed a rigid finger at his nose. "You wanna go out there and fuck them bitches, you go right ahead and do it! Bet I won't be here when you get back!"

"I don't wanna fuck nobody – except you." Their argument was as serious as it gets, but he couldn't wipe the smile off his face. It infuriated Nisha to no end. "Come on, now," The Champ said. "You know I don't want nobody else."

"I don't know what the hell you want! But I can tell you right now, you gon' end up with *nothing*, if you keep it up."

"Keep what up? I didn't do nothing."

She didn't have the patience to argue with him any further. She retreated to the bedroom and cried on her pillow while Lonzo laughed at late night cartoons on TV. When her tears finally stopped, and she was able to think rationally, Nisha wondered if this might be the end of their five-year relationship. There was only so much complaining and crying she could do before she had to accept the fact that the Lonzo she had now was not the same man who proposed to her six months ago. There was a chance he would return to his old self, but how much recklessness did she have to put up with while she waited for that to happen?

Unexpectedly, she found herself thinking about the last man who made her cry; her high school sweetheart, Ellis. He left to join the marines shortly after graduation. Nisha was so head-over-heels, she almost went with him. But she didn't like the idea of tossing and turning in a lonely bed, while her husband risked his life for an unjust war.

She decided to stay in Overbrook Meadows, and Ellis left. Nisha thought she found the perfect man in Lonzo, but it appeared she suffered the same fate. Night after night she found herself alone in bed, worrying about her man's safety. Unlike Ellis, Lonzo didn't have a noble cause to justify his actions. He was putting his fiancé through hell, so he could protect the interests of one of the most despicable men in the city.

He said it would be over soon, but she didn't know if she could put up with his foolishness for much longer. She wasn't sure if Lonzo was even worth the wait.

CHAPTER FIFTEEN
PATRICE AND
BIG BENJAMIN STYLES

Though her heart was tormented, by morning Nisha decided their troubles weren't great enough for her to leave. She made bacon and eggs for breakfast, and the couple settled their differences before Lonzo left for his part time shift at the warehouse.

"I don't want you to start drinking and smoking and doing stuff you never did, just because you're around those people. Lonzo, you taking a big enough risk as it is. I don't want you to get to the point where that lifestyle takes control of you."

He listened quietly, his shoulders slumped.

"You know you right, girl. I know you love me as much as I love you."

His words warmed Nisha's heart, but she didn't let her eyes show it.

"It do be a lot going on over there," Lonzo admitted. "I always come straight home after I get through with what I got to do."

"A lot going on like what?" Nisha wondered. "Drugs, women?"

Lonzo kicked himself for planting that seed when he was high last night. It was now destined to grow into a tall tree of distrust.

"I don't be messing with no women. I know it's hard, but you got to have faith in me, that I'm gon' do right by you. This will all be over when I have my next fight. We'll have enough money to

last us until my fight in Austin. I won't never work for Mr. Brown
again. I swear to God."

"Don't swear to God," Nisha told him.

"Alright, well I put that on my son," Lonzo said. "Just two
more months. You stay down with me, and we'll be straight for
the rest of our lives."

Nisha did her best to put her worries aside as the next few
days turned to weeks. The day after Easter, Lonzo and Fats
commenced a workout regimen that would continue until his fight.
His next opponent was a monster of a man named Benjamin "Big
Ben" Styles. By all accounts he was an absolute beast.

Big Ben was a native of Alabama. Legend had it he
whooped his first ass at the tender age of three, when a nurse tried
to give him a booster shot. Since then, Big Ben left a long trail of
busted-up people in his wake. The majority of those fights were
verifiable. Ben had a record of 27-4, with 21 of those wins coming
by way of knock out. He was 6'6" and nearly 240 pounds.

When Lonzo brought home a collection of his fight videos,
Nisha couldn't hide her angst as she watched Big Ben pummel one
boxer after the next. The worst video was a highlight reel of the
bruiser's knockouts. Nisha's heart started to pound midway
through the legalized massacre, but Lonzo was as cool as a
cucumber. He found fault with every boxer who fell before Mr.
Styles.

"He shoulda kept his hands up. You can tell he tired."

"He not jabbing back."

"He shoulda grabbed him, wrapped him up."

"That nigga can't fight."

"That nigga weak."

"Jab back, fool!"

"Nigga, move! Move your feet!"

"This nigga sorry."

After watching the tapes, The Champ formulated his
opinion of Big Ben Styles: "He ain't all that."

Nisha wanted to ask her man if he was smoking weed again. The tapes she saw gave her the exact opposite opinion. But she understood Lonzo's cockiness was essential to his success in the ring, so she kept her mouth closed.

On Saturday, May 29th, Nisha woke up at 7:15 am and found herself alone in bed. She checked the crib and saw Baby Lonzo was missing as well. She slid out of bed and crept down the hallway, hoping to catch Lonzo shadowboxing before he was aware of her presence.

She made it to the living room undetected, but her man wasn't exercising anymore. He sat on the arm of the couch with Baby Lonzo on his knee. Lonzo's chest rose and fell quickly. Sweat glistened on his body like oil.

The Champ was watching television. Nisha looked to see what was on, and her gut twisted up in a knot.

"That's him?" she asked softly.

Lonzo nodded and motioned for her to come closer. "Check him out."

On the screen was the ugly bear he was scheduled to fight that night. Big Ben had a thick neck like a tree trunk and a pudgy nose that had been broken at least once in his lifetime. He had wild hair and bushy eyebrows and a protruding brow that made him look like a Neanderthal.

Big Ben was on the news to promote the match, and he took offense when the reporter asked him what type of fight he expected from The Champ.

"Hold on, hold on," Styles said, shaking his massive head. "I gots to stop you right there." He had a raspy voice like a chain-smoker, but Nisha knew he wouldn't have made it this far in his career if that was the case.

"The only heavyweight champ I know," Big Ben said, "is Melvin Broadnax. That's the man with the belts around his waist, and that's the *only* man I'm gonna call *champ*. This, this *Alonzo*..." He screwed up his face and said the name with disdain.

"That man ain't no champ. He should be embarrassed to let people call him that. As a matter of fact, he should drop to his knees and *beg* Melvin for forgiveness, for having the audacity to go around calling hisself champ. That man's name is *Alonzo Ingram*, and that's the only thing I'll *ever* call him."

Lonzo sucked air between his teeth and nodded at the television. Nisha's mouth fell open and remained that way.

Realizing his interview had just gone from *blah* to *awesome*, the reporter grinned and egged Big Ben on. "So, you're saying you refuse to call Alonzo *The Champ*?"

"Not only do I refuse," Big Ben said, "but I ought'a whoop your tail right now 'cause you keep doing it!" He raised a huge fist and shook it menacingly. The reporter's eyes grew wide, and then he laughed.

"It's about *respect*," Big Ben continued. "If you ain't never had a championship belt around your waist, you *ain't* the champ. You can call yourself whatever you want, but you's a *lie*! You lying to America, you lying to your woman, and you lying to yourself every time you look in the mirror!"

The reporter couldn't hide his elation. "So, if Mr. Ingram is watching right now, do you have any words for him before your fight?"

"Yeah," Big Ben said and turned his bestial mug towards the camera. "Stop calling yourself *The Champ*," he warned, "'cause you ain't the champ! You just a wannabe. You *wanna* be the champ, but you ain't nowhere near it, so stop playing with yourself!

"You still got two cats standing between you and Melvin, and you ain't gon' get past neither of us. I know for a fact you ain't getting past me tonight. And after I whoop your ass, Lonzo – oh, excuse me. Is it alright if I say that on TV?" he asked the reporter.

"Yeah, that's fine."

"Alright." Big Ben faced the camera again. "After I whoop your ass tonight at Will Rogers, Lonzo, I want you to change your lame ass name! This is getting ridiculous. You ain't the champ, and you ain't never gon' be. Show some class, man! Have some respect for the sport."

With that, Big Ben ended his tirade, and Channel Six went to commercial.

"He just trying to get in your head, baby," Nisha said knowingly. "He want you to get mad, so you'll mess up in the ring."

Either Lonzo didn't hear her, or he didn't want to heed wise counsel. "He gon' call me The Champ," he said, staring at the television. "I guarantee you he gon' call me The Champ – *tonight* – in that ring. You'll see."

His countenance was dark. Nisha could almost see the heat waves rising off his scalp.

"You'll see," he said, sucking his teeth. "Everybody gon' see..."

The Champ ate a light breakfast and then went to the gym. Nisha started feeling stressed as soon as he left, but thankfully she had something to occupy her time nowadays.

Lonzo didn't want her to get a job until after her surgery, but he didn't know that for the past two months Nisha already had a job, sort of. She worked as a child care provider at her sisters' bootleg daycare. Shonda couldn't afford to pay for her services, but Nisha was doing it for the peace of mind, not the money.

She arrived at Shonda's home at 9:30 and got started on an arts and crafts activity with the bigger kids. At lunch time it was her task to serve the meals Shonda prepared and clean up after the kiddos when they finished eating. Nisha implemented story time at one, and at three she took everyone outside to enjoy the playground at a park down the street.

By five o'clock, she felt like she was at the end of a real work day. She sat on the couch with Shonda, while the parents came to pick up their big and little bundles of joy.

"I think I need a vacation," Nisha said as she slouched in the sofa.

"I can't approve no vacation time right now," Shonda joked. "You ain't even made it past your ninety-day probation period."

Nisha laughed.

"You ready for tonight?" Shonda asked.

"I guess so."

"I know Lonzo got this one," Shonda predicted. "That man he fighting is too ugly to win."

Nisha laughed. "You saw him on TV this morning?"

"No, but I saw him in yesterday's paper. What's his name, Big Ben?"

"Yeah. You shoulda seen him on the news. He was talking much noise."

"For real?"

"He's trying to get under Lonzo's skin. He was talking about there's only one person who should be called The Champ, and that's Melvin Broadnax."

"Who's that?"

Nisha rolled her eyes. "You don't know nothing about boxing, do you?"

"I ain't like you and Daddy," Shonda admitted.

"Melvin Broadnax is the heavyweight champion," Nisha informed her.

"Why *do* Lonzo call hisself The Champ?" Shonda wondered.

"Because he's the best. I guess he's trying to speak it into existence."

"What's Melvin's nickname?"

"The Undeniable."

"That sounds *tight*," Shonda said. "Why don't Lonzo use that name?"

Nisha stared at her and then shook her head. "I swear it feels like I'm still talking to one of the kids."

Someone knocked on the door.

"Come in!" Shonda yelled.

The door pushed open, and a fair-skinned woman with full lips and wide hips stepped inside. Nisha didn't know her, but somehow she looked familiar. The visitor looked around until she spotted one of the children.

"Come on, boy."

A four-year old hopped to his feet and ran out the door.

"Bye!" he yelled at Shonda.

"Whoa, whoa!" Shonda got to her feet and stopped the newcomer before she could leave. "Who are you? What you doing?"

"What you mean, '*What I'm doing?*'"

"Like I said: *What are you doing?*" Shonda reiterated. "You can't be coming up in my house, taking none of these kids."

"Obviously this *my* son," the woman said with plenty of attitude.

"Well, maybe that's something you want to tell me when you walk up in my house," Shonda offered, with the same level of aggression. "You ain't never dropped that boy off or picked him up before. I don't know you from a hole in the ground."

"My mama drops him off," the stranger said with a roll of her neck. "My name is *Patrice.* Now will you please back up out of my face?"

Shonda's eyes widened. She looked back to Nisha, who sat on the couch with a similar expression. Shonda slowly turned back to the visitor. Nisha saw her sister prop a hand on her hip, and she knew it was about to be on and popping.

"Let me tell you something, Patrice. This is *my house*, and *I'm* running things up in here. I been keeping your boy for three months, and I ain't never seen hide nor hair of you.

"If you wanna pick your son up, that's fine. If you wanna drop him off, that's fine too. But I can tell you what you *not* gon' do, and that's run up in my house with an attitude, like you running something. If you ain't got the common courtesy to acknowledge me when you knock on my door, I don't want that boy back over here."

"That's fine with me," Patrice said. "I didn't bring him over here in the first place." She looked around Shonda's unkempt home. "I bet this place ain't even licensed. I could shut you down with one phone call."

Nisha shook her head. She didn't know how this conversation went from zero to a hundred so quickly, but she knew her sister wasn't the type to tolerate such nonsense.

Shonda looked back and said, "Nisha, you'd better come get this heifer."

Nisha rose to her feet, and the visitor looked her up and down. Nisha didn't plan to fight the stranger, but Patrice's next words let her know they weren't so unconnected.

"*Nisha*? Didn't you used to work at the pharmacy?"

Nisha stopped in her tracks. "Yeah..."

Patrice nodded. "Mmm hmm. You worked with my sister, Toya..."

That sentence was like a light flashing in Nisha's mind. The reason Patrice looked so familiar was because Nisha had met her before; a long time ago, when she first started working for Dr. Coates. Also, now that she thought about it, Patrice and Toya were physically similar. They were both high-yellow with big, red lips. Both sisters had a head full of weave, and they were bottom-heavy, with thin waists and big asses that would make any brother do a double take.

"Yeah, I did," she said hesitantly.

Patrice nodded. "Mmm hmm. You the one go with that boxer..."

Nisha's eyes narrowed. Toya had a bad habit of saying inappropriate things about The Champ. She hoped Patrice was smarter in this regard, but no such luck.

"You know my sister's sleeping with him," Patrice said with a smirk.

In the split second it took for Nisha's blood to boil and for her fingernails to extend, becoming claws meant to scratch and tear high-yellow face until it wasn't pretty or smiling anymore, Shonda stepped between the women and chastised the visitor.

"What the hell you come over here saying some shit like that for? You better get your ass away from here, before both of us jump on you! We'll snatch so much hair out your head, you'll look like you got the mange."

"I don't wanna fight," Patrice said and backed out of the doorway, still smiling. Nisha's expression delighted her even more. "I'm just telling you what's going on," the witch said, "with my sister, and your man, at Mr. Brown's house..."

Nisha's heart raced, but her breaths stopped. Neurons fired uncontrollably, and her brain was filled with too much information. Normally she would never believe something like this, especially coming from a hood rat, but she thought about all the times Toya said things about Lonzo at work. She thought about the comments Lonzo made about the women who frequented Mr. Brown's.

She thought about the nights her man didn't get home until well past midnight. She imagined Toya and Lonzo making out, and it was over. In her mind's eye, she could see everything. She saw Lonzo holding Toya. She saw Toya sucking his neck. She saw Lonzo laying her down. She saw Toya's lips part and moan softly when she and Lonzo became one.

Nisha's body moved on its own accord. Shonda was ready for a fight a few moments ago, but the look in Nisha's eyes made it clear this wouldn't be a regular fight. Nisha wouldn't stop until there was blood, and plenty of it. It may feel good to pulverize Patrice in front of her son and the other kids who hadn't been picked up yet, but they couldn't give in to the devil so easily.

Shonda grabbed Nisha's shoulders and pushed her back towards the couch, while Patrice laughed in the background. Shonda was taller, but Nisha was bigger. She didn't resist much at first, but when Shonda yelled at one of the kids to, "Shut that door!" Nisha fought back with a sense of urgency.

With an inhuman growl, she shoved with all her might, and Shonda went flying across the room. Nisha charged the front door just as one of the kids slammed it closed. Nisha grabbed the doorknob, but Shonda was on her feet again. She wrapped both arms around Nisha's middle and pulled as hard as she could. Nisha held onto the doorknob with the same intensity. Her voice was calm, despite the deranged look in her eyes.

"Let me go, Shonda. Just, let me go. Shonda. Let go. Let me go..."

After what felt like an hour-long struggle, Nisha's hand slipped off the doorknob. She and Shonda crashed to the floor with a loud *BOOMP*! that rattled the windows and made Baby Lonzo cry.

Nisha tried to get to her feet, but Shonda's butt was planted on the floor, and she made sure it stayed that way.

"No, Nisha. I'm not gon' let you go. I'm not."

Nisha's struggles finally ceased, and she began to cry. Shonda relaxed her arms. Rather than restrain her, she hugged her sister tightly. She didn't let go for another minute. When she released her, Nisha shot to her feet. She grabbed her purse and headed straight for the door. Shonda didn't want her to leave, but she was sure Patrice was gone by then.

"Where you going?"

Nisha didn't answer, but she didn't take Baby Lonzo with her, so Shonda knew she wouldn't be gone long.

She somehow made it all the way to Lonzo's gym without a policeman pulling her over and deeming her unfit to operate a motor vehicle. When she walked inside, none of the boxers and trainers who were usually cordial wanted anything to do with what they sensed was about to be an atomic-size explosion. They gave her a wide berth as she made her way to the back of the building.

In the media room, Lonzo was laughing with Slick, who sat on the corner of a table with a toothpick dangling from his gold-laden mouth. Fats was there too. He sat in a small, plastic chair that could barely contain his humongous ass.

On the television, Big Benjamin Styles threw up his hands in victory after dropping a smaller man with an overhand right to the forehead. No one in the room was watching the video. That didn't surprise Nisha, because she knew Lonzo had lied about everything he ever told her. If it turned out there wasn't even a fight tonight, she wouldn't be one bit surprised.

All of the men in the room looked up at her at the same moment, and the conversation stopped abruptly. Nisha's face was red, her eyes puffy. She wasn't crying anymore, but there were dried saltwater stains on both of her cheeks. Her hair was unkempt. Her tee shirt was stretched and distorted because of her wrestling match with Shonda.

Lonzo rushed to her, assuming the worst. But behind his woman's big, wet eyes, he saw she was angry. Slick and Fats saw this too, and they hastily left the room.

"What's wrong?" Lonzo asked, his face almost as distraught as hers.

Nisha had been thinking about what she'd say for the last twenty minutes. Everything sounded so good in her head, but now that it was time to speak, none of her words seemed strong enough. She shuddered and stammered and hated herself for being weak.

"You, you, slept with Toya..."

Lonzo frowned and shook his head slowly. "What?"

She took his question as a form of stalling, and all the pain from the last thirty minutes rushed back with a vengeance. She breathed fire from her nostrils. Her body trembled. She swung her arm without full awareness of what she was doing. Her open palm impacted Lonzo's face with a thunderous **SMAK!** that hurt her as much as it hurt him.

He was stunned speechless. A trickle of blood leaked from the corner of his mouth.

The Champ's wide eyes narrowed, and he went after her with a quickness that caught her off guard. She couldn't stop a surprised scream from forcing its way up her throat as he grabbed both of her shoulders and shoved hard. She felt weightless in his grip. She didn't know if he lifted her completely off the floor, or if her feet were sliding on the carpet.

She impacted the wall with a **THUD,** and her head bumped the sheetrock. She saw a bright flash of white. This was the most pain Lonzo had ever caused her. The look in his eyes was the worst she had ever seen.

"*What the hell is wrong with you*?!" he bellowed.

She was scared to death but still angry enough to scream right back at him. "*You slept with Toya! Don't lie and say you didn't!*"

"*I don't even know who the hell that is!*" His face was very close to hers. She smelled Funyons on his breath. Blood continued to leak from the corner of his mouth, but she couldn't see the actual wound.

"The girl who worked with me at the pharmacy," she breathed. "I talked to her sister. She said y'all sleeping together!"

Lonzo's head cocked to the side, and confusion replaced his rage for a moment. He let go of her and backed away shaking his head. "I can't believe you'd come in here and pull some shit like this on my fight day." He rubbed his bleeding lip and fixed another hard look on his woman. "You crazy, Nisha. You jacked-up in the head. You know that?"

"No, you cheating on me! Her sister told me!"

"*I did not have sex with that woman!*" Lonzo spat. "*That bitch is a ho*! She been trying to get with me ever since you took that job!"

"This ain't about the pharmacy!" Nisha countered. "You been seeing her at Mr. Brown's house!"

"I saw her *one time!*" Lonzo yelled. "I only talked to her for like, one minute! *I didn't touch her!*"

"Yes, you did!"

"*You...*" A vein on the side of his neck bulged. His chest heaved. "You don't know what the hell you talking about, girl! I can't believe you come over here starting shit on my fight day! *I can't believe you, Nisha!* You acting like a goddamned fool."

She knew he was right about that, but "Why would she say that if you didn't do it?"

"*Bitches lie!*" Lonzo bellowed. "Especially *that* bitch! You know she messy as hell. Why would you believe something like that?"

Common sense tried to force its way into her mind, but she was too angry to listen to it. "I don't believe you."

"I don't give a damn what you believe!" Lonzo snapped. "Just get your ass out of here and let me do my thing. You wanna argue, we can do that shit at home! I can't believe you put your hands on me, girl..." He turned and tried to assess the damage in the reflection of a tinted window.

He spun again and spat more venom: "I got a fight tonight, you crazy ass girl! If this cut mess up my fight..." He trailed off, shaking his head in exasperation.

His words hit her like a sledgehammer to the chest. She wasn't sure if she believed what he said about Toya, but she felt bad about hitting him. It wasn't good for a boxer to enter a fight with an open cut on his face. Even in her angriest moment, she never wanted to do anything to hurt his boxing career.

She started to apologize, but he walked out of the media room, presumably to check himself in a real mirror. Nisha sat at the table and her tears flowed like blood. She knew Lonzo would come back and check on her after a while.

But he never did.

CHAPTER SIXTEEN
WHAT'S MY NAME?

Nisha didn't see her man when she left the media room. A few people tried to talk to her as she headed for the exit at the front of the gym, but Slick was the only person she slowed down for. The rapper wore a gloomy expression that made her feel guilty about her behavior.

"Hey... You okay?"

"I just wanna get out of here." She kept her head down, barely looking up at him.

"You know Lonzo wouldn't never cheat on you, right? I be with him all the time. I ain't never seen him do nothing like that."

Nisha was so stressed, her head hurt. She didn't know what to believe anymore.

"Is he okay?" she asked. "Is his mouth alright?"

"He'll be fine," Slick assured her. "Don't even worry about that."

"I don't wanna mess up his fight." She was on the verge of tears yet again.

"It ain't bad," Slick promised. "He ain't even bleeding no more. He just mad, that's all. But he'll be alright by the time the fight starts. You'll see."

Nisha didn't say anything. She exited the building and winced at the bright sunlight.

"You still coming to the fight, right?" Slick asked.

She stopped and looked at him. She couldn't miss Lonzo's fight, could she? If he was cheating on her, she'd be a fool to continue supporting him. But if he was innocent, she'd be a bigger fool for believing the rumor. She didn't know what to do. She shrugged.

"When this is all over," Slick said, "and you see them lying bitches for who they really is, you'll be glad you came." He reached into his pocket and produced a laminated VIP card.

"Thank you." She put the card in her pocket and gave him a hug before continuing to her car.

She made it back to her sisters' house at a quarter after seven. Returning to the scene where she literally went crazy was a little surreal. If she could go back in time, she wouldn't freak-out when that heifer pushed her buttons. Patrice and Toya lived to make other folks miserable. Nisha played right into her hand by responding the way she did. The fact that Baby Lonzo and a few other kids witnessed her breakdown, made it that much worse.

Shonda's boyfriend Blue was at the house when Nisha got there. There were four more people Nisha didn't know very well congregating in the living room. Everyone was animated about the fight, but an uncomfortable silence ensued when she walked through the door. Baby Lonzo rushed to his mother like he hadn't seen her in years. Nisha felt guilty for abandoning him when she was upset.

"Girl come in here!" Shonda called from her bedroom.

Nisha scooped up her son and hurried in that direction. Shonda closed the door behind her.

"What happened?" Shonda asked, her face filled with worry.

Nisha sat on the bed and shrugged. She looked dazed and confused. "He denied it. But I already knew he would..."

"Do you believe him?" Shonda was mostly dressed for the night, lacking only shoes and makeup.

"He never lied to me before," Nisha said. "But he didn't tell me he saw Toya at Mr. Brown's house. He said he only talked to her for a minute, but why was he talking to her at all? He knows she likes him."

"But you know he wouldn't cheat on you, right?"

"He told me women was throwing themselves at him," Nisha recalled. "I know if Toya met him somewhere where there was a bedroom, and nobody cared what they did, she would try her best to give him some ass. I think Lonzo would walk away...

"Him working for Mr. Brown is the real problem, Shonda. I told him to stop, but he wouldn't. I knew something bad was gon' happen. Even if he didn't sleep with Toya, I don't understand why he put hisself in that situation. He could've went to jail or got killed. Maybe that's why he kept going over there; he liked it. It was something over there he wanted..."

"But it's over now, ain't it?" Shonda asked. "You said he wasn't working for Mr. Brown no more after this fight."

"It don't matter if it's over *now*," Nisha said. "The damage is already done. He might've cheated on me. I don't trust him. I don't trust his decisions no more. I been asking myself – way before today – I been wondering if this the kind of man I wanna marry, somebody who will go out in the streets and commit crimes and hurt people when he knows he got a family at home that depends on him. Is that the kind of man I want my son to look up to?"

Shonda sat next to her and put an arm around her shoulder. "You wanna leave Lonzo?"

Nisha's eyes filled with tears. "I just want him to be a good man, like he used to be. I don't wanna have to worry about him going to jail. I don't wanna wonder if the rumors or true, if he slept with this girl or that one..."

"But he finna get paid," Shonda reminded her. "You been with him for five years. You can't leave him now that he finna get rich."

Nisha closed her eyes, realizing she was talking to the wrong person. "Shonda, if you can't see that I don't care about his money, then you don't know me at all."

Her sister frowned and thought about that for a full minute. "Do you still wanna go to the fight?"

"We not broke up yet," Nisha said. "I gotta be there for him."

By nine pm, Will Rogers' Coliseum was packed with boxing enthusiasts, fair-weather fans and curious spectators who couldn't believe Overbrook Meadows had raised an awesome prize-fighter, the likes of which no one had seen since Iron Mike or Holyfield.

Most of the lots were full, but Nisha didn't have trouble parking because her VIP pass offered valet services.

Shonda told her, "Girl, look at you, flashing your little card like you royalty. Don't you know it's only getting better from here? You big-time now. When you get to Austin, they'll probably put you in a luxury box with free food and everything. I know you ain't gon' leave that boy."

Nisha knew Shonda was trying to cheer her up, but that was nearly impossible. She showered and changed clothes before they left her sister's house, but Shonda didn't have many outfits her size. Nisha ended up wearing a pair of jeans and a tee-shirt to the fight. Neither fit her well. She knew she didn't look as good as she usually did when she went to the arena.

To make matters worse, Lonzo's groupies were out by the dozens. The public display of affection used to make her proud, but tonight she glared at each woman holding an affectionate sign. She looked into their eyes, to see if they held a secret of lust and betrayal.

Stop it, she told herself. *This is crazy*. But as soon as she let her guard down, she heard a voice she recognized, a voice that made her throat catch and her jaws clench.

"There them bitches go right there."

She turned slowly. Her heartbeats quickened as she looked upon a grotesque sight. Not only was Patrice standing in line ten feet behind them, but Toya was too. And even though Nisha's eyes filled with a dark rage that blacked out everything but the whores' faces, she couldn't miss the VIP card hanging from Toya's neck.

"Can't we go around these people?" Shonda asked. When Nisha didn't respond, she turned and saw what her sister saw.

Nisha handed Baby Lonzo to Shonda's boyfriend, just as Toya stepped forward with Patrice not far behind.

"Y'all tried to jump my sister today?" Toya wanted to know. She wore a tight, pink tee shirt with a pair of skin-tight jeans. Her breasts were awe-inspiring, her makeup was perfect, her hair immaculate. Despite everything else that was going on, Nisha regretted her decision to wear Shonda's clothes to the fight. If Lonzo appeared at that moment, he would surely choose Toya over his baby-mama.

"Bitch, ain't nobody tried to jump your sister," Shonda said when Nisha remained mute. "She the one come to my house starting shit."

"I went over there to pick up my son," Patrice argued. She stood next to Toya with both hands on her hips.

"Why you try to jump my sister?" Toya asked again, speaking directly to Nisha. "You was talking big shit at the pharmacy. What's up now? We both standing right here..."

"Bitch, you ain't said nothing but a word," Shonda said. She removed her earrings and kicked off her shoes with no hesitation.

A crowd began to gather around the women. They wanted action, but Nisha was still reeling from her reckless behavior earlier that day. She went after Patrice like an animal – in front of Baby Lonzo and a few more kids. And then she went to Lonzo's gym and made a bigger fool of herself.

She wouldn't let these tramps get the best of her again.

She calmed herself and asked Toya, "Did you sleep with Lonzo?"

Toya's lips were curled in a terrible sneer. She balled her fists and said, "What?"

"Did you sleep with him?" Nisha asked again. "You slept with Lonzo?"

The air between them became deathly quiet, even though there were hundreds of people outside. While she waited for a response, Nisha felt her heart ripping in two. It was so loud, she thought everyone could hear it. Every fiber in her being wanted to tear her former coworker's face completely from her skull, but she refused to move a muscle, unless Toya answered in the affirmative.

Toya looked at her sister, and then she looked at Nisha. She started to say something, but she didn't get a chance. As soon as she opened her mouth, Shonda filled it with a good, old-fashioned knuckle sandwich.

BAP!

The punch stopped *everything* for half a second. Toya stumbled back with a hand over her mouth. She growled, and Patrice charged forward with malice in her eyes. Nisha didn't want to fight, but it was either hit or be hit at that point.

The two groups of sisters went at it for what felt like a whole commercial break. With so much adrenaline flowing and hair-pulling and name-calling and people trying to break it up, it was hard to say who won. At one point Nisha grabbed hold of Toya's weave and pummeled her face repeatedly with her free hand.

But none of the blows made the pain go away. When the dust settled, Nisha knew that she had succumbed to what her father referred to as *niggerish behavior* yet again. To make matters worse, she never got an answer to her question. She still didn't know if Toya slept with Lonzo, or if Patrice invented the story.

The coliseum's security team didn't make it in time to intervene, and Nisha's group was able to sneak in before anyone pointed them out as the cause of the ruckus. They weren't sure if Toya and Patrice made it in as well.

Nisha was wild-haired and disheveled when she took a seat next to her father five minutes later, which shocked the hell out of Walter. She wasn't bleeding anywhere, but she cupped her wrist gingerly. The pain was back with a vengeance.

"Baby girl! What happened?" Walter took Lonzo Jr. from her arms and stared at her in wide-eyed confusion. "Did you get in a fight?"

Nisha nodded and started crying again. She shut down completely when her father tried to question her further. A few minutes later Shonda asked if she was going to go see Lonzo before his fight. Nisha shook her head and removed the VIP pass from her neck. She casually let it fall to the floor, where it was stepped on quite a few times before the night's festivities concluded.

The fights that evening were amazing. There was no doubt everyone got their money's worth.

In the first match, one of Lonzo's pals from the gym got decimated by a fiery Pilipino who landed a stunning fifty-four jabs in the first round. The second fight featured two middle weights with limited boxing skills. They made up for it with tenacity and dumb courage. By the end of the match, both sluggers were bruised and bloodied. The crowd gave them a standing ovation for their efforts.

In the third fight, another one of Walter's prospects wowed the crowd with his lightning speed in the first couple of rounds, but by round three he started eating uppercuts like they were candy. When he got knocked out in the fourth, Walter told his daughter, "I think I'm bad luck. Everybody I pick to win gets whooped up on..."

Nisha smiled, but she wasn't in the mood for his jokes. She didn't appreciate everyone else trying to cheer her up. What she really wanted was to go somewhere quiet, so she could be alone with her thoughts. But she had one more fight to watch before she could flee the arena.

After Walter's latest disappointment hobbled out of the ring, the lights went dim for the main event. The arena was fully packed. The fans stood and created an enormous ruckus. Women screamed, drowning out whatever the announcer had to say about Big Ben as the heavy-handed lummox sauntered to the ring.

And then Slick's song came on, and all hell broke loose. Flashes from professional and cheap cameras lit up the arena like fireworks. Nisha felt like she was at a rock concert. Fans young and old, black and white, sang along with Slick as he grooved to the ring, bobbing his head, swinging his arms. The Champ followed him with a shiny, red robe draped over his shoulders, the hood pulled ominously over his head, shading his face.

At that moment, Nisha had mixed emotions about her man, but she couldn't deny the electricity he brought to the venue. These people were in awe of him. When Lonzo climbed into the ring, hearts sighed. When Fats took his robe off, revealing his cut-up physique, the ladies swooned. People would remember where they were on this night just as they remembered when Tyson gnawed off a chunk of Holyfield's ear. They would save their ticket stubs and brag about it at work on Monday.

The fight started in typical Lonzo fashion, but from the first blow it was clear this wouldn't be another upset like the Veston fiasco. Lonzo was furious about the things Big Ben said in his interview, but he didn't let his emotions get the best of him. In fact, he allowed Big Ben to take the role of aggressor in the first round. Ben chased him around with jabs and hooks that were easily avoidable with Lonzo's quick feet and head movements.

When the bell sounded, Lonzo retreated to his corner with a menacing grin. Everyone knew they were in for a show.

In round two, Lonzo stuck with the same strategy: Big Ben pursued him, swinging for the fences with haymakers that would surely knock Lonzo's block off – but The Champ was always safely out of reach when the big fists flew by.

The second round was also when the taunting began. Lonzo grinned at his opponent. He dropped his hands to his waist and dodged punches. When Ben charged like a bull, Lonzo stepped around him like a matador and tagged him behind the ear. The referee rebuked Lonzo for throwing a punch to the back of the head. The Champ smirked arrogantly.

In round three things started to get ugly. Big Ben's offense wasn't a factor, so The Champ stepped up his game and took the fight to his opponent. He scored with stiff jabs to the mouth and nose. Styles was always available for a left hook to the jaw. By the end of that round, Lonzo was as fresh as a spring chicken, while Big Ben looked like he'd gone the distance with an old-school slugger. He spat blood with a foreboding look in his eyes.

Walter told his daughter, "This won't last much longer."

Nisha nodded, but she and her father's assessment was incorrect. By all accounts, Lonzo could've ended the fight in the fourth, but Big Benjamin Styles got under his skin with the trash-talk about his nickname. Lonzo wouldn't let him leave the ring until he taught him a lesson.

Rather than deliver the necessary combos to topple his opponent, Lonzo continued to jab Big Ben for most of the next round. Almost every punch landed flush, splitting soft lips, birthing a family of contusions on Benjamin's skull. When Styles started to block the jabs, Lonzo mixed it up with a hook or a straight right or a sickening uppercut to the gut.

Lonzo won round four by a two-point margin, and in the fifth he did something that was so out of character, Nisha and her dad were at a loss for words. He waded in with his usual jab-jab-hook combos, and Big Ben ate a dozen punches in a row.

He tried to grab hold of Lonzo, so he could catch his breath. The Champ broke out of the clinch roughly. He pushed the big man away and screamed something most of the audience couldn't hear past his mouthpiece and the noise in the arena. But Nisha had been with him for more than five years. She read his lips perfectly.

She was positive Lonzo asked his opponent, "*Who's The Champ?*"

Big Ben frowned, and Lonzo punched him in the eye. "*Who's The Champ?*" he yelled again.

Big Ben grimaced and tried to mount another offensive, but he was sorely outmatched. Lonzo bobbed and weaved like a hummingbird. He countered with a clean jab to the forehead.

"*Who's The Champ?*"

He hit him again. *BAP!*

"Who's The Champ?"

Mercifully, the bell rang, signaling an end to round five.

Nisha looked at her dad, and Walter shook his head and sighed. The rest of the audience loved Lonzo's new style of fighting and taunting, but true fans of the sport recognized his behavior as brutish, punkish and disrespectful.

Lonzo's taunting was reminiscent of one of Muhammad Ali's most infamous fights against Ernie Terrell. In 1967, Terrell disrespected Ali in a pre-fight interview. He repeatedly referred to him as Cassius Clay, refusing to use his new Muslim name. When they met at the Houston Astrodome, Ali made an example of Terrell by beating him thoroughly, often asking, "*What's my name?*" before he delivered a stinging blow to the skull.

There was no doubt Ali was the better fighter that night, but analysts criticized him for what they called "barbarous" and "unnecessary cruelty."

It was hard to believe The Champ would pull the same move more than five decades later, but the proof was dancing right before their eyes.

Lonzo started the sixth round with unquestionable dominance, and he continued to berate his opponent.

"What's my name?"

WHAP!

"I'm The Champ! Say it!"

PAP! PAP!

"Say my name!"

WOP! WOP!

Big Ben eventually backed into a corner, where he was struck relentlessly about the face and ears. The referee jumped between the fighters to save him from future brain damage. Benjamin Styles dropped to one knee with a torrent of blood leaking from multiple wounds. Lonzo threw his hands up in victory, and the crowd went crazy. But Nisha didn't feel good about what she had witnessed.

Lonzo's record improved to 18-1. His next fight was in Austin. For that bout, his purse would be no less than $300,000. Nisha was sure he wanted to go out and celebrate, but she no longer felt like it was their dream he was pursuing. She certainly didn't feel like pretending to be happy for him.

She hoisted her son with her good arm and asked Shonda to catch a ride with their father.

"What about the party?" Shonda asked. "Ain't we going to Pappadeaux?"

"I don't feel good," Nisha said. "I'm going home. Y'all have fun, though."

"What about Lonzo?" Shonda pressed. "Ain't you at least gon' say bye to him?"

Nisha felt she would say "Goodbye" to The Champ soon, but the parting she had in mind might be long-term.

"Tell him I'm tired. I'll talk to him when he gets home..."

CHAPTER SEVENTEEN
THREE BLIND MICE

Nisha grimaced as she pulled Baby Lonzo from his car seat. She propped him on her hip and rubbed her wrist warily. She wondered what was going on in there, with her lunate bone and the blood vessels that weren't supplying it with oxygen. She wondered if her surgery would cost more now that she reinjured herself. She wondered what Toya was going to say before Shonda punched her in the mouth.

She was pretty sure it would've been a denial. Then again, Toya was vindictive. If she slept with Lonzo, she might admit it for the shock value alone. She might also lie for the same reason.

Nisha shook her head and sighed. A part of her wanted to pack her things and head to her father's house. Her optimistic side wanted to change clothes and meet up with Lonzo and their friends at Pappadeaux.

The only thing she was certain about was this had been her worst day *ever*. She didn't think things could go further south, but there were more storm clouds heading her way. In fact, the turmoil Nisha experienced up to this point was nothing compared to the evil that waited inside her apartment.

She reached her doorstep with quickened breaths because of the two flights of stairs. She flipped through her keys while trying to juggle Baby Lonzo and her purse. Her key slid into the lock effortlessly, but there was no need to unlock it. The door pushed open, as if it hadn't been closed. She frowned and removed her key. She cocked her head and stared at the doorknob.

Did she leave it open? When was the last time she'd been home? Did Lonzo stop by sometime during the day? Nisha didn't think much of it, but if she had, she would've noticed the light shining through the now open door. She would've seen the long crack in the doorframe.

Instead, she walked inside and stopped cold in the living room. There was a lot to process. Her brain raced to keep up with her eyes.

The first thought that came to her mind was *burglary*. But that wasn't right, because burglars usually take things. She didn't see anything missing. Everything was accounted for, except it was shattered or shredded or stomped or sliced.

The flat screen television lie on the floor with a huge, boot-size hole mid-center. Every cushion on the couch was cut, with its innards spilling like intestines. The glass coffee table was shattered. Papers, crushed picture frames and cracked CD's were everywhere. Someone even threw the cordless phone at the wall hard enough to break through the sheetrock. It remained partially implanted.

Nisha's heart shot up her throat. Every hair on her body was rigid. She reached back blindly for the doorknob and spotted movement out of the corner of her eye. A dark figure approached quickly from the kitchen. As her eyes widened with terror, she saw a second person coming from the hallway.

She screamed. She groped madly for the doorknob but couldn't find it. She turned and saw that she was standing three feet away. She had closed it behind herself out of habit. From inside the apartment, she realized the doorframe was ripped almost completely off the wall.

She raced for the door, but the man coming from the hallway was closer now. He touched her arm. She jerked away from him violently.

"*Stop!*"

"Shut up," he said at almost the same time.

Undaunted, Nisha grabbed the doorknob. She yanked hard, but only managed to open it a foot before the intruder kicked it closed again. His foot impacted the wood less than a foot away from her hip, and she screamed again.

She retreated to the corner where one of her end tables once stood. The shattered glass crunched under her feet. She wrapped both arms around her son; holding him close to her chest. The man from the kitchen drew closer still. The one who kicked the door watched her with an almost bored expression. Nisha was terrified to see a third man hurrying from the bedroom.

"Leave me alone!" She screamed frantically. *"Get out of my house!"*

"Goddammit, I told that bitch to shut up," the one from the hallway said. His skin was mud brown. His eyes were small. His lips were big. He reached under his shirt and produced a pistol. It was black on the bottom, chrome on top. "I gotta shut you up?" he asked. He pointed the gun at her face.

Nisha cried out again. This time she didn't mean to. Knowing he would back up his threat with deadly force, she turned away from him, shielding Baby Lonzo with her body. Her only hope was that maybe, after he shot her, he wouldn't roll her over to check to see if he hit the baby. Maybe they would run away and let her die and let Baby Lonzo live.

She squeezed her eyes shut and waited for the inevitable. Her heart was like thunder. She moaned softly, *"Please, please, please,"* to God or her assailants or anyone else who cared enough to heed the cries of the innocent.

"Want me to do her?" the voice on her right asked.

"You can if you want," someone further away said.

Nisha heard the gun cock.

"Naw, don't do it," a third voice said. "Say, turn around," the same man said.

"No, please," Nisha begged. Her body shivered. Baby Lonzo struggled to loosen her death grip.

"Turn around, ho," the first voice said. Nisha knew that was the big-lipped man with the gun. She heard him cock the weapon again, or maybe he un-cocked it. "I ain't gon' hurt you."

It was too late for that. The men hadn't harmed her physically, but if she lived through this, the psychological scars would last decades.

"I'ma do it," Big Lips said.

"Ain't worth it," the nice guy said. "Turn around, girl."

She shuddered. Her breaths were hot and heavy. She thought it was a trick. They wanted her to turn around, so they could shoot her in the face. But they might also shoot her for not turning around. She took a deep breath and turned slowly.

The first person she saw was Big Lips. The gun was still in his hand, but it was down to his side now. He wore all black. His hair was styled in a short, nappy afro.

The second intruder was the nice guy who told them to spare her life. He was tall and dark-skinned, with a neat goatee. He was handsome. He was the kind of guy she might've been attracted to, if they met under different circumstances.

The third man was short and lumpy. He had chubby cheeks and dead eyes that probably never revealed what was on his mind.

Now that she got a good look at all three of them, Nisha knew they would execute her. She was a liability. But Nice Guy's next words revealed they expected to carry out this break-in without violence.

"What you doing here, gal? Ain't you supposed to be at the fight?"

Nisha shook her head. Her face was slick with tears. Baby Lonzo looked around in wonderment, but he didn't have the good sense to be afraid.

"Where Lonzo at?" Big Lips asked. "Why you ain't with him?"

"Answer that man," Nice Guy instructed when Nisha didn't respond.

"*We, we had a fight,*" she cried. Her face was twisted and ugly. "*He mad. He mad at me.*"

"Yeah, well, we mad at him," Nice Guy said.

"That's why we to' up yo shit," Lumpy stated the obvious.

"If he keep messing around in Como," Nice Guy said, "he *will* get dealt with."

"Best believe," Big Lips said.

"This shit here," Nice Guy said, waving a hand around the wrecked living room, "this just a warning."

"Lonzo know who it's from," Lumpy said.

"If we wanted him dead, he'd be dead by now," Nice Guy said.

"Fuh sho," Big Lips said. "Ain't nothing but a thang."

Nisha watched the men one at a time, growing more upset as they spoke. The realization that this was all Lonzo's fault made it worse than some random act of ignorance.

"*Please,*" she said. "*Please, just leave.*"

"Shut up," Nice Guy said. "Why don't *you* leave?"

Nisha inhaled sharply. She didn't think she heard right, but she wasn't sticking around for clarification. She turned to the door. Her path was blocked by Big Lips. Nisha looked back to Nice Guy with large, hopeful eyes, and he told his cohort, "Move, nigga. Let her go."

Big Lips moved out of the way. Nisha held her breath and took slow, steady steps towards freedom. She expected to be struck in the back of the head at any moment, but she made it to the door and pulled it open with no interference. Before she stepped outside, Baby Lonzo twisted in her arms and yelled, "Bye!" to one of the intruders.

Nisha was so startled, she let out another rattling scream. She threw a trembling hand over her mouth and kept moving.

"Wait," someone said.

Nisha ignored him. She walked onto the breezeway and saw the beautiful moonlight. One of her tormentors spoke again.

"Hold on, gal. Lemme, lemme see that baby. That's Lonzo Jr., ain't it?"

The voice was laced with humor. Nisha hoped it was a sick joke. She quickened her pace.

"Let us holler at Lil' Lonzo!" Nice Guy taunted her. They laughed. "Come on, don't be like that. Lil' man wanna play."

Nisha didn't breathe at all until she made it to the stairwell. She descended quickly, taking two steps at a time. Big Lips came out onto the breezeway and monitored her retreat.

"You better run!" he yelled. "Tell your bitch ass nigga to stay outta Como!"

Somehow she made it to her car. The parking lot seemed to be tilting beneath her feet. The door was locked. She fidgeted for the right key, and the keychain fell to the concrete. Nisha whimpered as she bent to retrieve it. She looked up from her crouched position and saw Big Lips was still watching her. He smiled. Nisha thought his teeth looked like fangs.

She snatched her keys from the asphalt and pressed the button to unlock it. She jerked the door open and sat behind the wheel with Baby Lonzo in her lap. With everything else that went wrong today, she knew the car wouldn't start. The intruders would have to come down to help her. One of them would ask to hold Baby Lonzo while they figured out what the problem was.

But the car started right up. She threw it in REVERSE and backed out of her parking spot going way too fast. She slammed her foot on the brake just in time to avoid colliding with a parked Mustang. She threw it into DRIVE hard enough to break the gearshift.

Before she took off, she looked up at her apartment one last time. All three goons were standing on the breezeway. Big Lips waved goodbye. Nice Guy blew her a kiss.

Nisha didn't know what life had in store for her, but she knew she would never come back to this place. In her mind's eye, she would always see those men standing on the breezeway, smiling down at her.

She stomped the gas pedal and peeled out with one hand on the steering wheel and the other supporting her baby. The child laughed when she hit a speed bump hard enough to blow a tire. She marveled at how sweet and innocent he was. She hoped he would never know how his daddy put their life on the line by working for a creep named Mr. Brown.

Nisha didn't attempt to call the police during her escape. She hit the freeway and went straight to her father's house. In her state of panic, she forgot Walter and the rest of her family were out celebrating Lonzo's victory. She pulled into her father's driveway a few minutes after midnight, and an icy chill rolled down her spine. She didn't see any lights on in her childhood home, but her sixth sense was blaring. She wondered if it was wise to enter alone.

The odds of another muscle crew targeting Walter were slim, but after the horrific encounter she just endured, she wasn't in the mood for gambling. She turned her car off, but decided it was best to wait there, with the doors locked, just in case.

She laid Baby Lonzo on the passenger seat and fished her cellphone from her purse. She had seven missed calls. She heard the phone ringing when she was on the freeway, but she didn't remember hearing it that many times.

Rather than listen to her messages, she called 911 to report the break-in, vandalism and intimidation. The operator took the address and said she'd send the police. Nisha also gave the woman her father's address, so the police could come and get a formal statement.

She called her father next. Walter was at Pappadeaux with Lonzo, Shonda and a few dozen more people who wanted to bask in The Champ's glory. Nisha didn't want to ruin their night, but all festivities came to a halt when she gave Walter the grim news.

"*What?* Oh my God! Where, where are you now, baby girl?"

"I'm at your house. But I don't wanna go in. I'm scared it might be some more people in there."

"We'll be right there," Walter promised. "Hold, hold on a second..."

She heard him speaking excitedly, and then she listened to the commotion from a multitude of shocked voices. There was shuffling on the line, and then Shonda had the phone.

"Nisha! You okay? Girl, what happened?"

"Somebody broke in our apartment. I'm alright, just scared. They didn't hurt me."

"They broke in while you was there?"

"They were already there when I got home," Nisha said, hoping she wouldn't have to tell this story a hundred times.

"I called you," Shonda said. "Why you didn't answer the phone?"

"I was on my way to Daddy's. I couldn't get to it."

"I knew you shoulda came with us," Shonda said. "If you wou – hold on a second. Lonzo wanna talk to you."

"Wait–" But her sister was already gone.

"Baby! You alright?" The Champ was near panic. "What the hell happened over there?"

Nisha tried to keep her emotions in check, but hearing the concern in his voice was like a slap in the face. "I don't wanna talk to you. This is all your fault."

"What? What's my fault? What you talking about?"

"They came because of *you*! All that stupid shit you got going on finally caught up with you. They tore up our apartment, pointed a gun in my face. All 'cause of you, Lonzo! I had the baby with me. They could've..." Her eyes welled with tears. She squeezed them shut and brought a hand to her mouth.

"*What are you talking about?*" Lonzo nearly screamed. "Why you talking like that? How you figure it was 'cause of me?"

"Because they said it!" Nisha snapped. "They said you messed with somebody in Como, and they was doing this to get you back. They told me to tell you to stay out of Como. They said it was a warning..."

She sniffled. Lonzo didn't say anything.

"Now, are you gonna tell me you don't know anything about it?" Nisha asked. "I know it has something to do with Mr. Brown. You gonna say you don't know nothing about it?"

"They, they pointed a gun at you?"

"Me *and* the baby! Because of you!"

"Baby, calm down. I'ma, I'ma take care of this. If them ho ass niggas–"

"Take care of it how?" she wondered. "Go back and start some more mess in Como? Ain't you done enough already? I was lucky to make it out of there. They almost killed me!"

"Why didn't you come with us tonight? You shoulda been here with me."

Nisha shook her head. "I don't want to be there with you," she breathed. "You ain't nothing but trouble, Lonzo. Everything about you is *bad*."

"Don't start talking like that."

Her phone beeped, indicating she had an incoming call. She was glad for the interruption. "I gotta go."

"Wait. Where you going?"

"Somebody's calling me. I think it's the police."

"Alright, well, we on our way," Lonzo said. "Your dad's coming straight to you, but I'll probably check on the apartment first, to see if they still over there. Or do you want me to come with Walter?"

"I don't care."

"Baby, are you alright? You sound like–"

She hung up on him and took the other call.

The police called to verify Walter's address and said a unit was in route.

Nisha listened to her voicemail while she waited. One message was from Shonda:

"Girl, you shouldn't have left like that. Everybody's happy, but you could tell Lonzo was hurt when Daddy told him you went home. We're on our way to Pappadeaux. You need to come, Nisha. You need to be here for your man."

Another was from Walter:

"Hey, baby girl, I hope you're feeling better. You know we need to talk about what happened when you got to the arena tonight. We're headed to the restaurant. I got Shonda and her boyfriend and some more folks with me. I probably won't stay too long. If you wanna call me tonight – no matter what time, I'll be here for you. Don't shut us all out, Lanisha. We worried about you."

The last call was from Lonzo:

"Nisha. Man, what the hell is going on with you? Why you leave before I came out? Shonda say y'all got into it with Toya and her dumb ass sister. That ain't even like you, to be fighting like that. I told you I didn't mess with that girl. Why you don't believe me? We getting ready to go out to dinner. Your pops is here, and Reggie, and your sister is too. It don't even feel right without you coming with us. I guess I'll holler at you when I get home. I love you, girl."

Nisha frowned. In the midst of fearing for her life, she almost forgot about Toya and her insufferable sister Patrice. Thinking about them now only served to harden her heart against the man who promised to fulfill every one of her dreams.

She wished there was a way she could avoid Lonzo completely, at least tonight, but she knew he would rush to her side. His cape was fluttering in the wind, and he had a big "S" on his chest. But how can Superman fix a problem he caused? That's like an arsonist trying to put out his own fire. No thanks, sir. You've already done enough.

Walter was the first to arrive. He had Shonda in the car with him along with her boyfriend Blue and three more people. Seconds later, a Fleetwood pulled to a stop in front of the house. Lonzo's cut man Gillespie got out followed by Fats, Lonzo's brother Leo and a few more of Lonzo's friends from the gym.

Walter said Lonzo and Reggie went to check on the apartment and answer whatever questions the police had. He unlocked his front door and ushered everyone inside. Nisha was obliged to recap her harrowing tale from start to finish. When she was done, all she wanted was to get some rest, but there was no time for that. Two uniformed officers arrived, and they wanted Nisha to tell her story again – except this time she had to follow them downtown and meet with a composite artist.

Nisha wanted to do all she could to make sure her assailants were brought to justice, but more than that, she needed this horrible day to end. She started crying, and her father shoed everyone out of the living room. Some of the visitors weren't familiar with the house, and they had no idea where they should go.

"It don't matter!" Walter yelled at them. "Just get out of here! You can go stand outside, for all I care."

When they were gone, he took a seat next to his youngest child and put an arm around her shoulder.

"Why you crying, baby girl? What's upsetting you? Is it all these people?"

"I just, I wanna *lay down*," she whined. "I'm tired. I feel like I been arguing with people all day…"

"You don't wanna talk to the police?"

"I do. But I don't wanna be there all night. I'm real tired, Daddy. I been through a lot today."

Walter nodded. His eyes were soft and compassionate. "I understand. Tell you what; I'll run you down there and make sure they let you go in thirty minutes. I'll get rid of all these people, so you can rest when we get back. You and Lonzo can stay here as long as you want.”

Nisha reluctantly pushed herself off the couch and grabbed the baby’s diaper bag. “Okay,” she said with a sigh.

“That’s my girl.” Walter hefted his sleeping grandson and followed her to the front door.

CHAPTER EIGHTEEN
EYE TO EYE

Walter kept his promise to get her out of the police station as quickly as possible, but he couldn't provide the solitude she needed when they got back to the house. They pulled into the driveway at a quarter till two am. Fats and Gillespie were gone. Most of Lonzo's other followers had hit the dusty trail. But Shonda was still there with her boyfriend Blue. Lonzo's brother Leo was dozing on the couch. He woke up and said he was leaving when Walter and Nisha walked through the door.

"Mmm. How'd it go down there?" he asked, stretching his back.

"They said they would do all they could," Walter told him.

"It sho' is a mess, when you can't even have peace in your own home," Leo noted. "What would possess somebody to do something like that, tear up all your stuff for nothing?"

Nisha knew exactly why the thugs trashed her apartment, but she couldn't tell the police, and she didn't think it was a good idea to tell Lonzo's brother. Either way, she didn't feel like talking. "I don't know."

"I hope they catch 'em," Leo said. "Y'all don't deserve that."

Nisha nodded, her expression downcast.

"Alright, y'all take it easy," Leo said and headed for the door. "Tell Lonzo I said congratulations again."

"Okay," Nisha said. "Be careful." She walked him out and then asked her sister, "Where's Blue?"

"He sleep in the other room." Shonda lounged on the loveseat with no shoes or socks, her hair wrapped with a handkerchief.

Walter handed Baby Lonzo to his mother and yawned. "I'm going to bed. I'm too old to be staying up this late."

"Thanks for taking me downtown," Nisha said. She kissed him on the cheek.

"You got anything to eat?" Shonda asked her father.

"I made spaghetti last night. You can heat it up, if you want." He rubbed his spine and shuffled down the hallway.

"You hungry?" Shonda asked her sister.

Nisha shrugged. She hadn't eaten anything since lunch yesterday.

"Come on," Shonda said. "You shouldn't go to sleep hungry."

She heated the spaghetti, and she and Nisha ate in the kitchen. Lonzo called during the meal. He said the police were finished with the apartment. He and Reggie were on their way to Walter's house.

"What it look like?" Nisha asked him.

"Damned near as bad as a fire," Lonzo said. "They broke pretty much everything they could. They cut up the mattress, sliced all the clothes in the closet. Them niggas smashed the crib, pissed in the dresser."

Nisha shook her head. Her appetite was immediately gone.

"We'll be alright though," he said. "That's material stuff. We can get it all back. Did the police come over there yet?"

"Yeah, I had to go to the station."

"Did you, what'd you tell 'em?" Lonzo wanted to know.

"What you mean?" Nisha said, though she knew what he was asking.

"About why they came. Did you tell 'em?"

"No."

"Alright. That's good, baby. You know I'ma take care of this. Don't worry. Me and Reggie will be there in a minute."

"Alright," Nisha said and disconnected.

Shonda waited a few beats and then asked, "They on their way?"

Nisha nodded. She twirled her fork in her spaghetti, and then pushed the plate away.

"How's your apartment?" Shonda asked. "Everything's messed up?"

She nodded. Her eyes were red from crying. Her pain was so palpable, it broke Shonda's heart, just to look at her.

"You think the police gon' find them?"

"I don't see how they can, when they don't have all the facts," Nisha said. Shonda looked confused. Nisha told her, "I couldn't tell the police, but those guys were getting Lonzo back for something he did."

Her sister's eyes widened. "How you know that?"

"They told me. They said for me to tell Lonzo to stay out of Como. They said he knew who sent them."

Shonda was dumbfounded. "What, what he do? What kinda stuff Lonzo into?"

Nisha shrugged. "All I know is he works for Mr. Brown. He beats people up, the ones who can't pay their debts..."

"And they came back like *that*?" Shonda asked in a hushed voice. "What, why would they do that? Don't they know Mr. Brown gon' get them back even worse?"

"I guess they don't care," Nisha speculated. "Maybe they think they're bad enough to take on Mr. Brown."

Shonda shook her head slowly. "What kind of man think he can go against Mr. Brown?"

Nisha thought about that and decided she didn't want to know. The person Shonda was talking about had to be crazy – or powerful. The thought of Lonzo seeking revenge against such a person was ridiculous. She shuddered, thinking about all precarious paths The Champ's bravado might lead them down in the next couple of days.

She washed the few dishes involved with their late-night snack. Lonzo and Reggie arrived while she was putting the plates away. Lonzo wore black slacks with a shiny, red button-down. His shirt was un-tucked, and the top three buttons were open, revealing a sexy glimpse of chest flesh that would've made his woman's mouth water on a different day.

He gave her a hug, and she stiffened. Lonzo looked back at Reggie, who made a quick, if not discreet exit.

When they were alone, Nisha broke away from him and took a seat at the kitchen table. The Champ took the chair across from her. She could smell the Versace cologne he put on after his fight. He looked fresh and handsome. There was a small cut above his left eye, but this was nothing like his appearance after the Veston debacle.

Lonzo put his elbows on the table and took a long, slow breath. He rubbed his chin and asked, "Why you get in a fight?"

Nisha didn't want to cry again, but thinking about his infidelity made her chest hurt. "I didn't wanna fight. Toya was mad because her sister said we tried to jump her. I asked if she slept with you, and Shonda hit her before she could answer. The next thing I knew, we was fighting."

"Why you ask her that after I told you we didn't do nothing? How come you don't believe me?"

"Why she have a VIP pass?" Nisha's eyes filled with tears. She wiped them quickly. "It was just like mine. Where she get it from?"

"I don't got nothing to do with those passes. I don't know who makes 'em, and ain't no way I can keep up with who they give 'em to."

"Did you give it to her?"

Lonzo looked her dead in the eyes. "I did not give that girl a VIP pass, Nisha. I didn't do nothing with her. I swear."

"Why'd you talk to her, when you saw her at Mr. Brown's?"

Lonzo shook his head and sighed. "It wasn't nothing like you thinking. She said something to me, and I looked back and said, 'Don't you work at that pharmacy?' or something like that. And she said, 'Yeah,' and then she said she be watching my fights.

"She said I coulda won my last fight, if I woulda kept my cool. So, you know, I stopped, to hear what she had to say. But she didn't say nothing else about the fight. She started grinning, asking how long I was gon' be there, and stuff like that. That's when I knew it was time to bounce. Yeah, I know she was flirting, but I didn't go along with it. I told Reggie to give me a ride, and I came home."

"Why you didn't tell me about it?"

"'Cause I know how you are. I didn't want you getting all mad over something that ain't really nothing. I don't tell you every time some girl smile at me or try to give me her number. That shit ain't even worth talking about."

Nisha watched his eyes and his mannerisms. "Alright."

"Alright, what? You believe me?"

She nodded. "Yeah. I believe you." She let go of the pain Patrice's lie had caused, but she didn't feel better. "I still don't know if I can trust you."

He frowned. "Why not? What's wrong now?"

"If you ain't sleeping with nobody else, that's one thing. But you still do a lot of stuff I don't agree with, Lonzo. I don't think you make good decisions. I don't, I don't know if I can be with somebody like you."

His face went slack. "What you talking about? Everything I do is for you. I take care of you."

Nisha was shaking her head before he was done speaking. "No, you don't, Lonzo. You take care of *you*. You do what *you* think needs to be done. I told you a hundred times not to go work for Mr. Brown. If you would've listened, I never woulda got into with Toya, and our apartment wouldn't be messed up. Those people could've killed me."

"Stop saying that. They just wanted to scare you. They wasn't gon' hurt nobody."

Her anger grew quickly. "Don't tell me what they wasn't gon' do! You weren't there! You didn't have a gun pointed at your face. It was just me and the baby, and I heard that man ask his friends if he should shoot me. One of them said, 'Go ahead.' The other one said, 'Naw, don't do it.' *That's* how close I came to getting killed, Lonzo!"

She wiped her nose angrily. Lonzo's eyes narrowed. He nodded.

"That's okay. We gon' get them niggas." His bottom lip quivered. "Point a gun at my woman? Yeah. We gon' take care of the problem. You ain't gotta worry about that." His eyes were like fire.

"Lonzo, I don't want you to get nobody back – especially if you're gonna run around saying you're doing it for me. If you wanna do something for me, sit yo ass down somewhere."

He frowned. "Sit my ass down? Man, you *tripping*."

"No, Lonzo. You tripping! How many times I gotta tell you *'I don't want it?'* I don't want your money. I don't want you to pay for my surgery. I don't want you to work for Mr. Brown, and I don't want you to *avenge my honor* – or whatever it is you think you're doing. *Why won't you listen to me?*"

"I am listening to you!" he shouted back. "But you ain't making no sense! Them niggas wrecked everything we have. *Everything*! And they put a gun to yo face. You wanna let them get away with it?"

"What do you wanna do? What does big, bad Lonzo wanna do about it, huh?"

"Don't play with me."

"I'm not playing! You think this is a joke?"

"Naw, I think you don't know what's going on. You can't run away when somebody does something to you. My grandmama taught me that a long time ago. That's how I got to this point in my life. If somebody hit you, you hit 'em back *harder*."

"Well that's what I need now, Lonzo. I need you to walk away. I need you to get out of it, all of it, *right now*. That's the only way we gon' make it. I can't go through no more of this with you. No more long nights worrying about you. We not gon' make it like that. I'm telling you right now: *We not gon' make it*."

"You gon' leave me? Is that what you saying? You gon' leave me for standing up for myself?"

"You're not standing up for yourself," Nisha reasoned. "You did something to those people *first*. They're the ones standing up to *you*!"

He rose from his seat and paced the room with his hands on his hips. Nisha used to be a down-ass chick. When did she become such a lame?

Reggie appeared in the hallway. He took a deep breath before stepping into the room. Lonzo glared at him. Reggie was flustered, but he stood his ground.

"What you want?" Lonzo snapped.

"Bad news, cuz. Some more shit happened..."

Lonzo's sneer was replaced with concern. "What, what's going on?"

"It's Slick," Reggie said. "He got shot, man. They tried to kill Slick."

"Shot?" Lonzo's mouth fell open.

"In the back," Reggie informed him. "He at the hospital. They don't know if my nigga gon' make it out of surgery. If he do, he prolly won't walk again. We gotta go, man."

Nisha was stunned silent. She watched Lonzo go through a myriad of emotions before fixing hard eyes on his fiancée.

"You see that? You see what happens when you let shit go?"

"That don't mean you got to do something," Nisha argued.

"What? Slick been down with me since day one. They probably did that 'cause of *me*!" His voice caught on the last word. His body was tense, his vision blurry.

He turned and stormed out of the kitchen. Reggie followed him. Nisha got up too. The men were exiting the house when she entered the living room.

"Wait!" She followed them out, but Lonzo was done listening. He jumped into Reggie's car on the passenger side. Reggie climbed in behind the wheel. Shonda came outside in time to see them back out of the driveway. She put an arm around Nisha's waist and squeezed tightly.

"It'll be alright," Shonda said, but that was a big, fat lie. She knew it and Nisha knew it, and if Lonzo had a lick of sense, he had to know it too.

CHAPTER NINETEEN
COOL DOWN

Nisha thought she was in high school again. She didn't know what day it was, but she knew it was too early for school. She rolled away from her father and buried her face in the pillow. As usual, Walter was persistent. He shook her shoulder and continued coaxing her.

"Baby girl. Wake up. It's something you need to see."

She rolled over lazily and squinted at the sunlight squeezing through her curtains. She was in her old bedroom, but something wasn't right. Her father was more aged than he was when she was seventeen. Plus today was Sunday. There was no school on Sunday.

She sat up and gradually realized she was an adult, and she didn't live in this house anymore. Then again, maybe she did. She couldn't go back to her apartment, because three goons tore up everything of value and peed in the dresser.

"Come on," Walter said.

Nisha threw her sheets aside and got up to follow him. She still had on the jeans and tee-shirt she wore to the fight yesterday. That wasn't comfortable sleepwear, but she didn't remember going to bed last night.

Walter led her to the living room, where Shonda and Blue were watching television. According to the clock, it was nine am. Nisha thought her sister looked worried. Come to think of it, her father was worried too.

"Sit down, baby girl," Walter said.

Nisha sat next to her sister with a confused expression. Walter remained standing. Everyone was watching television.

Nisha looked that way too. There was a Ford commercial on. It ended after a few seconds, and Channel Six News resumed its morning broadcast. Star reporter Chad Collins wore a charcoal blazer with a light blue shirt that matched his eyes.

"Welcome back," he said. "Before the break, I told you we had bad news in the world of boxing, and for the fans in Overbrook Meadows. Alonzo Ingram, better known as 'The Champ,' was arrested earlier this morning for charges that will include possession of illegal firearms."

As he spoke, a picture of Lonzo appeared in the corner of the screen. It was a closeup of The Champ smiling after one of his victories. Sweat dripped from his face. He still had his mouthpiece in. Nisha thought it was a great picture. The photographer captured the fire that forever burned in his eyes. You could also see a light-hearted, almost carefree beauty in his smile.

"This arrest," Chad continued, "occurred hours after Ingram defeated Benjamin Styles in his 19th professional bout. Ingram improved his record to eighteen and one with last night's victory. He is currently one fight away from a shot at the heavyweight title. Insiders say this arrest will almost certainly derail his championship dreams.

"Also last night," Chad said, "a member of Ingram's entourage, a rapper named Brashad Cook, who uses the stage name *'Slick,'* was gunned down in Como, a west side neighborhood. Cook was shot in the back by unknown assailants. At this time, his condition is stable.

"The police have not yet made any connections between Cook's shooting and Ingram's arrest. But one member of the force, who spoke on a condition of anonymity, said they are most-likely related. We are waiting for an official statement from the police department.

"What we know for sure," Chad continued, "is this is a serious blow for Overbrook Meadows' boxing community. Ingram's fight at Will Rogers last night was sold out. Analysts have ranked him among the top five heavyweights in the world. We look forward to more developments. Gabriella..."

The view switched to a split screen of Chad in the studio and a female reporter who was standing near a busy interstate.

"Wow, that's sad news," Gabriella said. "But you know what's *not* sad, Chad? *Bluebonnets*! They're in full bloom all across the Lone Star State, making for a beautiful commute, wherever you're going!"

Walter turned the television off and took a seat next to his daughter.

But Nisha got up, without speaking. She went to the bathroom to brush her teeth and get ready for what was sure to be another long day.

A call to the county jail confirmed Lonzo was indeed arrested and was charged with illegal possession of a firearm. Not surprisingly, Reggie was arrested as well and faced an identical charge.

Nisha hoped Lonzo got arrested before he did anything stupid, but she wouldn't know for sure until she talked to him. In the meantime, his bail was set at $20,000. Fats promised to get him out as a soon as possible.

While they waited, Walter took his daughter to the mall to get a few new outfits for her and the baby. After lunch, he wanted to check out the damage at her apartment. Nisha didn't see the point, but Walter promised not to let anything happen to her. He was the only man she had total faith in at that point.

The apartment was as bad as Lonzo described, and it was starting to stink. Nisha took careful steps through the debris, not wanting to touch any of the items she was fond of two days ago. She scavenged a few sentimental keepsakes, but for the most part everything was ruined. Walter said it would be alright. He said everyone needs to start from scratch at least once in their lifetime. It keeps you humble, and it makes you more appreciative when you put your life back together.

They went to the hospital after that to check on Slick.

Slick's room was on the 2nd floor of Jackson Memorial's Trauma unit. Nisha almost broke down when she saw all of the machines hooked up to him. But Walter already coached her on how to be strong, no matter how bad things looked. He said Slick would feed off their energy.

Nisha brought him flowers and balloons from the hospital's gift shop. She left them on the nightstand and approached the bed. Slick looked fatigued and ashen. His lips were chapped, his hair unkempt. The smell of death clung to his frail body. She touched his shoulder, and his head slowly rolled in her direction. He opened his eyes and blinked a few times.

"Hey," Nisha said. "What you done did to yourself this time?"

He smiled weakly. Even his gold teeth had lost some of their luster. "They got me," he said. His voice was low and hoarse. "They tried to get me in the car, but I ran. They shot me in the back."

"The doctors said you're gonna be okay," Nisha reported.

"Yeah. When I first got hit, I was scared to death. My whole body went numb from the waist down. I passed out. I knew I was gon' be in a wheelchair. But when I got out of surgery, I could move my toes. The doctor said the bullet nicked my spine, but it didn't hit my spinal cord. They said I'll be able to get out of bed, one day..." He took a deep breath, nearly exhausted from the short spiel.

"I heard Lonzo got arrested," he said. "I feel real bad about that. I know it was 'cause of me."

Nisha thought that was a strange thing to say. It was more likely Slick got shot because of Lonzo.

"He made his own choices," she said. "You shouldn't feel bad about that."

"But I know he was doing that for me," Slick insisted. "Lonzo ain't never messed with no guns. He don't need 'em."

"You don't need to worry about him," Nisha said. "You need to worry about getting yourself better."

"I was supposed to be there for him," Slick mused, "when he made it to Austin. I was supposed to lead him to the ring. We was gon' be on TV. *Regular* TV." His eyes glistened. "Everybody was gon' see us. That was gon' be our big moment. I probably would've got noticed, and I could've got a record deal."

He looked away dreamily. Hot tears rolled down his cheeks. Nisha promised her dad she wouldn't cry, but she couldn't help it. She found tissue in her purse. She wiped Slick's face and reached to hold his hand. His fingers were cold to the touch. The doctors said he was stable, but Nisha wondered if he might die after all. The bullet that entered his back damaged his lung and intestines.

"You got three months before Lonzo goes to Austin," she said. "You'll be better by then."

She knew she was giving him false hope, both about his condition and Lonzo making it to Austin. But it's okay to encourage sick people.

"You're still gonna get signed," she said with a grin. "You know getting shot is good for a rapper's career."

Slick smiled too. It was one of the most pathetic things Nisha had ever seen.

She and Walter stayed with him for thirty minutes, until two techs came to take him downstairs for X-rays. Walter helped them roll Slick's bed out of the room, and then he and Nisha headed home.

Fat's bonded The Champ out on Sunday, but Lonzo didn't come by Walter's house that day. Nisha didn't see him until Monday afternoon. He showed up wearing blue jeans and a pristine white tee-shirt. The outfit was new, but Nisha knew he was the same, old Lonzo. His humble posture and sheepish demeanor didn't change that. She stepped outside and talked to him on the porch, rather than invite him inside.

"When'd you get out?"

"Yesterday," he said. "Around six. I was gon' come see you then, but I had to take care of some stuff first. I bailed Reggie out."

Nisha was expressionless. Lonzo put his hands in his pockets and looked down at his shoes.

"I guess you was right," he said.

"About what?"

He looked up at her. "Really? You want me to say it?"

"No, I'm serious," Nisha said. "I told you a lot of stuff. What do you think I was right about – you not working for Mr. Brown, not hanging around Reggie, not getting caught up in that stupid revenge stuff? What was I right about?"

"All of it. It's just, sometimes you gotta see for yourself. You know? You gotta bump your head before you see that what you're doing is wrong."

Nisha shook her head. "No, you don't, Lonzo. It's okay to learn like that when you're a kid. But when you're grown, sometimes you have to listen to what people are telling you. You don't always have to try it for yourself, because instead of bumping your head, you could lose your life."

"Ain't nobody lost their life."

"I went and saw Slick yesterday."

Lonzo winced.

"Why did he get shot?" Nisha asked. "Was it because of you?"

"Naw. It's some people in Como trying to make a move against Mr. Brown. That's why they went after us, too. It ain't personal. They wanna hurt Mr. Brown."

"What's gonna happen with your fight in Austin?"

Lonzo sighed and shrugged. "It's, it ain't a definite no more. The promoters are tripping, 'cause if I go back to jail, they'll lose a bunch of money. They wanna take me off the ticket. But Fats is doing everything he can to keep my fight date."

"Do you have a lawyer?"

"Yeah. I hired one today."

"What's he saying?"

"He said it looks bad, you know, 'cause they caught us red-handed. But I might be able to beat it, 'cause of what's been going on."

"What do you mean?"

"You know, how our apartment got messed up. And then Slick got shot the same night. My lawyer says I can tell the judge I felt like my life was in danger; that's why I had that pistol. If that don't work, I can prolly get probation, since it's my first offense."

"Did you do what y'all left to do?" Nisha wondered. "Did you get your revenge?"

Lonzo shook his head. "We got arrested before we did anything. I haven't done nothing to them niggas. I'ma let it go, like you told me."

She nodded.

"I went to the apartment today," Lonzo said. "Me and the homies took everything that wasn't messed up. It ain't much, but we got some stuff. I paid some crackheads to throw everything else away. I gave the keys back to the manager. She wasn't tripping about us breaking the lease..."

Nisha nodded.

"I got us a new apartment," Lonzo went on. "It's in Meadowbrook. It's nice, two bedrooms, like you said you wanted. I don't got too much furniture in there yet. I got a bed and a TV. You and Baby Lonzo can have the bed, and I'll sleep on the floor, until we get him his own bed. He prolly too big for another crib..."

He chuckled nervously. Nisha was unmoved. Lonzo sighed and asked the most important question. "So, are y'all gonna come back today, or you wanna wait until I get his bed, or what?"

"We not going."

Lonzo didn't seem shocked by that. "Why not?"

"I don't wanna live with you," Nisha said. "I think we should back up. Take a break for a while."

"What's *a while*, Nisha?"

"I don't know. We need to figure out where we're going, whether it's a good idea for us to be together. I got doubts, Lonzo. I don't know if you want a girl like me. And I don't, I don't know if I wanna be with a man like you."

"What doubts?" Lonzo remained calm. Nisha didn't expect that. "Why you got doubts about me all of a sudden?"

"It's not all of a sudden, Lonzo. You been doing stuff, for a long time... Stuff I tried to tell you not to do. You don't never listen to me. Sometimes you act like a different person, somebody I don't even know."

"When, Nisha? When I act different?"

"Your last fight," she said. "The way you was yelling at that man."

"I won."

"Showboating don't got nothing to do with winning. You wasn't boxing that night. You was acting like a thug, straight off the street."

He smacked his lips. "Whatever."

"Yeah, whatever."

"You said I been acting different for a long time."

"How far back you want me to go? What about what happened with Dr. Coates? I told you to leave that man alone, and you ran your bad ass down there and beat him up."

"That was different."

"No, Lonzo. It's not different. It's who you are. You're a hot head, a loose cannon. You want me to put myself and our son in a dangerous situation, and I'm telling you I can't do it."

"What dangerous situation? Ain't gon' be no danger. I got us a new place. Don't nobody know about it."

"*You're* the danger, Lonzo. Don't you see that? It don't matter where we go. If you're there, then we got the same problem."

"So, what is you saying?" he asked, showing signs of stress. "You don't wanna be with me no more? You don't wanna get married?"

Nisha's heart fluttered. She looked down at her engagement ring. Her brain told her to give it back, but her soul begged her to keep it. "Lonzo, I don't know what I wanna do." Her eyes glossed over, but she refused to cry. She wanted to be strong.

"I need to know you can change," she said. "I need to know you're not some dumb boxer who only thinks with his fists. If you want me to put my life in your hands, I have to know you'll make the right decisions for our family – not go out in the streets and commit crimes whenever you need money. I don't want a man who'll jump in a car to do a driveby. I thought you was different. That's why I fell in love with you."

The Champ listened and didn't immediately respond when she was done speaking. "I thought you said you was gon' be down with me, 'till the last bell," he said at length.

Nisha remembered telling him that. It was the night he proposed to her.

"Now they trying to put me in jail and take away my fights, and you wanna leave?" he said. "Is that how it is? You wanna leave when I'm at my lowest?"

"Sometimes people don't show who they really are until they're at their lowest," Nisha countered. "You may be a good man when everything's going good, but I don't like who you turn into when times get hard. Because that, that's when I depend on you the most."

He watched her eyes, and she watched his. She didn't know if their relationship could survive a separation, but it was out of her hands at this point. She told Lonzo what was needed to make things right. Either he could change, or he couldn't. Only time would tell.

"I'm going back in the house," she said and opened the screen door.

"Wait." He reached for her but didn't touch her. "How long is this gon' take, for you to trust me again?"

"That's up to you."

"How you gon' know if I changed, if you don't spend no time around me?"

"I'll know," she assured him.

"What about my son? I can't–"

"You know you can see him anytime you want. He gone to the store with my dad, but you can come get him later."

Lonzo shook his head and sighed. "I don't like this. We been together for five years. Am I, am I supposed to wait for you? I ain't had no sex since I started training for this last fight. What I'm supposed to do while I'm waiting on you? I got needs."

His comment made Nisha's body grow frigid. She thought she had enough strength to get through this, but her vision blurred. Tears spilled from both eyes. She looked down at her hand again. This time she removed her engagement ring and offered it to him.

"Here. You can have sex with somebody else."

Lonzo's eyes widened. He backed away, refusing to accept it. "Naw, Nisha. I don't want that. I'll, I'll wait for you. I was just asking."

She closed her fist around the ring, squeezing tightly. "I gotta go."

She entered her father's home and pushed the door closed. She sat on the couch with her hands in her lap and listened to her own heartbeats, to the ticks from Walter's grandfather clock, to Lonzo's footsteps retreating from the porch.

When her father returned thirty minutes later, she was sitting in the same position. Walter knew Lonzo had been by. From the looks of it, things didn't go well for The Champ. But Nisha put her ring back on before she got up to help with the groceries, so maybe there was hope.

CHAPTER TWENTY
A NEW MAN

The bluebonnets of spring decorated Central Texas' landscape throughout April and most of May, but the state flower could not flourish under the heat waves of summer. By June the flowers were choked out by wild clovers. Some thought the colorful weeds were just as beautiful.

On the Fourth of July, Baby Lonzo surprised his mother by not only announcing that he, "Gotta go potty!" but also running to the bathroom on his own, closing the door behind himself and pulling his trainers up properly when he was done with his business. At 18 months, Walter took that as a sign they should stop calling him "Baby Lonzo."

"How about Lonzo Jr.?"

Nisha thought that was a great idea.

Monday, July 5th was Nisha's first day back to work since her days at the pharmacy. Her new title was file clerk. She worked for an accounting firm downtown. Her new boss was an aged Jewish fellow. Mr. Cohen provided decent medical insurance, which was good because Nisha still needed surgery on her right wrist.

She wore her old splint for a couple of weeks after the fight with Toya, and the pain subsided. But she couldn't lift more than fifteen pounds with just her right hand. Thankfully, there was no heavy lifting involved with her new job. No one at the office suspected she was hindered in any way.

Lonzo Sr. preferred Nisha didn't work until after she had surgery, but the couple hadn't moved back in together, and his concerns weren't as important as they once were. They remained engaged, but she still had doubts about their long-term success.

Lonzo swore he didn't go back to work for Mr. Brown or do anything else illegal. He said the crime lord let him go with no strings attached, and the goons from Como were done harassing them, but Nisha feared the damage was already done. Whenever she let her guard down and agreed to go on a date with him, she found herself looking over her shoulder, wondering if Nice Guy or Big Lips or Lumpy might be following them.

Lonzo thought her fears were silly. Nisha warned him not to tell her how long it should take for her to "get over it."

Walter and Shonda thought it was only a matter of time before she and Lonzo were lovey-dovey again. Deep down, Nisha felt that way too. Every week Lonzo waited on her went a long way in proving his devotion and commitment to their family. Every day he didn't go to jail or to Mr. Brown's house helped even more.

Lonzo paid her a visit after her first day of work. He brought a bouquet of roses for Nisha and a new toy for his beloved son. Lonzo Jr. went crazy over his mechanical T-rex. Lonzo Sr. went crazy over the tight, black slacks Nisha wore to the office. He gave her booty a squeeze in the living room. She batted his hand away playfully.

"Stop, boy."

He sat up on the couch and grabbed her hips. "Come sit over here with me."

Nisha giggled as she plopped down on the sofa. Lonzo snaked an arm around her waist. The other hand groped her thigh.

"I think I need to sit over there," she said, pushing his hands away. Her man was like a horny octopus. "You can't be doing all that at my daddy's house."

"I been begging you to come to the apartment all week," Lonzo replied. "Why you tripping?" He wrapped both arms around her and smooched her neck.

She pulled away, even though his kisses sent lightning bolts from her jugular to her toes. "For real," she said grinning. "You gotta quit."

"Alright. But you know you wrong, girl. We haven't did nothing since before my last fight. That was damned near three months ago."

"Your last fight was on May 29th," she corrected him. "That was only a month and..." She counted in her head. "Six days ago."

"But we stopped having sex two weeks before that fight," Lonzo recalculated.

"That's still not three months."

"But yo ass done got so *fat* since then," he whined. "I can't keep my hands off it."

"What you saying? I got fat?" She'd gained seven pounds since their separation, due to the carefree lifestyle at her father's house (and Walter's good cooking), but she didn't think it was noticeable.

"Naw you ain't fat. You look good!"

"I gained a little weight," she confided.

"It must've all went to your *ass*!" he exclaimed. "Stand up, baby. Let me look at it."

"No," she said with a grin.

"Come on. It's my birthday."

"No, it's not!" She laughed. "This is my daddy's house, Lonzo. Not a strip club."

"Your daddy's not here."

"He'll be back in a minute."

"Well, when you get up, I'm gon' look at that ass. You have to get up for something sooner or later."

She giggled. "You a pervert."

"Naw, I'm just a man with needs."

She understood that. When she put a freeze on their sexual relations, she didn't think they'd make it. It was bad enough she wouldn't move into the new apartment. But The Champ didn't give up on her. He visited regularly, courting her like he did when they first met. The only difference now was they had tasted the forbidden fruit. It was hard not to give in to a quickie.

"When you gon' come home?" he asked. He leaned back on the sofa and watched her affectionately.

He wore jeans with a blue tee. It didn't take much to make him look good. His physique was as trim as ever. He bought a few pieces of jewelry with his fight money. He now had real diamonds in his ears. He sported a flashy, Cuban link chain.

"That's not my home," Nisha told him. "I've never lived in that apartment."

"Yeah," Lonzo said. "But I wanna make it a home. The only thing I need is you and our son. We should get married too – No, I wanna wait 'til after my fight in Austin, so I'll have enough money to give you a big wedding, like them people on TV."

"Ain't you getting a little ahead of yourself?"

"I know we getting back together."

"You haven't even gone to court for your pistol case. Your fight in Austin could get cancelled."

"My pastor told me to think positive."

"Your *pastor*?" She gave him a look.

"I been going to church, sometimes."

"With who?" Nisha's doubtful look remained.

"My grandma."

"When?"

"On Monday and Wednesday night. I can't go on Sunday, 'cause I don't wake up early enough. But I can catch them night services."

"You been going to church?"

"Yes ma'am. What's the problem?"

"I don't believe you."

"That's okay. Pastor says you don't go to church to please other people. You do it for your own personal relationship with the Lord."

She almost laughed at him. She had to fight to keep it in.

"Yeah, I got you thinking," he said. "You see I'm different now. I'm a new man. So you should wanna give me some." He grabbed a boob and leaned in for a kiss.

She pushed him away laughing. "You ain't no different!"

"Yeah I am. You should see how different my dick–"

The front door opened, and his mouth snapped shut. He sat up straight and then jumped to his feet when he saw Walter had a few bags of groceries.

"I'll get those for you, sir." He took the bags from him and headed for the kitchen. "You want me to leave these on the counter?"

"Yes," Walter said with a grateful smile. "Thank you very much, young man." He grinned at Nisha. "You don't see too much of that nowadays, respectful black men who wanna help out..."

"I see Lonzo's biggest fan has arrived," she quipped.

"Just calling it like I see it," Walter said.

Lonzo returned from the kitchen and headed for the front door. "I dropped those bags off for you, sir. I'm gonna take off now. I gotta pick up my grandmama for church in a little bit."

"Church?" Walter couldn't hide his surprise. "You're spiritual, courteous *and* about to be the heavyweight champion of the world?" He looked at Nisha with one eyebrow raised. "Sounds like a good catch to me."

She rolled her eyes and got up to see The Champ out. "Well, maybe *you* should go out with him," she told her dad.

Lonzo laughed good-naturedly. He stepped out onto the porch. "You have a good day, Mr. Elder. I'll see you later Miss Nisha."

Her eyes widened. *"Miss Nisha?"*

"Yes, Ma'am. You have a nice day." Lonzo skipped down the steps and walked stiffly to his car.

She closed the door and looked at her father. Before he could continue his matchmaking, she told him, "Both of y'all are full of it."

At work the next day, she was in a great mood, and the morning hours flew by. At lunchtime she chose Subway over McDonalds, despite Lonzo's affection for the weight she'd gained.

When she returned to the office, she noticed a bouquet of roses on the receptionist's desk. Their secretary, Mildred, was married with four children. Nisha thought it was awesome her husband kept the romantic fires burning after so long.

"Wow. Those are nice!" she said as she walked by. "Is it your anniversary?"

"No," Mildred said. She hefted the vase. "These are for you."

"Really?" Nisha beamed like she won a pageant. The vase was beautiful. There were two dozen long-stem roses inside, half of them pink, the rest white. She held them under her nose. The scent was delightful. "Who are they from?"

"Not sure," Mildred said. "I was gonna look at the card, but you've only been working here two days. I didn't want to get in your business like that."

"It's okay. You could've looked at the card. I don't care."

"Oh, well in that case, it doesn't say who they're from," Mildred reported. "The card just says: *To Nisha, With Love.*"

Nisha laughed. She could already tell she and Mildred would get along fine.

"You don't know who they're from?" Mildred asked with a smile.

"My fiancée probably. Not sure why he didn't put his name on the card. I can't see Lonzo sending flowers without wanting to take credit for it."

"He has good taste," Mildred said. "A vase like that costs a hundred dollars."

"How do you know?"

"I've been working as a secretary all my life, for a lot of different companies. I've had a lot of flowers dropped off at my desk, and those are the prettiest."

Nisha's smile grew even bigger. "Thank you."

She toted the expensive vase to her desk, wondering what possessed Lonzo to purchase such a gift. He brought her flowers before – a bouquet yesterday as a matter of fact. But he wasn't the type to go all out. The roses he gave her yesterday came from Walmart.

This level of sucking up was unnecessary, because Nisha thought she might move in with him as early as this weekend. She placed the flowers on her desk and grinned at them for the rest of the day. When she got off, she toted the vase to her car, fully aware of the jealous stares she garnished from women in the parking lot.

She picked up Lonzo Jr. from her sisters' house on the way home. Shonda was busy with the kids, but Nisha wouldn't leave until her sister followed her outside to see the gift.

"Lonzo gave you those?"

"Yeah. Can you believe it?"

"He want you *bad*," Shonda surmised. "You know you gotta give him some for that, don't you?"

"No, I don't," Nisha said with a chuckle.

"Yes, you do. It's a rule."

"Girl, what are you talking about?"

"Everybody know the rules. If a man buy you lobster, some shoes, a purse or some flowers like that, you gotta give him some."

Nisha cracked up.

"Yeah, go ahead and laugh," Shonda said. "Bet you won't be laughing when he pull his thing out."

Nisha imagined Lonzo showing up at Walter's house later today.

Did you get my flowers? he'd ask.

She'd reply, *Yes, thank you very much.*

And then he'd drop his pants. *Cool. So you know what time it is...*

The thought made her laugh harder.

She was still chipper when she got home. She wanted to show off her roses again, but her dad was out running errands. She placed the vase in the middle of the dining table and then got started on dinner. She heard the doorbell while she chopped onions for homemade chili.

She assumed it was Lonzo, coming to collect his reward. Her smile was delightful as she skipped through the living room. But when she opened the door, her smile disappeared. Her eyes grew large, and her mouth fell open.

"Oh my God..." she breathed.

Her visitor was tall and handsome, with brown skin like butter toffee. His hair was shaved close to his head. He wore no beard or moustache. His eyes were serious. His smile was stunning.

The visitor had a strong jawline that hadn't changed much since their high school days, but from the neck down he was a totally new man. He wore a golf shirt tucked into a pair of Dockers. His shoulders were broad. Nisha saw the outline of his hard pecs. The muscles in his arms definitely hadn't been there seven years ago. Overall, she noticed thirty new pounds of flesh, all distributed in the most visually pleasing areas.

"Ellis... I don't believe it," she said with a hand over her mouth.

"Well, believe it," he said. His voice was deeper than she remembered. This was not the same boy who took her virginity on prom night and broke her heart shortly afterwards.

Ellis was now a grown man.

"Did you get my flowers?" he asked.

Nisha thought she might faint. She gripped the doorknob so hard, her knuckles turned white. "Ye, yes," she said, barely above a whisper. "I, I got them."

CHAPTER TWENTY-ONE
SERGEANT MAJOR JIMMY ELLIS

Jimmy and Nisha met at William Joseph Middle school. They had several classes together in the sixth grade, but they didn't know each other well. Jimmy had a crush on a girl named Arista Epps back then. Nisha was being pursued by a boy named Chris Tucker. Chris had a big nose and most of his pants were high water. Nisha didn't really like him, but she liked the attention he gave her. She didn't realize she was leading him on until Walter sat her down one day and they had a talk about puppy love.

In the 8th grade Jimmy and Nisha were paired for a social studies project. They developed a mutual crush that made working together difficult, but they pulled it off and got an A on the assignment.

The following year, they attended Finley High. At the beginning of their freshman year, Jimmy asked his teachers to call him by his last name (Ellis). A lot of the students continued to call him Jimmy out of spite, but Nisha never disrespected him in this regard. She caught up with him after class one day and struck up a conversation.

"Hey, Ellis, why'd you change your name?"

He stopped and smiled when he saw who it was. "Hey, Nisha. I didn't change my name. I just want to use my last name from now on."

"Yeah, but why?"

"'Cause some kids mess with me," he said. "They call me *Jimmy Crack Corn...*"

At fourteen, it was hard for Nisha not to laugh. "You should tell them, '*And I don't care*,' when they say that," she offered with a giggle.

"Do you know anything about that song?" Ellis asked.

Nisha shook her head. "No."

"It's about a slave singing about the day his master died," Ellis informed her. "I looked it up."

Nisha felt embarrassed for making light of it. "Oh. I guess it is a dumb song."

"They try to fix it up now," he continued. "They changed the word 'master' to 'boss.' But if you find the original version, it says '*master*.'"

"You studied that for a class?" she asked.

"No. I looked it up when people started calling me *Jimmy Crack Corn*."

Again Nisha had to stifle a snicker.

"You think that's funny, don't you?" he asked.

She shook her head, but he was smiling. She nodded and said, "A little."

"Your name's funny too," Ellis said. "It means *old*."

"Nuh uhn," Nisha said. "*Elder* means my family were the oldest members of their tribe, back when they were handing out names. People looked up to my ancestors. They were probably the leaders."

Ellis smiled. "Where'd you hear that?"

"My daddy told me. He likes to study the meaning, I mean the origin of names."

Ellis was impressed. He approached his locker, only then realizing she was following him.

"Why don't you use your middle name instead of your last name?" she asked.

He shook his head, grinning. "My middle name is *Ophelia*," he confided.

Nisha laughed out loud this time, fully convinced this was a joke.

But it wasn't.

She caught herself, and her eyes grew wide. "Oh, I'm sorry. I thought you was kidding."

"I got named after my grandma," Ellis explained. "My full name is Jimmy Ophelia Ellis. I can either be *Jimmy Crack Corn* or *Ophelia* or *Ellis*."

"You made a good choice," Nisha observed.

"Plus it will get me ready for the military," Ellis said. "Everybody uses their last name in the marines."

"You're going to the marines?"

"My dad's a marine, and my uncle's a marine, and my grandfather was a marine."

"That don't mean you have to be one."

He stared at her like she was speaking French. "How come?"

"Because you can be whatever you want to be."

Ellis shook his head. "I'm gonna be a marine."

"You're gonna be a marine because you want to, or because you feel like you have to?"

He opened his mouth to respond, and the tardy bell rang. Luckily, they were both headed to lunch.

"Aw man. The line's gonna be long," Ellis predicted.

"I brought my lunch," Nisha replied smugly.

"Well, I'll see you later," he said. He slammed his locker closed and started to take off running. He stopped and jogged back to her. "Nobody here knows my middle name. Please don't tell anybody."

"I promise."

He watched her eyes, and then he turned and sprinted for the cafeteria.

The next day he followed her after they were dismissed from math class. He didn't say anything for a full two minutes. Nisha thought he was weird, but when they reached her locker, he asked, "Do you have a boyfriend?"

She shook her head.

"Will you, do you want to be my girlfriend?" Ellis asked.

She frowned and then nodded. "Okay."

He smiled brightly. "Okay."

They stood there awkwardly for a moment, and then he took off again.

"Bye!"

"Bye," Nisha said.

The rest of their freshman year was filled with goofy encounters like this, but towards the second semester, their puppy love matured into something resembling a real relationship. Ellis caught up with her almost every passing period, so he could carry her books and walk her to class. He ate lunch with her, and he walked her to the bus stop each day.

They only held hands once that year, but that was enough to keep the fire burning in their hearts throughout summer break.

They kissed for the first time at the homecoming football game their sophomore year. Ellis saved his allowance for a month, so he could buy her a mum. They shared their first slow dance at a homecoming party later that night. Nisha was so nervous, she felt sweat accumulating in her armpits. She would've been embarrassed, but Ellis' forehead was slick with perspiration.

They didn't express their love verbally until Finley High hosted a Valentine's dance one year later. Nisha was nervous that night, but it was a different kind of nervousness. She had reached sexual maturity, and the butterflies danced both in her belly and further south.

After going with the same boy for three years, Nisha's friends thought she might spread her wings and experience someone new her senior year, but Ellis was the only one for her. By then they were the longest lasting couple at Finley High, which was remarkable considering their maturity level and the vast number of temptations at school. Nisha knew Ellis as well as she knew her sister. Ellis considered Nisha his best friend. Even Walter had come to accept that his daughter was going to marry her high school sweetheart.

On prom night, Nisha wore an emerald green dress that was strapless and silky. Ellis couldn't take his eyes off her cleavage when they danced at the ballroom. They didn't drink alcohol at an after party, but they participated in another prom tradition.

They made out in the front seat of a Mustang Ellis borrowed from his big brother. They didn't stop kissing when his erection was visible through his slacks. Nisha moaned in appreciation when he reached between her legs. He almost shot his load when she unzipped his pants and touched his naked manhood for the first time.

She had time to back out when he asked if she wanted to sit in the backseat instead, but everything seemed so right. Nisha knew their lovemaking would be monumental. It was the culmination of wants and desires that had been marinating for years, since the day he confided that his middle name was Ophelia.

She gave herself to him, mind body and soul. Ellis was as gentle as a paper boat riding a moonlit wave. When he tore her hymen and told her he loved her, she cried and said she loved him too. Their intimacy took them to a new level of consciousness and understanding.

From that moment on, she knew they would be together forever. But as graduation neared, reality delivered a vicious backhand that left her reeling in a pool of despair. Over the years, she tried to forget most of the tear-filled nights, to save her from a mental breakdown, she supposed. But she would never forget the afternoon of June 23rd, one month after she and Ellis left Finley High School for good.

He got a call from his recruiter that day. He rushed to Walter's house to make one last plea for Nisha's hand in marriage.

"Come with me," he begged. "We can still be together. We can go to the courthouse right now. You can come with me, if we're married."

"Ellis, I don't want to move to North Carolina," Nisha reasoned, her face wet with tears. "Stay here with me. We can go to college. You don't need the G.I. Bill."

"I'm not doing this for college money. I'm doing this because it's my destiny. I told you that."

"It is not your *destiny*," she argued. "Just because your father went doesn't mean you have to."

"Yes, it does." He'd been telling her the same thing for years.

Nisha was at her wits' end. "No it doesn't! You don't have to go! Stay here with me!"

"Come with me!" he countered. "You can live on the base. We can have a family."

"My family is *here*," Nisha said. "I don't want to live on a base while you run around fighting some dumb war. I don't wanna worry about you getting killed. I can't live like that. I need a man who'll come home to me every day."

"Nisha, I could stay here and get hit by a truck tomorrow. Nothing is promised. You never know what's going to happen."

"You're not going to get hit by a truck!"

"I'm not going to get killed in the war either! I'm gonna make it. Everybody in my family made it."

"That's stupid!"

"My plane leaves in two weeks. If you love me, you need to get on it with me."

"If you love me, you'll stay here with me!"

"I already signed the papers!" Ellis was exasperated. "I am *enlisted*, Nisha. Right now! I already joined the marines."

She threw her hands over her face and ran to her room crying. It was the worst pain she ever felt. Life as she knew it would never be the same. Ellis waited in the living room for a few minutes, and then he left the house with tears staining his cheeks as well. He got on the plane without her fifteen days later. That was the beginning of the end for them.

He wrote letters once a week, and she responded every time, but beneath the kind words they penned, there was an unspoken resentment on both sides. She could never forgive him for leaving her, and he could not forgive her for not going with him. Six months later, Ellis was sent to South Korea, and his letters stopped coming.

They never officially broke up, but it was obvious he'd moved on with his life. Nisha had to be coaxed into doing the same. It was Walter who dragged her to a fight one night, because he was tired of watching her mope around the house. While there, Nisha saw a cocky, young boxer whose record was only 3-0, yet he had the audacity to call himself The Champ.

Ellis waited patiently in the doorway while Nisha regained her composure. She then threw herself at him with a full body hug that nearly toppled him.

"Ellis! I missed you so much! What are you doing here! Why didn't you call?"

He laughed and hugged her back. "I missed you too, Nisha. I was going to call, but I thought I'd surprise you."

She backed away from him grinning brightly. "You look so different! Where'd you get all these muscles from?" She squeezed his arm affectionately.

"You know how it is," he said. "They get you all cut up in boot camp, keep you on a strict diet."

"What are you now? A Lieutenant General Major," she kidded.

"Close," Ellis said. "I'm a Sergeant Major."

She raised an eyebrow. "Mmmm. Sounds important. Are you still in Korea?"

"I just left Pakistan."

"What brown people are we bombing now?" she asked sarcastically.

Ellis chuckled. "Don't tell me you're still a bleeding-heart liberal..."

"Yeah, you probably don't want to talk politics with me," she said with a smirk.

"*Okay*..." Ellis said with a roll of his eyes. "Moving right along..."

She shook her head and laughed.

"So, what's been up with you?" he asked. "I hear you're a mommy now."

Nisha's eyes widened. "Who told you that?"

"Of course I did a little research before I came over here."

"What kind of research?"

"This is a big city," Ellis said, "but it's not that big if you never move out of your childhood neighborhood. I know you have a little boy. I know you worked at Dr. Coates' pharmacy. I know you recently moved back in with your father. I called him this morning. He's the one who told me where you work."

Nisha was impressed. She was also surprised her dad helped Ellis out. She would've sworn Walter was on Lonzo's payroll. Speaking of which...

"If you did so much research," she said, "I'm sure you heard about my baby-daddy..."

"That's all anyone talks about. I wouldn't have come over here, except your father said you and Alonzo were split up. Is that true?" He looked down at her engagement ring.

Nisha hid her hand subconsciously. "I can't believe he told you that. My dad's the main one who's been telling me to go back to Lonzo."

"Really?" Ellis cocked his head. "He told me he was staying out of your love life."

"My dad told you that?"

"Yeah, this morning."

Nisha chuckled. "So *now* he wants to stay out of my love life..."

Ellis shrugged. "So, was he right about you and Lonzo? Are y'all broke up?"

Nisha suddenly felt like she was in a tanning booth. She wiped her brow. "We, um... We're taking some time apart," she admitted.

"Oh, well, I can't say I'm sorry to hear that. Does that mean you can go out with me? I would love to catch up."

She hesitated for a moment before saying, "Yeah. That would be cool."

She knew Lonzo wouldn't approve, but they were technically separated. Besides, she hadn't seen Ellis in seven years. Considering the depth of their high school romance, they had every right to get reacquainted. If Lonzo had a problem with it, he should've thought about what he was risking when he went back to work for Mr. Brown.

And who said Lonzo had to know?

"Can you pick me up in an hour?" she asked.

"Great," Ellis said. "I'll see you then."

Nisha thought she'd have to take Lonzo Jr. to her meeting (which was nowhere near a date) with an old friend, but her father came home fifteen minutes after Ellis left. Nisha asked if he could watch her son. Walter said he'd be happy to.

"What's the deal with you?" she asked before she went to her room to find an outfit.

"What are you talking about?"

"Yesterday you wanted me to get back with Lonzo. Today you hook me up with my ex-boyfriend."

"I didn't hook you up," Walter said with a chuckle. "I just told him where he could find you."

"And you told him me and Lonzo were split up."

"Ellis is a very respectful man," Walter explained. "I don't think he would've contacted you, if he thought you and Lonzo were living together."

"That's what I'm talking about. You could've discouraged him, if you wanted..."

"I'm not going to interfere with your personal life, Nisha. Lonzo is gonna be the heavyweight champion. Ellis is a decorated war hero. If some crackhead came looking for you, I'd tell him to get lost. But either of these guys could offer you a great life."

"Um, I'm still with Lonzo. Me and Ellis are just friends."

Walter shrugged. "That's not my concern, baby girl. Either one of them can be whatever you want them to be."

Nisha turned and left the room with a confused expression.

Ellis rang the doorbell again forty-five minutes later. Nisha answered wearing a white blouse with a tight, black skirt that was probably too sexy for a casual outing with her first love. Ellis had also changed into khaki slacks with a dark blue button down.

She liked how his clothes were the perfect size and he wore them neatly. The military influence was evident in all aspects of his character, from the way he walked to the way he talked.

His rental was a 2019 Navigator. He opened the door for her when she got in and when she exited the vehicle at an upscale French restaurant called Mille Fleurs. Nisha had never been there before, but Ellis felt right at home in the classy environment. He pulled out her chair and made their wine selection with perfect French.

Nisha was reluctant to try many of the delicacies, fearing she would get sick and ruin the meal, so Ellis ordered her *entrecote au poivre,* which was a grilled rib eye flambéed with brandy. While they dined, the couple talked about the good old days at Finley High and the ups and downs they'd experienced since graduation. The conversation inevitably returned to Nisha's iffy relationship with Lonzo.

"I don't mean to keep bringing this up," Ellis said, "but why are you still wearing an engagement ring, if you're not together anymore? I'm pretty sure I could take him, but I don't want some crazy boxer to run in here and attack me because I'm on a date with his woman."

Nisha grinned. "You think you could take him?"

"I'm pretty sure," he said with a straight face.

"Have you ever seen Lonzo fight?"

"No, but that's the difference."

"What's the difference?"

"A fighter wants to *fight*. A marine wants to incapacitate you, as quickly as possible."

A chill rolled down Nisha's spine, but it wasn't uncomfortable. Rather, she was impressed with everything about Ellis, from his speech to his dress to his accomplishments.

"Alright, I'll tell you what's going on with Lonzo," she said.

"I'd love to hear it." He propped his elbows on the table and leaned closer.

Nisha took a deep breath and told the whole story from start to finish. It was strange, considering she hadn't seen Ellis in so long. But for some reason, she felt like he was still her best friend, and she could tell him anything without worrying about how he would respond.

When she was done, he watched her for a moment before saying, "Wow."

She shook her head. "Nuh-uhn. You gonna have to do better than that."

He chuckled. "That's a lot, Nisha. I'm actually at a loss for words."

"You need to find some."

He laughed. "What do you want me to say? Do you want an observation? A critique? An opinion?"

"Sure. All of the above."

He rubbed his chin and smiled at her. "I think you're an exceptional woman."

She smiled back. "Thank you. But what does that have to do with my story?"

He shook his head, grinning. "I'm saying you're an exceptional woman because of what you've been through, what you've put up with..."

She took a sip of her wine.

"I think you should've left when he hit your boss," Ellis said. "Another good time to leave was when he went to work for *Mr. Brown*. And then when he started coming home late and getting high–"

"He only got high once," Nisha interrupted.

"The fact that he wasn't coming home at a decent hour is enough," Ellis said. "You don't deserve that, to be waiting up all night, wondering if he's dead or in jail. And when those people came to your apartment..." He shook his head. "That *definitely* should've been the last straw."

"It was," Nisha said. "That's when I left."

"You left, but you haven't *left*. Even after his arrest, you haven't fully broken it off with him. You're still wearing his ring, hoping he'll do right, so y'all can get back together."

Nisha started to feel like her decisions were stupid. She reminded herself that Ellis had an ulterior motive. "What do you want," she asked, "to swoop in and save me from my terrible life?"

He nodded. "If it was that easy, I'd have you on a plane tomorrow."

Nisha's heart froze. She was kidding, but he was serious. "I haven't seen you in seven years. How come you haven't found someone else since then?"

"A marine's life is not as glamorous as it may seem," he informed her. "I travel all over the world and see a lot of great things, but I rarely settle down long enough to find the kind of woman I would like to have a meaningful relationship with. A lot of soldiers force the issue and end up with spouses they can't stand and babies they never see. I never wanted that. If I couldn't find a woman I loved as much as I loved you, I wouldn't waste my time."

Nisha blushed. "But we haven't seen each other in a long time. I know you don't expect to walk in and pick up right where we left off..."

"I don't have any expectations," he replied. "I'm here for three weeks. I hoped I could see you, and I hoped you'd still be the beautiful, funny and amazing woman I knew in high school. You are. You're the only woman I've ever loved. I would like to see you again, but as far as picking up where we left off, it would be foolish of me to expect such a thing."

Nisha agreed that it was foolish, but at the same time, the possibility had a fairy tale feeling that would make any woman's heart flutter.

When he dropped her off an hour later and gave her a nice, warm hug, Nisha's heart quivered even more.

She felt like it was prom night all over again.

CHAPTER TWENTY-TWO
THE FINAL CHAPTER
IN THIS CORNER

On Friday Nisha was in a rush when she picked up Lonzo Jr. after work. Shonda had his things ready, but she wouldn't let her sister leave until Nisha told her what the big deal was.

"What are you talking about?" Nisha asked.

"You called me from work and told me to get all his stuff ready. You ain't never did that before. What's going on? Why you in such a hurry?"

Nisha was at the front door, but she stopped to answer Shonda's questions. "I had to work late. Now I'm in a rush to get ready for my date tonight."

"Date? With who? Lonzo?"

"No. Ellis."

"*Ellis*? You still talking to him?"

Nisha frowned. "Yeah. Why not?"

"I thought he just stopped by to say, 'Hi.'"

"No, we went out when I saw him on Monday."

"And you're going out with him again? Have you been talking to him since then?"

"I talk to him every day," Nisha informed her. "Last night we were on the phone 'til two in the morning." She smiled wistfully.

Shonda frowned. "What do you think, you're in high school again?"

"No, but it feels like that sometimes. When we go out, I feel things I haven't felt since we were in school. It's weird. We were talking about that last night."

"You went out with him more than once?"

"He took me to lunch Wednesday."

"He picked you up from your job?"

Nisha nodded. "We went to Pappadeaux."

"*Pappadeaux*?" Shonda was seriously vexed.

"It's just a restaurant," Nisha said. "I know it's Lonzo's favorite, but it's not like he proposed to me there."

"Speaking of Lonzo, how does he feel about all this?"

Nisha shook her head. "You know I haven't told him."

"He doesn't know Ellis is back in town?"

Nisha shook her head again. "He'd be tripping, if I told him."

"You know I usually got your back," Shonda said, "but don't you think Lonzo got a right to trip? You not just going out with an old friend. You're going out with your *first love*, a man you was about to marry."

"We just catching up."

"At two o'clock in the morning? Come on, Nisha. You know I'm not stupid."

Nisha sighed.

"What's really going on with y'all?" Shonda asked. "Are you trying to start something back up? You know you can't go back in time. The past is the past."

"But who said it has to stay in the past?" Nisha wondered. "I like Ellis. We were always good friends. I don't think we shouldn't be friends just because I'm with Lonzo."

"You're not with Lonzo. Y'all are separated. So maybe you're starting to think this would be a good time to try something new – or in this case, something *old*."

"I don't see nothing wrong with that."

"It's not wrong," Shonda argued, "if you tell Lonzo about it. You know he don't want you to see your old boyfriend. Just 'cause y'all not living together don't mean it's okay to go out with somebody else – unless you both agree to it. How are you supposed to figure out if you want to be with Lonzo if you got Ellis on your mind?"

Nisha knew her sister was right, but, "Shonda, you know how it was when me and Ellis broke up. I always wondered if life would've been different, if I had left with him. I'm older and smarter now. I think I owe it to myself to at least think about it."

"You can't pick up where you left off."

"I know it's not that easy," Nisha agreed. "But, it's not that hard either."

Shonda couldn't believe it. "Ellis look as good as Lonzo?"

"It's not about looks," Nisha said. "But yes, Ellis is fine as hell. And he's a lot more stable than Lonzo."

"But Lonzo finna be a millionaire."

"I don't care about his money. But since you brought it up, Ellis is doing very well for himself too. He's not a millionaire, but he's been in the marines for a long time. He's a master sergeant. He don't have no dependents."

"You really been thinking about this," Shonda noticed.

"I am. Ellis is just, so different than what I'm used to. He never would've done any of the bad things Lonzo did."

"Have, have y'all slept together?" Shonda asked. "You sound like you in love."

"We haven't slept together in seven years."

"But are you still in love with him?" she pressed.

Nisha considered that. "We're just getting reacquainted, Shonda. Now, I gotta go." She opened the door and ushered Lonzo Jr. outside.

"I think you need to tell Lonzo about this," Shonda advised her.

"Me and Ellis are just friends," Nisha insisted, but there was no use lying to her sister about it. Shonda could spot trouble from a mile away. She knew Nisha was wading into waters that were much too deep.

For her third date this week, Nisha pulled a new dress from the closet that still had the tags on it. She bought it at the mall yesterday, specifically for this occasion. It was solid black with spaghetti straps and a scoop neckline that put her puppies on display. The stretchy fabric accentuated her ass, hips and waistline.

She wore a pair of stylish sandals she also bought yesterday to replace the many pairs of shoes lost in her vandalized apartment. She usually styled her hair in an easy ponytail, but tonight she wore it down, in loose curls. She also put on a little lipstick and mascara, something she hadn't done in months.

When Ellis showed up at seven o'clock, he stared at her for a few of seconds, his smile growing by degrees.

Finally he said, "If I would've known you'd turn out like this, I never would've gone to boot camp. You look absolutely amazing."

Nisha couldn't remember the last time someone called her *amazing*.

"No, you had to follow your dreams," she said. "It was your destiny to be a marine."

"Well, it's a good thing life allows us to hit the rewind button sometimes," he replied, "even though I don't deserve a second chance."

Nisha hadn't decided if he was getting one, so she didn't say anything.

Ellis wore a gray, casual suit with a black shirt and no tie. His wingtip shoes had a crisp shine. He said he wanted to take her somewhere *nice*, but he didn't say where. Nisha didn't care about the particulars. The sun was starting to set on what had been a beautiful day. The night was filled with promise.

He gave her a hug and opened the door of his rental for her.

"Do you like Indian food?" he asked.

"I don't think I've ever had it."

"Good. Then you can have your first experience with me."

"I already had my first experience with you," she said slyly.

Ellis chuckled. His smile was as cute as it was in the eighth grade. His eyes twinkled in the dappled sunlight. "Do you remember that night?"

"A girl never forgets her first. What about you? Do boys forget theirs?"

Ellis shook his head. "No. Well, I know I never have. As a matter of fact, I've been thinking about it a lot, in the last few days..."

Nisha didn't know how to respond to that. Ellis let her off the hook. He closed her door and walked slowly around to the driver's side, giving her time to blow out a pent-up breath and wipe the perspiration from her forehead.

He took her to The Taj, and they dined on tandoori tiger prawns, chicken tikka and lamb vindaloo. It was relatively early when they left the restaurant, so he took Nisha to her favorite park for a twilight promenade.

She liked the Arlington park because there was a huge duck pond in the center surrounded by a looping sidewalk. In the middle of the pond were three intricate fountains. There were no children screaming in the nearby playground and no cyclists cutting calories at that hour. It was just her and Ellis and a forest of pecan trees.

They walked quietly for a while, listening to the nocturnal wildlife, admiring the glow of the lamplights on the water's dark surface. Nisha wished the moment could last forever, but she and Ellis weren't kids anymore. They knew their friendly dates were much more than that, and at some point, they had to make adult decisions that would affect more than just the two of them.

"So," she said, but Ellis began speaking at the same time.

"Sorry," he said.

"No, go ahead."

"No, you," he said, and they both laughed.

"You probably want to say the same thing I do," Nisha guessed.

"About how we need to talk about what's going on?"

She nodded.

"Well," Ellis said, "let's talk about it."

They rounded the corner on the biking trail, heading back the way they had come. The moon was full. This natural illumination, coupled with the florescent glow from the park's lamps, provided enough light for Nisha to see her date clearly. His expression was serious. His eyes hopeful.

He told her, "I don't think there's any secret how I feel about you. But in case you're wondering, I like you, Nisha. I like you a lot. I'm, I would even say I still love you, as much as I did when we were in school. I still believe you're the only girl for me."

Nisha took a deep breath and let it out slowly. She felt a scattering of goose bumps sprout on her arms.

"Do you think that's weird," he asked, "for me to still love you after all this time?"

She took another slow breath. She shook her head and spoke softly. "No."

"I think you have feelings for me too," Ellis said. "Do you?"

Her eyes were large. She nodded.

"When we were young, that's all we needed," Ellis said. "When I was your man, and you were my girl, we didn't give a damn about what anyone had to say about it. But we're grown now. Things change. You have a child, and I have a commitment to the marines. I have to leave in a couple of weeks. I'm going to Bridgeport, California. There's a Mountain Warfare Training Center there. My days in Afghanistan are over, but it's my job to train the next generation."

Nisha listened and walked. Her throat tightened to the point that she found it hard to swallow. She knew what he was going to say next. Part of her was thrilled, but mostly she was terrified.

"I want you to come with me," Ellis continued. "I left you behind seven years ago, and I've regretted it ever since. We have a chance to turn back the hands of time. Except now we're older and smart enough to make the right decisions."

Nisha's head was spinning. Ellis watched her expectantly.

"This..." She sighed. "Whoo. This, it's a lot."

"I know it is." He stopped walking and took both of her hands in his. "I know you have things you have to deal with..." He turned her left hand over and trailed off as he stared at it. "Your ring..." He gave her a puzzled look. "What happened?"

"I took it off." She looked up at him. Her eyes glistened.

"You broke it off? You gave it back to him?"

"I took it off today," she said, "before you came." She looked away. She felt guilty when she removed her engagement ring before their date. She didn't know what she was doing anymore. Her life was in limbo.

"If you took it off," Ellis said, "then you must feel the same way I feel."

He waited, but she didn't respond.

"I don't want to pressure you," he said. "I'll be in Overbrook Meadows for two more weeks."

Nisha didn't think that was enough time to make a decision of this magnitude. She had never been to California. The thought of living there was scary. And there was something else that bothered her.

"Wait, I thought I couldn't live on the base with you unless we were married."

Ellis smiled. "Nisha, what do you think this is all about? Why do you think I came back to Overbrook Meadows?"

She had no idea. "To see your mom?"

He chuckled. "No. I came for you. I still want to marry you, as much as I did seven years ago. I want to give you the lifestyle you deserve. I'll raise your son as if he's my own. I would never let harm come to you."

Her eyes widened. She felt lightheaded. She brought a hand to her head and took a wobbly step to the side. Ellis took her into his arms.

"Are you okay?" he asked. "You, you don't have to make a decision today. I just want you to think about it. Can you do that for me?"

She nodded and her world gradually came to a standstill. She giggled. "I, I think I almost fainted."

"Because you're shocked or overwhelmed with joy?" Ellis asked. "Or, jeez, I hope you're not feeling disgusted..."

"No," she said. "The first two."

"Shock *and* joy?" He grinned. "That's great."

Nisha nodded. "I'm excited. Ellis, you don't know how happy I am that you came back into my life. But, I don't think I can go..."

"You told me that seven years ago."

"I know."

"What's stopping you this time?"

She tried to think of a good reason that did *not* involve Lonzo. She couldn't come up with one. "I, I don't know."

"I'm not giving up until you come up with a better excuse."

Nisha nodded. "I th—"

Before she could finish her sentence, he leaned down and kissed her. His lips were soft and warm. The feel of them on her mouth reignited passions she hadn't felt since they were eighteen. The feel of his hand on the small of her back and his other arm around her waist felt so familiar, so right.

She closed her eyes. The smell of his cologne blended with the smell of water from the pond, creating a totally new scent that would forever reside in her fondest memories.

He backed away and kissed her again, very softly, and then once more on the corner of her mouth. When he released her, Nisha thought she might fall into an abyss of fear and regret, but the concrete beneath her sandals held her up, for now.

"You ready to go?" he asked.

Nisha didn't want the night to end, but she nodded. It was after ten, and the park had strict hours of operation. They climbed into the Navigator, and Ellis dropped her off twenty minutes later. Her father was still up, waiting for her in the living room. He told her Lonzo had been by.

"What'd you tell him?"

"I told him you wasn't here," Walter said. He looked like he wanted to say something else, but he didn't. He just got up and went to bed.

Nisha turned the living room light off and went to check on her son.

When someone rang the doorbell one minute later, she assumed Ellis had forgotten something. She kicked off her pumps and yelled, "I'll get it!" as she rushed to the living room.

She unlocked the door and pulled it open without checking the peephole. If she had checked, she would've had time to ready herself or at least stop her eyes from bulging when she saw Lonzo standing angrily on the porch.

She wasn't sure why his eyes were red, his fists were balled, or why his chest rose and fell like he'd been shadowboxing, but it wasn't hard to put the pieces together. Plus Lonzo had never been the subtle type. As soon as he opened his mouth, she knew the gig was up.

"Who the hell was that?" he growled.

Nisha played dumb. "Who?"

"*You know what I'm talking about*!" Lonzo barked. He closed the distance between them with one quick step. Nisha backed away. Lonzo pursued her further, stepping boldly inside the house.

"Stop," Nisha said. She knew he would never hurt her, but The Champ was an imposing figure.

Lonzo looked over her shoulder, and, without looking back, Nisha knew her father had come to her defense.

Lonzo fought hard to keep his composure. "I'm sorry, Mr. Elder, but me and Nisha need to talk."

"I don't want no mess at my house," Walter said.

"I just wanna talk to her."

"It's alright," Nisha said, though she wasn't sure if it was. Her heart raced. The hairs stood on every part of her body. "I'll go outside."

"I'll be right here," Walter said.

Lonzo backed out of the house and waited for her on the porch. She followed him timidly and pulled the door closed. He watched her every move. His nostrils flared. He crossed his arms over his massive chest and stared at her like she was a whore.

"Lonzo, you need to calm down," she warned.

"Who was that nigga?"

"What are you talking about?"

"I was parked down the street," he said and pointed.

Nisha looked and saw his ugly Buick squatting against the curb four houses down. He must have run to Walter's house, rather than drive, which explained his breathing. Nisha wondered why he was parked there in the first place.

"Who was that?" Lonzo asked again.

"It, it don't matter."

"Yes, it do matter! I got a right to know!"

She had never been more afraid of him. Her voice rattled when she spoke.

"Lonzo, you need to calm down and lower your voice. You're scaring me."

"Why won't you tell me his name?"

"It was Ellis."

Lonzo's face changed as his brain raced to remember what she had told him. "The one you went to high school with?"

She nodded.

"What he doing over here?"

"We just went out, to catch up. He got back in town on Monday."

"This was your first time seeing him?"

Nisha's body grew cold. She shook her head.

Lonzo was so angry, there was a nervous tick on the left side of his face. Somehow he managed to keep his cool. "You been talking to him, on the phone?"

Nisha's teeth rattled. She nodded.

Lonzo brought his hands up. Nisha cowered, but he put the heels of his fists against his own temples and rubbed hard. He shook his head.

"Why you do me like this?" he moaned.

"I didn't do anything, Lonzo. I just–"

"You told me you loved that man," he recalled. "You said you was gon' marry him, but he left to go to the army."

"That was a long time ago."

"So, what's he doing back over here? Why he coming back now?"

"We just went out to eat. It wasn't–"

"*Don't lie to me! Stop lying to me, Nisha!*"

"*Stop yelling at me!*" she cried.

"Why can't you tell me the truth?" Lonzo spat. "Is he, did he get married?"

She shook her head reluctantly. "No, Lonzo. He not married."

"He still wanna be with you?"

She shook her head. She wanted to lie, but she couldn't do it, not with him staring into her eyes. She wiped her nose and nodded.

Lonzo shook his head furiously. He looked around for something to kick or throw but thought better of it. "You told him about me, that we was engaged?"

Nisha nodded. Her eyes filled with tears. She wiped them away nonchalantly. The move nearly cost her everything. Lonzo's eyes grew as large as half dollars. He grabbed her wrist and stared at her hand in shock.

"*Where's your ring?!*"

Nisha tried to yank her arm away, but his grip was strong.

"*You took your ring off?!*"

"Stop!" Nisha screamed. "*You're hurting me!*"

The door flew open, and Walter charged like a linebacker. Lonzo let go of Nisha's arm, but her father was primed for battle. He stepped between them and shoved Lonzo hard with both hands. Lonzo stumbled off the porch but regained his balance before he fell to the ground.

"*Let her go!*" Walter yelled, a full three seconds after the fact.

Lonzo looked up at them with tears in his eyes. Nisha screamed. She backed away and tried to disappear behind her father.

"*She doing me wrong!*" Lonzo cried. His voice cracked. Spit flew from his mouth. Tears rolled down both of his cheeks. "*She doing me wrong, Walter! Can't you see?*"

"I don't know about all that," Walter said. "But you not finna hurt her, especially not at *my* house!"

"*I don't wanna hurt her,*" Lonzo cried. His arms hung limply. Nisha thought the expression on his face was the worst she had ever seen on him or anyone else. He looked like a war-weary soldier standing over the corpse of his best friend. Every vein in his neck and face bulged. "*She doing me wrong, Walter! Why she doing me wrong?*"

Even in his protective state, Walter couldn't help but feel compassion for the boy. His features softened, and the fire in his eyes faded into a look of concern.

"Y'all need to talk about this in the morning," he suggested. "Everybody mad right now. You need to go home, Lonzo. Just, go home..."

The Champ wavered in indecision. He took a shuddering breath and tried to calm himself. He wiped his face stood up straight, so he would at least resemble the man Nisha promised to never leave.

"Can I, can I talk to her before I go?" he asked.

"I don't think that's—"

"Go ahead," Nisha said. She took a step to the side, so she and Lonzo could see each other fully. Her face was a mess with tears that looked worse than normal because of the mascara she wore for her date with Ellis.

"Reggie, he took those charges," Lonzo stated. He still looked terrible, but his voice was almost back to normal. "Reggie took the pistol charge for me. He said all the guns was his, so they dropped my case."

Nisha was surprised by this revelation, but she was too numb to show it. Reggie was a career criminal who was destined for the penitentiary. Taking the rap for Lonzo's gun was an unexpectedly noble thing to do.

"So my fight in Austin is still on," Lonzo continued. "If I win, I'm fighting for the championship. I'm guaranteed two million for the title fight. Even if I don't win, I'm getting two million. I don't know what that other cat is offering you, but I can give you the same things, Nisha. I can give you more."

He sniffled. "For the last couple of months, I been changing for you, 'cause that's what I thought you wanted me to do. I told Mr. Brown I wasn't never working for him no more, and he said it was cool. He don't mess with me. Even tonight, when I saw that dude over here, I didn't run up and whoop his ass like I wanted to. I ain't no hot head. I ain't like that no more.

"If you wanna be with me, then go put your ring back on and tell that fool to get lost. If you wanna be with him, then tell me to get lost. I'm not gon' sweat you no more. I been waiting on you for a long time. You said you was trying to get your head right, but you lied, Nisha. You been going out behind my back. You been messing with my head."

She shook her head in denial, but Lonzo didn't want to argue anymore.

"I'm coming back tomorrow morning to see my son," he said. "If you got my ring on, then we back together." He coughed. "I won't say nothing else about that other nigga. But if you don't got my ring on, you can give it back to me, and we'll go our separate ways. You can go live your life however you want. I'm through sweating you."

With that, he turned and commenced the lonely walk back to his car. Nisha and Walter remained on the porch until he started the bucket and drove away, and the street was quiet once again.

Nisha felt guilty for her role in the drama. Walter's look of disappointment made her feel worse. She wanted to explain herself, but her dad shook his head and went back inside. Nisha followed, wondering what destiny the new day would bring.

She had a choice to make. She knew she couldn't listen to only her heart this time. But she couldn't rely solely on her intellect either. The only way she would put her ring back on was if her heart, mind and soul were all on the same accord, compelling her to remain in The Champ's corner.

She had all night to think about it, but she made her decision before she fell asleep at midnight.

EPILOGUE

TWO MONTHS LATER
BRIDGEPORT, CALIFORNIA

"Hey, Sarg! You not gonna watch this?"

Jimmy Ophelia Ellis looked away from the cue ball and saw one of the new recruits waving him over.

"The main event's about to start!" McIntosh shouted. "This guy's from your hometown. You don't wanna see this?"

Ellis frowned. He liked boxing, but he didn't like it today. He didn't watch any of the Saturday night fights up to this point in the evening. He knew he probably shouldn't watch the main event either, but McIntosh would wonder why he didn't support his hometown hero. Plus, in a way, Ellis wanted to know if Nisha made the right decision.

He threw his pool stick across the table and said, "Hey, man, we'll have to finish this some other time."

"You always find a way to get out of it when you have no hope of winning," his opponent, Sergeant Peters, said. "I'm starting to wonder if you're a scrub."

"Watch your mouth, son," Ellis told him. "You know I'll wax the floor with your sorry ass any day. When I get back, we'll drop some money on the table. See how much shit you're talking when your paycheck's in my pocket."

Peters laughed good-naturedly. "I'll be waiting right here, Sarg."

Ellis wiped the pool chalk from his hands as he made his way to McIntosh and the other boxing fans. The owner of Lucky's Pool Hall had a 48-inch flat screen mounted above the bar. The television was the newest and most flashy piece of equipment in the dimly lit and smoke-filled building.

"What are you doing over there?" Corporal McIntosh asked. He slapped Ellis on the back and pushed him towards the bar. "What you drinking?"

"Nothing," Ellis said. "I'm good."

"Let me buy you a drink," McIntosh offered. He was a big man. A red head with a shiny face.

Ellis looked up at the television. He was starting to feel anxious, a little queasy. He had been in a funk all day. He took a seat next to his friend and told the bartender, "Gimme a whiskey double."

"How come you don't wanna watch the fights?" McIntosh pressed. "You not rooting for Ingram?"

"Why," Ellis asked. "He any good?"

"*What*?" Another soldier sitting two spots down stood and fixed a disbelieving look on him. "What do you mean *Is he any good*? Don't you know this man's about to be the next in line to fight for the belt?"

Corporal Friday was from Dallas, and he had relatives in Overbrook Meadows. Ellis never met him in their pre-military days, but sometimes they got together and discussed their familiar stomping grounds.

"He gotta win this fight first," Ellis said.

Friday shook his head in disappointment. "Man, I can't believe you're selling out like this! I been following The Champ since *day one*. He put Overbrook Meadows on the map. I'm surprised you haven't met him. He be all over the place." Friday was slim and bald. He had a big nose and big ears and a big mouth that was rarely closed.

"Naw. I never met him," Ellis said with a frown. The bartender brought his shot, and he downed it in two gulps. He grimaced. "Gimme another one."

"I never met him either," Friday said, talking over McIntosh's head. "But I done seen so many of his fights, I feel like we cousins or something. I know a bunch of people that's related to him." Friday took his seat with a big smile on his face. He rested both forearms on the bar and leaned forward enthusiastically. "This is gon' be the *shit*! It's been a long road, but my nigga finally made it. He on TV!"

Ellis looked back up at the television in time to see Ingram's opponent enter the ring. The venue for tonight's fights was the Frank Erwin Center in Austin. The arena could hold 50,000 fans. The place was packed.

Tonight, Ingram was fighting a well-toned brother named Quincy Nichols. Nichols was as black as oil, with fuzzy dreadlocks he had tied back. His record was 23-1, with fourteen knockouts. According to the broadcasters, his only loss came by way of a split decision most people thought should've gone the other way.

After Nichols got settled in his corner, the arena was bathed in an eerie darkness. A smooth bass line played on the loudspeakers.

"Uh oh!" Friday sat up in his seat. "Here it come. Here it come!"

The lights began to flash, and a huge spotlight swung to one corner of the building, where The Champ made his entrance. The crowd began to roar. Ingram had a huge entourage of trainers and other staff. The guy leading the pack didn't look like he had anything to do with boxing. The thin man had a big chain around his neck. He rocked back and forth rhythmically. Ellis thought Lonzo was foolish to associate with such riffraff, but the man raised a microphone to his gold-laden mouth and started to rap. And he was good.

"The Champ is here!
Now which one of y'all suckers didn't know that?
When you see these lights
When you see these fights
You now Lonzo's coming
Better bring your Kodak
'Cause, The Champ is here!"

"Yo, yo!" Friday jumped to his feet and pointed at the screen excitedly. "That's Slick, y'all! I know that dude! He used to go with my sister! This is a new song!"

"Who?" a soldier on the far end of the bar asked.

Friday was barely able to contain his enthusiasm. "That rapper, man! He been rolling with Lonzo since he first started fighting. His name is Slick! He went out with my sister for a while, but she ended up getting pregnant by some other dude. But, but, but that nigga, he was supposed to be *dead*, man! He got shot, like *nine times*! Everybody said he was gonna die. He was in a wheelchair for a year!"

McIntosh checked out how animated the rapper was and called bullshit. "That sonofabitch wasn't in no damn wheelchair! Look at him. Ain't nothing wrong with him."

"For real!" Friday insisted. "He got healed. They say it was a miracle. I had heard that he, um, he went to one of those Baptist churches down south, way in the boondocks. You know, where they be messing with snakes and screaming and dancing and shit. They say Slick let one of those snakes bite him on the spine, and the preacher prayed for him, and he jumped right out that wheelchair and started jumping around and shit."

Ellis shook his head, grinning. McIntosh refused to believe Slick was ever even shot.

"Bullshit, Friday! Why you always making stuff up, man?"

"I swear!" Friday said. "He got shot, like, ten times!"

"You just said it was *nine*!" McIntosh said, laughing.

"Oh, well, I know it was a bunch of times."

"Get the hell outta here," another bystander named Douglas said. "The man got shot *one time*. It was in the back, but the bullet didn't hit his spine. He was in rehab for two months. Nobody thought he was gonna make it, but, as you can see, he wasn't hurt too bad."

"How you know?" Friday asked him.

"I read about him in Hip Hop Weekly," Douglas said. "They say Slick is the next big thing. He just got signed to Interscope. Now, where you get *your* information from?"

"He heard it through the grapevine," Ellis said, and they all laughed.

"Whatever," Friday said. "I know the dude personally. I ain't gotta—"

"Man, could you shut the hell up, so we can watch the fight?" McIntosh said.

Friday sat down, nodding. "Yeah, that's cool. I was just, I was just saying..."

The announcer gave the particulars for the fight, indicating the winner would go on to fight Melvin "The Undeniable" Broadnax for the heavyweight championship. Lonzo's trainer removed a shiny, red robe from his shoulders, and The Champ rolled his neck and loosened up his arms.

Ellis watched him carefully, subconsciously sizing him up. This was totally unnecessary because Nisha made her decision two months ago. But Ellis wondered if she sometimes regretted her choice. Lonzo was handsome, Ellis couldn't take that away from him. His muscles were well-defined, stunning, really. The Champ stared at his opponent with malice and confidence, and Ellis felt a chill roll down his spine. He shook it off and downed his second shot. "Gimme, gimme another one of those."

The fight started with a feeling-out period for both fighters. Lonzo danced around, throwing jabs and double jabs to see how Nichols would react. He was fast. Ellis was great at hand-to-hand combat himself, but he had to admit Lonzo was a lot quicker than him. Nichols followed The Champ around anxiously, trying to land a few jabs of his own, but Lonzo's head movement was as speedy as his hands. He bobbed and weaved effortlessly. Friday was on his feet again.

"Aww, he got him. He got him, y'all..."

Ellis agreed that Nichols was probably out-matched, but no one was prepared for what happened next. At just fifty-two seconds into the first round, Lonzo lowered his head and cut the distance between the two. He caught Nichols with a jab to the nose, quickly followed by a hook to the jaw. Nichols raised his fists, and Lonzo went downstairs for a beautiful combo to the gut that made Ellis wince.

Nichols' eyes bulged. He lowered his elbows to protect his ribs, and before his trainer could yell at him, Lonzo came back upstairs with a right hook-left hook-uppercut combo that was so fast all Ellis saw was sweat flying off Nichols' head. Lonzo grunted and finished him off with his signature punch, another devastating uppercut to the temple. Nichols' head snapped back, and his mouth went slack. His arms fell limply to his sides as he drifted slowly to the canvas.

Lonzo could've hit him a few more times during the descent, but The Champ was gracious in victory. He backed to his corner and waited stoically while the official gave the countdown. When the ref shouted, "*TEN!*" all hell broke loose, both in Austin as well as Lucky's Pool Hall.

"I told you! I told you!" Friday jumped up and down like he was the one who earned a shot at the title. "Didn't I tell you?! Didn't I tell you he was gon' knock him out?!" He ran up and down the bar slapping everyone on their shoulders. "Didn't I tell you that was my man? Lonzo ain't no joke! That boy gon' be the champion. I'm telling you! He going all the way to the top!"

Everyone at the bar was excited about the amazing display of skill and courage they just witnessed, but Ellis kept his mouth closed. He watched the screen in awe, wondering what the hell just happened. He watched all the replays and still couldn't believe it. He knew Lonzo was good, but what just took place in Austin was *greatness;* there was no doubt about it.

Ellis' eyes were transfixed on the screen when the announcer raised Lonzo's hand in victory, and a broadcaster thrust a microphone under his chin.

"Awesome fight, Champ! Your next match will be for the heavyweight title! Did you think things would go so easily tonight?"

Lonzo was a little out of breath. Sweat glistened on his face and chest, but his smile was big and beautiful. "First off," he said, "I wanna give thanks to the Lord Almighty, who gave me the strength to be here and the ability to accomplish my dreams. I wanna thank my grandmama too, because she raised me and made me everything I am today. I gotta thank my trainer. Fats been with me through thick and thin."

The audience applauded. Cameras flashed in all directions.

"It's been a long road," Lonzo told the reporter. "It wasn't easy to get here, and this fight wasn't easy. Nichols is an awesome competitor. I have to give him his props. I won, but that dude can fight."

This brought another hearty round of applause. Ellis shook his head, growing more impressed by a man he thought he had all figured out. Lonzo might not be a smart guy, but he was well-spoken and charismatic. He had raw talent that made men respect him and a bright smile that made the ladies swoon. Ellis knew the endorsement deals would come rolling in. Lonzo could sell anything from Nikes to deodorant to Subway sandwiches.

"What do you think about Broadnax?" the reporter asked. "Do you have a strategy in mind for your heavyweight bout?"

Lonzo's trainers crowded around him, all of them smiling like kids on Christmas morning.

"I don't have a strategy for Broadnax yet," Lonzo said. "But I'm gonna do what I always do: Hit the gym. Train hard. Study the films. Eat right, do right and train some more. I'm The Champ. He may have the belt right now, but I've been telling people since day one: *I am The Champ.* When you go into a fight with that state of mind, you can't lose. Who can stop you, when you know you're the best?"

"What do you think—"

"Hold, hold on." Lonzo cut the reporter off and looked around the ring. "Where my son at? Who got my... Come on! Bring Lonzo Jr. up here."

The camera angle stayed on Lonzo and the reporter, but the view widened when a beautiful woman approached with a two-year-old in her arms. The boy was as cute as a button, wearing miniature boxing trunks and a red tee shirt that had, "THE CHAMP" printed in bold, white letters.

But it wasn't Lonzo's son that held Ellis' attention. The woman carrying the child was none other than Lanisha Elder. The sight of her made Ellis' heart hurt all over again.

"Come on, boy," Lonzo said, reaching for his son. He propped the toddler on one hip and leaned to give his fiancée a kiss on the lips. "I love you, baby."

Nisha said something back to him. Ellis couldn't make it out because she didn't have a microphone, but he didn't need to hear her to know she was the happiest woman on earth. Her smile told the whole story. Her eyes glistened as she joined the rest of the world in admiration of The Champ.

Lonzo continued speaking to the reporter, but Ellis wasn't listening anymore. From the moment Nisha appeared on the screen, she was the only thing that mattered. She took a step back to give Lonzo room to shine, but Ellis' eyes remained glued to her. He reached for his third shot blindly and downed it in one swallow.

He sighed. Apparently she made the right decision. But according to Nisha, it never was about the riches or the fame. She said she chose Lonzo because he was the father of her child, and she knew he was a good man. She said they had their ups and downs, but she was sure there would be more sunny days in the future than rainy ones. Even if there was more rain than sunshine, she said she was willing to take that risk and stick it out with The Champ.

She told Ellis all of this the day after they shared what he thought was a meaningful kiss at the park. Ellis dropped her off that night with his heart high in the clouds. The next morning, Nisha called and said she couldn't see him anymore. She said what they had was in the past, and it was too late to go back.

Ellis knew he shouldn't feel bad about her decision. He gave it a good fight. He popped up out of the blue, after seven long years with no contact, and he *almost* had her. He almost convinced her to come with him this time. But, in the end, she made the same decision she made when they were eighteen.

"Damn, dude. You crying?"

Ellis looked over and noticed McIntosh was watching him queerly. Ellis's eyes were blurry. He thought he'd be okay, but he blinked, and a fat tear rolled down his cheek. He wiped it away and shook his head. He coughed.

"Naw, man, it's just... I got, it's just my allergies."

McIntosh narrowed his eyes and looked up at the television. His gaze returned to Ellis. "You didn't want Ingram to win?"

"I, uh..." Ellis sighed. "I had my money on the other guy."

"You, you need a loan?" McIntosh asked. "Jeez. How much did you lose?"

Ellis chuckled. He shook his head and slid off the barstool. "I'm alright, man. It's all good. The uh, you know, the best man won." He dug in his pocket and came up with five twenty-dollar bills. He dropped two on the bar and headed for the pool tables, confident he wouldn't lose twice in one night.

"Where you at Peters?"

"I'm right here!" The man he was playing earlier met him at the table. "You ready for this ass whooping?"

"You got your piggybank?" Ellis waved his money in the air.

Peters pulled out his wallet. "I sure do."

Ellis found his pool stick. He looked around the bar reflectively. "Hey, Peters, what's say next weekend me and you go to the city, see if we can find us some women folk? I'm sick of hanging around this place."

"What's a matter, Sarg?" Peters asked. "Getting lonely?"
He grinned, unaware of how right he was.

"Everybody needs somebody," Ellis said with a seriousness
that gave his friend pause. "A man can be anything he wants, with
a woman by his side."

"Alright," Peters said. "Next Saturday we're going to the
big city." He tossed three twenties on the table. "But you might
not have no gas money after I take you to school."

Ellis placed his money on top of his friends. "I can't wait to
shut you up. Rack 'em up, son. Let's see what you got."

KEITH THOMAS WALKER

ABOUT THE AUTHOR

Keith Thomas Walker, known as the Master of Romantic Suspense and Urban Fiction, is the author of more than two dozen novels, including *Fixin' Tyrone, Life After, The Realest Ever,* the *Backslide* series, the *Brick House* series and the *Finley High* series. Keith's books transcend all genres. He has published romance, urban fiction, mystery/thriller, teen/young adult, Christian, poetry and erotica. Originally from Fort Worth, he is a graduate of Texas Wesleyan University. Keith has won numerous awards in the categories of "Best Male Author," "Best Romance," "Best Urban Fiction," "Best Young Adult Romance," "Best Duo," "Book of the Year," and "Author of the Year," from several book clubs and organizations. Visit him at www.keithwalkerbooks.com.